AFFLICTED

A NOVEL

FAYLA OTT

F
Ott

In loving memory of Reverend Wallace Strawn, and his wife Debbie.
I'm forever grateful for their lives of service to the cause of Christ.

Acknowledgements

I want to thank my Lord and Savior for the privilege of writing this story. I'm both humbled and honored that He'd choose me. I especially thank Him for giving me the strength and discipline to finish it.

I'd like to thank my husband, Cliff, who was my main support as I worked on this novel. He listened to me brainstorm, discuss characters and scenes, and even listened as I whined about the woes of writing. He has always believed in me and my dream to write novels. That means more than he knows. I couldn't do this without him.

To my boys, Seth and Luke. Seth acted as my personal barista on many days, making me endless amounts of coffee, and he also listened to me brainstorm and offered some great feedback. Luke's signature hugs gave me a boost on those frustrating days when I wanted to bang my head into my laptop.

To Marcia Nelson, my travel buddy and friend. She made my research trip to Salem a fun adventure. I'm so thankful not only for her companionship, but for her enthusiasm for this story. Also, her experience as a library director is an asset to me as an author. She has offered many helpful tips and suggestions.

Thanks to my pastor, Dan Spencer, for loaning me his Biblical reference books on demons and spiritual warfare. This part of the book needed to be researched carefully for spiritual protection, so I appreciate his help and guidance.

I'd like to thank the kind people of Salem, Massachusetts, for their assistance in guiding me as I explored the area's historical sites and museums, and restaurants and shops. They were hospitable and eager to help in any way they could. I thoroughly enjoyed my stay in their town. More specifically, a huge thanks to Salem Food Tours and our tour guide, Karen Scalia, for a delightful experience. Karen went above and beyond to ensure I gathered the right information relating to my research.

To my launch team, Carol Roberts, Melody Shampine, Lisa Haislip, Brooke Cox, Britney Beasley, Robin Blizzard, Kelly Johnson, Ginger Young, Nicole Knight, Marguerite McBride, Laura Williams, Karla Carson, Joy East, Linda Wall, Susie Delozier, Jamie Taylor, and Sarah Terry. They were a big help for the launch process. Not only have they encouraged me, but they were helpful in suggestions and comments. Their assistance in marketing is extremely valuable.

Thanks to all my friends and family who support my writing endeavors. You encourage me more than you know.

There is no fear in love; but perfect love casteth out fear: because fear hath torment. He that feareth is not made perfect in love.
I John 4:18 (KJV)

For we wrestle not against flesh and blood, but against principalities, against powers, against the rulers of the darkness of this world, against spiritual wickedness in high places.
Ephesians 6:12 (KJV)

A Short Guide to Character Names/Titles

Goody   An abbreviated version of Goodwife, a title used to address a married woman, or a woman who has been married. The modern term is "Mrs."

Goodman   A title used to address a man. The modern term is "Mr."

Magistrate   A term used to address a high official of the court.

Reverend   A term used to address a minister.

Pronunciation guide

Demons:
Sonnellion: S-aw-n-eh-l-ee-oh-n
Carreau : Car-reau,
Verrier: Ver-rier
Belias: Be-li-as
Angels:
Raphael: Raf-ay-el
Uriel: Ur-i-el
Semiel: Sa-may-el
Raguel: Ra-gel

Note: There are a few characters who have identical first names in the story. To honor the real life victims or heroes, their names were not changed. However, in each scene, there is a last name present, or a specific circumstance, to help the reader identify the character.

CHAPTER ONE

January, 1692
Salem village, Massachusetts

Sonneillon, the first of the four dark shadows, moved boldly through the trees that surrounded Salem Village. Behind him, Carreau, Belias, and Verrier crawled with anticipation, hungry for this new mission. They didn't know what was planned, only that it was of high priority. It had to be, with Sonneillon personally escorting them to the site where they were assigned to wreak havoc. Sonneillon stopped. He spread his enormous, red, reptilian wings in front of the other creatures, blocking their view from anything other than his impressive span. He enjoyed doing that. It reminded the lower hierarchies who was in charge. It was the same reason he walked and they crawled while in his presence. He smirked before he turned around. The movement of his wings in the moonlight mimicked flames of fire flashing before them. It had the intimidating effect it always did. Sonneillon saw it in their eyes. He gave them a hard stare as a bonus.

Belias belonged to the lowest order of the demon hierarchy. He cowered beneath Sonneillon's stare. Sonneillon reveled in his fear. Next to him, Carreau and Verrier stood as a team. They were from

1

the same order, but it didn't mean anything. Either of them could unleash wrath upon the other in seconds, if threatened in any capacity. Sonneillon knew how to keep them in line, and he'd be sure to for this assignment. Everything had to be in order.

"Lucifer has commanded us here to this village. Check out your new mission." Sonneillon pulled in his wings and stretched his clawed hand in the direction of the small spread of houses and scanty structures. Carreau and Verrier spewed obscenities, spitting on the ground in front of them. Their pride controlled them. Belias remained silent. Sonneillon knew it wasn't from allegiance, but from fear. That was good. He worked well with fear.

"This is the important mission? A handful of people in a pathetic little village who mean nothing to anyone?" Verrier said.

Sonneillon seized him by the throat, and squeezed until his eyes bulged. He slung him to the ground and then looked at the others. Carreau sneered at Verrier who was coughing and gasping big gulps of air.

"Need I remind you of the time you were assigned to a little boy named David? The one who slayed the giant, and whose Psalms are now read and recited by Christians everywhere? Let's see…what did you say then, Verrier? Ah, yes. You said that a little boy couldn't possibly be a real threat. When will you ever learn, you filthy piece of swine? There are no insignificant Christians. Every prayer uttered, every act of faith, every single step of obedience and allegiance to the Christ will cost us a victory. Lucifer has his reasons for sending us to this 'insignificant' crummy little village and its neighboring town."

He reached down and lifted Verrier by his head. "And-you-will-do-your-job!" Sonneillon tossed him aside again, then turned to Belias and Carreau. "Is that clear?" His hot breath singed their faces. They bowed and nodded as a humiliated Verrier crawled back to stand next to them.

Sonneillon turned back to the village. "What makes this mission easier is that we have actually been invited to Salem. Take a look."

The vile creatures arrived in a house where they saw a group of young females engaged in rituals they knew all too well. Sonneillon filled them in on all the details of their purpose there. As he talked, and Lucifer's plan unfolded, the three subservient demons grew more excited and hungry for the evil that they would begin to inflict on the poor souls in Salem Village.

～

The Parris parsonage grew darker, and large shadows danced on the walls from the flames of the fire. Tituba whispered in a foreign tongue, and the girls leaned in to hear, as if getting closer would grant them an interpretation.

Lydia shrank back. She wished she hadn't come. She was scared of Tituba, the slave that Reverend Parris brought with him from Boston, along with her husband, John Indian. Tituba had shown them strange rituals, activities Lydia knew would get them into trouble. During their last meeting, she had danced for them, and moved in such a way that Lydia blushed. She had never seen anyone move that way. Dancing was strictly forbidden in Salem Village. So was fortune telling, which brought them together today. Tituba had promised them a fortune telling session. She said she could reveal the names of their future husbands. Lydia shivered. Fortune telling was witchcraft, and witchcraft could get them hanged. She looked around the room at her companions. Reverend Parris' daughter, little Betty Parris, looked as frightened as Lydia. Her cousin Abigail Williams lived with her, and made her do whatever she said. Lydia wished Betty could live with her. They'd be great sisters. She never had a sister. Or a brother.

"Lydia!" Ann Putnam's sharp voice snapped her out of her

thoughts. Ann summoned her closer. Lydia complied. They all did what Ann said. Even the older girls who ranged from sixteen to nineteen. Ann was the youngest of their group at just twelve years old. Somehow the younger girl commanded a following from her peers. Lydia had seen Ann's mother, Goody Alice Putnam, manage to draw the same response from many women in Salem Village. Abigail often tried to dominate the group, but ultimately Ann won them over again. Abigail and Ann often fought the battle of their strong wills. Lydia longed to be like them.

Tituba held out the glass of water and started chanting something unintelligible. The chants sent shivers up Lydia's spine. Mercy Lewis asked, "Are you sure this will show us the identity of Ann's future husband?"

"Shhh!" Tituba whispered. She put the glass down in the center of their circle and reached down beside her to pick up an egg one of the girls brought from their hens. She cracked the brown shell and separated the yolk from the egg white. Picking up the glass again, she dropped the egg white into the water. She held up her dark slender hand, motioning for them to wait for it to settle. Then, she looked down into the glass. Her brown eyes widened and she stilled.

"What?" asked Ann. "Whose face shape is it?" She grabbed the glass from Tituba's hand. Lydia elbowed her position between the girls to stare at the contents in the glass. She jumped back, along with the other girls. The gasps of those around her echoed her own terror at seeing the shape of a coffin in the glass.

Death.

Death for whom? Ann? Her future husband? For all of them? Lydia looked to Tituba, hoping she'd clarify. A log in the fire crackled.

Mavis Walcott spoke first. "It's the sign of the devil!"

"Hush! It's no such thing!" Ann said. Her shaky voice belied her conviction.

Tituba just stared at the glass, its contents partially spilled from the sudden drop to the floor. She picked it up, held it out and chanted something similar to her earlier ramblings. She swayed back and forth, holding the glass over her head. The girls watched, both fascinated and fearful.

Finally, she spoke in English. "Death is coming to Salem Village." She held out the glass and swept it in front of their faces. "Death is coming. And you will partake in it."

Ann reached out and slapped Tituba in the face. Tituba didn't flinch. She just stared a solemn gaze.

"I told you she's a witch!" Mercy exclaimed.

"Ann, this isn't fun anymore. I'm going home." Mavis stood up, smoothed her waistcoat, and walked toward the door.

"No one is going anywhere until we make a pact." Ann said. Mavis sat back down.

"A pact?" Abigail asked. "What kind of pact?"

"A blood pact. We will tell no one what happened here today. No one can know." Ann pricked her finger with a pin from her petticoat, then passed it on, so each girl followed suit. Tituba refused to prick her finger. Mercy Lewis sighed, then gave the pin back to Ann, who grabbed Tituba's hand and pricked her finger. Tituba still stared at her motionless.

Lydia's finger stung, but she was glad they were making the pact. As she pressed her finger next to each girl's finger, she hoped no one would tell what happened. She pictured her father's rage, and she shivered. What would he do if he knew she had participated in such acts? Lydia feared for Tituba, too. Although Tituba frightened her, she didn't want anything to happen to the slave. But what if she was a witch? Didn't she deserve to die? Did Lydia deserve to die, too? After all, she had been listening to the stories and playing the devil's games. God's wrath would be on them all.

Ann instructed the group to hold hands. "We are joined by blood and by this promise to each other. We will not tell a living soul what transpired here today. Our blood binds us to this promise. Now, let's swear to it."

The girls had no idea they were being watched. As they began to recite, "I swear on my blood and the blood of those around me that I will not tell a living soul what we saw here today", the creatures retreated to gather their minions. Sonneillon couldn't wait to get started. He looked back at the girls. Their eyes reflected fear, even those of their bold little leader. This was going to be fun. The people of Salem village and Salem town would never be the same.

The Reverend Samuel Parris led his wife Elizabeth to the door of the parsonage. He looked at the woodpile. It was dwindling fast. His flock still refused to do their duty for their shepherd. Anger surfaced, but he calmed himself for his wife's sake. He would save his emotions for the next committee meeting. His anger was certainly justifiable as it classified as righteous indignation. How dare these people who call themselves Christians not tend to the needs of their minister and his family? No matter how much he preached against neglecting one's faithful duties, week after week, he received only a small portion of his salary, and he resorted to ordering his slave John Indian to chop his firewood, although his contract clearly stated that particular duty fell to the congregation. He knew the villagers wanted to drive him out. They did not care for his traditional theology and strict policies, but God needed him to purge these people of their evil tendencies. He would be faithful to his duty, even if they would not. He did have a few supporters. The Putnams had managed to influence a group of followers on his side. John Putnam and his wife wanted the church strong for their own reasons, but at least he had someone to stand with him on church matters such as attendance and giving. If he hadn't had faithful tithers, he would have had to leave Salem village by now.

He and Elizabeth entered the parsonage to find the group of girls in a circle around his slave Tituba.

"What folly is this?" he asked. "Betty, Abigail, why are these girls here?" He stared at his daughter and niece. They stared back with wide eyes. Ann Putnam stood up.

"Hello, Reverend Parris."

"Why, Ann. I didn't see you here. Perhaps you could enlighten me on why you girls are not at home, tending to your household obligations. It is the late afternoon, is it not?"

"Yes, sir, it is, and we all must be going to do just that. We wanted to check on Goody Parris. We had heard she wasn't feeling well and we thought to cheer her up today. But when we arrived, your Betty told us her mother was out on visits with you, sir. So Tituba was kind enough to let us sit by the warm fire for a bit before we go."

Ann smiled the smile of her mother. Reverend Parris wasn't fooled. He knew Alice's persuasive tongue all too well. Ann had inherited her gift of manipulative speech, but he had the gift of a keen eye and ear and neither had missed the signs of guilt from the other girls. The gasps when he and his wife opened the door and their wide eyes contrasted the calm, gentle tone of their friend. He looked at Tituba. She would not meet his eyes, and he could have sworn she had hidden something under her skirt. He could not afford to anger Ann's parents, though. Without them as his allies, he would surely have to leave Salem village.

"Well, of course. You girls warm yourselves before you go. This winter chill has its way of gripping your soul like the devil himself. Tituba, you should bring in more wood for the evening. Where is that husband of yours?"

"He's splitting wood for the woodpile, Reverend. He said he'd better do it now before another snow comes." The Reverend noticed she held her skirt as she walked to the door. He also noticed how the girls watched her.

"Ann, did you harm yourself, child?" His wife pointed to Ann's apron, a smear of blood visible on the front.

"Oh, yes, but it's just a finger prick from my sewing needle. No real harm has come to me. Well, I'd better get on home and help mother with the chores. Thank you, Reverend. The fire was most helpful. Goody Parris, I am glad you are feeling better. Come along, girls. Let's be on our way. Goodbye, Betty and Abigail!"

She briskly put on her wrap, and the other girls followed her to the door. It struck Reverend Parris how readily these girls jumped up to follow her. Again, he was reminded of her mother, Goody Putnam. He looked at his own daughter and niece, who busily attended to his wife to help her get settled. Of the two, Betty was the most congenial, while Abigail possessed a more determined spirit. He had to watch her, for the devil liked stubbornness. He would also have to watch Betty. She was heavily influenced and in the presence of both Abigail and Ann Putnam, the devil could easily win her over. If he could win one over, he could easily get to a whole village. Samuel Parris wasn't about to let that happen.

⌒⌣

Outside, Tituba stacked wood into the crook of her arm. Ann stopped in front of her, bringing her face close to hers, and gave her a pointed look. She held up her bloody finger. "Remember the pact, Tituba."

As the girls followed Ann down the pathway away from the parsonage, Lydia heard Tituba whisper, "Death is coming. You can't stop it. It is already here." When she looked back, Tituba was gone.

CHAPTER TWO

Lydia shut the door and turned to face her father.

"I just came from the Reverend Parris' house." She began to unbutton her coat. Her stiff fingers ached from the cold, so she struggled to release the buttons from the tight holes.

"Why?" he asked. He bent over the fire, added more wood, and stirred the orange coals with the iron poker.

"The girls and I finished our study early, so we decided to stop by and visit Goody Parris, but she was out with the Reverend. Tituba invited us to get warm before we started home. I'm sorry, Father, but we started talking and didn't realize the time until the Reverend and Goody Parris arrived."

He looked up, his eyes searching hers. Could he know she was lying? She figured it best to stick with the story Ann had told Reverend Parris.

"Get busy with supper. I have to spread more straw in the barn for the stock. It's going to get even colder tonight."

He put on his coat and left her alone. She was often alone in their modest house. Her mother had passed away with scarlet fever when Lydia was only four years old. Her father had built this house not long after he and her mother married. He had planned to add on to it as more children came, but the fever changed everything.

The kitchen and sitting area were one large room, the keeping room, and adjacent to that was a smaller room with its own fireplace where Lydia slept. In the back of the house was a small lean-to. It was originally intended to store food and supplies, but her father slept there during the warmer months. They did store many of their canned goods in there, along with barrels of apple cider, and in the summer, the garden vegetables filled baskets around the walls, but her father took up the remaining space with his small bed. In the winter, he slept in the big room near the fire.

Lydia would like to think he gave up the larger sleeping room for her benefit, but she knew it was because he couldn't bear to be in there since her mother passed.

He wasn't a cruel man. He had only used the whip on her a few times; however, he was distant. Goody Nurse had told Lydia that she had contracted the fever first, and her mother tirelessly cared for her. When her mother took ill, Lydia began to improve. She often wondered if her father had wished that she'd died instead of her mother. Lydia missed her mother terribly. She often visited her gravesite just to feel close to her.

She picked up the potholders from the peg under the mantle and then placed the Dutch oven with the day old beans on its hook over the fire. The heat burned her chapped face. She pulled back.

Was she bound for the hot fires of Hell now? She had been playing the devil's games. She had heard the sermons about the lake of fire. Lydia often had bad dreams about her mother suffering in that lake of fire. When she was five, she overheard some of the ladies talking about her mother. They said she was stricken with the fever because she had done something to make God punish her. Didn't Reverend Parris always preach that the fires of Hell were created for the sinners?

Why did she go along with Ann's plan to get Tituba to show them the fortune telling game? She had been curious, though, and fascinated about their future. Death and Hell! That was their future, now.

The door opened, and the bitter cold rushed at Lydia. Her father latched the door and stuffed straw under it. He turned and nodded at the fire.

"Mind the beans, that you don't scorch them this time."

"Aye, Father." She stirred the pot, trying not to scrape the bottom too much since she had scorched them the evening before. A few minutes later, she scooped some onto a plate, making sure to give her father the only remaining piece of salt meat. She placed the brown bread on his plate, and filled his mug with cider. The thought of eating churned her stomach, so she just put a sparse amount on her own plate, hoping her father wouldn't notice. She couldn't stop hearing Tituba's voice, warning them of death. Whose death?

A knock at the door interrupted the usual silence between her and her father at evening meal. Lydia hoped whoever it was wouldn't want any food. All that was left were the black beans that had stuck to the bottom of the pot. The bread was gone and the barrel of cider was getting low as well. Lydia would have to make more bread tomorrow. As for the cider, it was probably half frozen in the back room. Lydia had planned to ask her father to help her bring it into the keeping room to thaw overnight.

The visitor knocked again. Lydia looked at her father. She wasn't permitted to answer the door when it was dark. He scraped his plate clean, gulped the last of his cider, and rose to remove the straw and unlatch the door. Lydia knew he wasn't thrilled about an intruder at this time, either.

Lydia hurriedly removed the plates from the table. Maybe they wouldn't have to offer their guest anything after all.

Her father opened the door and a worn leather shoe pushed its way in to block the door from shutting again. A raspy voice addressed her father.

"Goodman Knapp. It be a cold night. Might my little girl and I warm ourselves by your fire for a bit?"

Not Sarah Good! She silently pleaded with her father to turn the beggar away. She would want food for sure!

"Goody Good, we were about to turn in."

"It would only be for a minute. My Dorcas can't feel her toes. If you could just let us warm up for a bit, and then maybe let us sleep in your barn on some straw. We'd be on our way first thing in the morning." She coughed a deep, crackled cough. Lydia's father surprised her and probably Goody Good, too, when he agreed to let them in for a moment.

The rank odor filled the room as soon as they stepped inside. Lydia hid her gag with a small cough before greeting them.

"Good evening, Goody Good. Dorcas."

Sarah Good only nodded and pulled the little girl to the fire. She rubbed the child's hands between hers, then reached down and pulled off the girl's shoes and rubbed her toes the same way. Dorcas stared at Lydia, but said nothing. Her matted, brown hair covered one eye.

Sarah leaned over the fire and peered into the hanging pot. "Are ye going to throw out the charred beans, girl?"

Lydia looked at her father. He nodded.

She scooped the black beans onto a plate. "I'm sorry, but we have no bread left."

Sarah didn't seem to hear her. She and Dorcas started scooping up the beans with their dirty fingers and shoving them into their equally dirty mouths. When they finished, Sarah didn't even ask for more, but just scooped the remaining black beans onto the plate and they shoved those into their mouths as fast as they did the first helping.

She looked up at Lydia when they finished. She sucked her fingers clean while she stared. Lydia squirmed under her piercing gaze.

"Looked like your friend Ann Putnam and those other fine friends of yours had a bone to pick with that slave of the preacher's today. Didn't I see you with them outside his house a bit ago? Seemed to me like all wasn't so fine and dandy with you girls and that slave."

Lydia's heart jumped. What had she heard? "I don't know what you mean, Goody Good. We were just saying goodbye to her."

"Humph." Goody Good obviously didn't believe her, and she wanted Lydia's father to see that she didn't believe her.

"Where is your husband tonight, Goody Good?" her father asked, after Sarah wiped her mouth with the sleeve of her tattered coat.

"At Goodman Hanson's farm."

Lydia had heard about Goodman Good. Some said he was a lazy, no good man who couldn't care for his family. Goody Nurse and Goody Easty said that he and Sarah had suffered many trials and that life had been hard on them. Lydia wondered what evil they had committed to bring about such a hard life. William Good worked between the neighboring farms, taking jobs whether big or small, but apparently it wasn't enough to pay for lodging for him and his family. The three traveled and knocked on doors, asking for any help they could get to survive each day. Often Sarah and little Dorcas traveled alone since William usually slept at the farm where he worked. Most didn't want to put up all three at once.

"Do you have any cider to wash down our supper?"

Lydia didn't like Sarah's tone. She acted as if Lydia owed her something. She should be grateful her father let her in.

"There will be no cider tonight, Goody Good." Her father answered. "There's a bucket of water there by the hearth. Take your fill and then I'll walk you to the barn. You'd best put those shoes back on the child, such as they are. We have an old quilt you can use, and there's plenty of straw." He looked at her a moment before speaking again. "When daylight comes, I expect you and the child to be gone." He picked up the candle as if hurrying them along.

Sarah said nothing. She cupped her hand and drank from the bucket and then offered some to Dorcas. They soon followed her father out to the barn. Lydia breathed a sigh of relief when they were gone. Sarah Good was known for her short temper when she didn't get her way. She had even cursed some in Salem village for not letting her stay in their barn or have any food.

Lydia dumped the bucket of water, and filled it with fresh, clean snow to thaw by the fire. Then, she shook some straw around the room, hoping to rid the space of the rank odor the two homeless visitors had left behind. She looked down and saw Dorcas' small footprint embedded in some ash dust on the floor. Somehow, she didn't feel so relieved anymore.

⌒〜

Outside, Sarah Good snuggled her baby girl next to her chest. She doubled the quilt over them, trying to ignore the straw sticking through her clothes. The straw would keep the cold earth from reaching through their clothes and freezing their already dry, chapped skin. Last evening, they had spent the night at the Winston place without the owner's permission. The barn had no piles of straw and Sarah had feared they'd freeze before morning, without even a quilt for cover. Sarah awaked to discover something large moving against her. She jumped up, ready to attack whatever it was that threatened her and her daughter in the middle of the night, but she had been amazed to find that it was the Winstons' horse. He had somehow broken free of his rope, and had lowered his large frame to lie next to them. His warmth was welcome and probably kept her and Dorcas alive. Perhaps Providence was looking favorably upon them after all.

She looked down at her sleeping daughter. Of course, if Providence truly cared about them, she'd have a nice home with a warm fire, beds, blankets, and food. She'd have a working farm to provide their needs and they'd never be hungry or cold. No, God cared nothing for her and little Dorcas. Even her husband fared better than they did. Oh, he gave her money occasionally, but mostly he worked for lodging and food for himself, which did his wife and daughter no good. Sarah knew it wasn't entirely his fault that they were in this state. Her no good husband before him had died and left her with all of his debts. Poor William had married her and thus inherited those debts as well. Now, they were looked upon as beggars, and no one wanted to associate with the likes of them. She saw the way that uppity girl Lydia looked at her and Dorcas. She had been disgusted with them. Sarah also saw the fear in her eyes when she mentioned seeing her with the other girls and that slave outside the Parris house. She had been right. They had been up to something. She grinned with a thought as her eyes fell shut. Now wouldn't it be something if those girls got into trouble? And wouldn't it be something if they brought a few of these pious village folk with them? One could only hope…

Just outside the house, the ugly creatures watched. Their red eyes weren't visible to Goodman Knapp as he knocked the snow from his boots before going back inside.

"Let me go to the girl! She's already full of fear. I could have her loyalty in a matter of seconds." The demon started for the house. Belias cursed and pulled him back.

"You fool. Sit still. We can't touch her. We can only discourage her and encourage her fear."

"Why? Why can't we touch her! She's ripe for possession!"

"She has the prayer cover." He pointed to the winged figure on the roof. He was alone, but he had great strength.

The little demon cringed and shrank back. "Who? Who prays for her?"

"Don't even think about it. That warrior won't be a match for the likes of you. She is in Sonneillon's hands."

That silenced the demon. Belias grew weary of these pawns he had to supervise. He wanted a bigger job. A bigger job like the prayer warrior Rebecca Nurse, or her sister Mary Easty. He'd even settle for some of the other assignments. Instead, he had to watch over this pitiful little girl with so many limitations attached. Belias hoped he'd be in charge of the Parris household. Instead, Verrier and Carreau were in charge of afflicting all of the children. He wished he could see the look on that proud minister's face when his own daughter starting acting deranged.

The demon next to him danced from foot to foot, eager to pounce at the order. He looked to the barn. "What about those two? What can we do with them?"

"We use them."

"Will they be the afflicted or the accused?"

"Both," Belias answered.

⸎

Semiel watched Belias and the little demon from the roof. He didn't worry about the smaller demon, but Belias was strong, so Semiel stood in his fighting stance, ready. He had no idea why he had been ordered to guard this girl, but he sensed this duty held great significance to the kingdom. If only more Christians prayed for each other. Semiel knew evil brewed in Salem, and when there were little to no prayer warriors, evil increased at a fast rate. Semiel had already seen many larger demons in the area, so evil was increasing. He just hoped God's people recognized it before something terrible happened to this place.

CHAPTER THREE

Betty Parris screamed into the darkness. Abigail sat up next to her in bed and shook her cousin. "Hush up, Betty! You'll wake the house!" She yanked her hands back. Betty's nightgown was soaked. Did she soil herself? No, that was sweat. Abigail touched her forehead. Betty's hair clung to it, and she smelled damp skin. "Betty!" Although she couldn't see her cousin's face in the dark, Abigail knew her eyes were wide in fear. That is how they often looked these days.

"Betty, stop breathing so hard!"

The small voice struck fear in Abigail. "I'm not." Betty's shaking hand grabbed Abigail's arm and spoke again. "I'm not breathing hard, Abigail."

She froze as the hot breath now touched her neck from behind and she knew that could not be Betty's breath. She jumped and twisted in the bed. Terror sucked the breath from her lungs and she couldn't move or speak. All she could do was stare at the red eyes in front of her. Suddenly, she was on the floor. She wasn't sure how she got there, but the dark figure loomed above her. He floated over her listless form and she forgot about Betty as she struggled to get up. The creature's dark shape obscured his face, but his red eyes bored into hers. He smelled like rotten eggs. The creature spoke over her face, but the voice sounded inside her head.

"Submit to me and you shall have what you seek."

She tried to scream, but his hand moved, and took her breath.

"Submit to me. Now."

A warm pulse spread throughout her body, and she slipped into darkness. She never noticed the second creature hovering over her cousin a few feet away.

⁓

Dr. William Griggs cursed the worn soles in his shoes with each step he made in the cold and soggy snow. He'd do penance later. Right now, he was both annoyed and intrigued by the Reverend Parris' summons for him to call upon the house. The note had simply stated, "Your expertise is needed immediately for the observance and assessment of the children." Reverend Parris wasn't in the habit of requesting anything of the village members, but rather demanding what he wanted. Dr. Griggs was no exception. In the few times he had been to examine the reverend's wife, he had noticed the disdain in the minister's voice when he spoke to him. The Reverend had no reason to be haughty by material means. William knew of the troubles he had with the church and the dispute over his salary. He had also heard that the reverend had inherited money in the past, but lost it in various investments in the farming industry. When his agricultural and trading endeavors failed in Barbados, he had decided to become a minister. William wondered how long the Reverend Parris would last in Salem village. The people in the village weren't the easiest to lead, and he was afraid the reverend was making the situation worse with his harsh demeanor and superior attitude.

He reached the parsonage just when his toes felt detached from his body. He took a deep breath and knocked. Tituba the slave opened the door. Dr. Griggs noted the fear in her dark eyes. Curious. He stepped inside.

"May I take your hat and coat, Doctor?"

"In a moment, Tituba. It might take some time for me to warm up." He blew his warm breath into his stiff hands, then vigorously rubbed them together.

She nodded, and walked over to the reverend's study door and knocked softly. The slave was quite beautiful in an exotic way. Her skin was much darker than the fair- skinned women he had been accustomed to, but she wasn't the same color as the Indians, nor did she quite favor the Africans. He figured she was a mulatto of some sort, though from what two races, he didn't know. She had soft, brown, wavy hair. She had pulled it up into her cap, but some tendrils managed to escape and fell to the side of her face. He tried not to look at the way her apron fit across her breasts. He already had to do penance for the swearing. He didn't need to add lust to the list.

Reverend Parris came out to greet him.

"I appreciate your promptness, Doctor. Warm yourself by the fire, then we will go up to the girls."

Dr. Griggs felt more than heard the hurried command. Nevertheless, his body craved the fire and he stepped up to the hearth and sighed when its warmth greeted him. Reverend Parris wasted no time in clearing his throat after only a moment, moving the doctor out of his momentary trance to follow him up the narrow, cold stairway. Warmth greeted him once more when they reached the top. The only window in the room was quite small, and it was covered to keep out the cold. The fire was the only light and the flames cast shadows on the walls. The girls were lying on the bed, and they appeared to be sleeping peacefully. The doctor was tempted to ask why he had been summoned when the reverend motioned him closer to the bed. Startled, Dr. Griggs stood rigid when he looked closely at the faces glowing in the firelight.

Betty Parris' eyes fixated on the ceiling. Dr. Griggs waved his hand over her eyes. She did not move, nor did her eyes blink. She was white, except for the purple hues circling her eyes. He looked at Abigail. Her eyes were closed, but her lips were moving.

He walked to the other side of the bed, and leaned in to see if she mouthed anything audible. Her whispers grew quieter as he got closer. He leaned in until he could feel her hot breath on his ear. Her hands reached up and grabbed his throat. With surprising strength, she yanked his head around so that his eyes were inches above hers. Hers were red. They actually glowed like fire. She increased her grip and restricted his air. Her strength resembled a large man's. Trying not to panic, he wrapped his hands around hers and pulled. She laughed, but it was not Abigail's laughter he heard. Reverend Parris grabbed the doctor and pulled, but her grip on his neck was fierce and the doctor saw death in her eyes.

He twisted and squirmed to free himself while the reverend pulled, thinking this just might be his end. Then he spotted it. A Bible lay on the small table next to the bed. He raised his weak hand and frantically pointed to it. The reverend picked up the Bible and started reading from the Gospel of John. His voice shouted, "In the beginning was the Word, and the Word was with God, and the Word was God."

Abigail released him and screamed, covering her ears. She shook her head, back and forth, until she closed her eyes again, her lips moving silently, just as they were before. Dr. Griggs fell to the floor, coughing and gasping.

Reverend Parris walked over to a chest in the room and opened it. He pulled out some rope and began binding Abigail's hands to the railing. Obviously, it was not the first time he had taken such measures with his niece.

When he finished, he looked up at the doctor. Dr. Griggs nodded. "It's for the best." He stood up and walked back to Betty, keeping his distance. He could still feel the burn of Abigail's grip on his neck. "Has Betty been violent?"

"No. At least not to others. She either lies there, just like she is now, or she scratches herself until she bleeds. Look there. Under her sleeves." He pointed to her nightdress. The doctor pulled up her sleeve and almost recoiled from what he saw. Long, deep lines of red marked her arm. Her nightdress sleeve partially stuck to her scratches with dried blood.

"Does Abigail have these?"

"No. Their symptoms are as different as they are. Abigail's anger is directed at others while Betty's is directed at herself."

"Any other symptoms?"

"Yes. They have gotten down on their hands and knees and barked like dogs, they have muttered strange words, and sometimes they choke for no reason at all."

Dr. Griggs rubbed his neck. "Has Abigail hurt anyone else?"

The reverend nodded. "Tituba."

"I'll talk with her later. Reverend, it's probably best if Abigail remains as she is until we can figure out how to help her. You'll have to use caution while feeding her and tending to her needs."

"What about when she is acting in normal behavior?"

Dr. Griggs had a hard time picturing the girl on the bed as normal, but he sympathized with the reverend. "I'm sorry, but you'd better not take any chances for now. As for Betty, does she ever come out of her trance?"

"Occasionally, but when she does, she acts skittish and feeble." He sighed. "Doctor, let's get to the matter, shall we? What is this madness? What sort of disease causes this behavior?"

Doctor Griggs rubbed his neck again and gazed at the girls one more time. He looked up at the reverend, dreading the reaction that was sure to accompany his answer.

"Reverend, this is no physical disease."

"What do you mean?"

"I'm afraid your children have been bewitched."

~

Tituba heard John Indian outside, splitting firewood. She wished the parishioners would fulfill their promise to provide the firewood. Her husband had to work hard enough at Ingersoll's tavern without coming home to the tiresome task of chopping and splitting firewood in the freezing temperatures. Better yet, if only the reverend would see to the firewood himself. Tituba almost laughed at that thought. The arrogant minister would never reduce himself to such a menial task.

The doctor and the reverend hadn't come down yet so she pulled on her wrap and stepped out into the cold to meet her husband. A large, dark man, he stood tall above her as she approached him. Despite the cold, sweat ran from his temple.

"Tituba! You should be inside where it's warm. I'll be in shortly."

"I figured I'd better warn you. The doctor is inside, upstairs with the girls. I heard some kind of commotion earlier. John, what if—"

"Hush, woman! I told you not to speak of it."

"But John, if those girls speak up about what we did here, I'll be hanged for sure!"

"Nobody's going to be hanged. You hear? Nobody. Now since you're out here, gather some of that kindling and bring it inside. We're going to need it in the morning, and it might as well be inside now rather than out here in the wet snow. I'll bring more wood to dry out for tomorrow. Go on. You will fall ill with only that little wrap around your shoulders." He resumed splitting the logs with the long-handled ax. Tituba knew she shouldn't say any more. Often, there were ears lurking about in Salem Village. It wouldn't do for anyone to hear that she had anything to do with whatever afflicted the girls of the Parris household. Tituba opened the door and stepped back inside. The keeping room was still empty. She stacked the kindling, and then began to prepare for the evening meal. She hadn't told John that she'd been having nightmares. Each night it was the same dream. There was a hill, and many people lying on the ground, blood spilling from their bodies. In every dream, she'd walk up the hill, but as she came closer to the lifeless bodies, they'd rise up, and point their really long fingers at her. She would run down the hill, screaming, before she woke up.

Why, oh why, had she listened to that Ann Putnam? She and Abigail had a way of manipulating others into doing just what they wanted them to do. Tituba should have known better, but she had missed the rituals since leaving her home in Barbados, and the girls enjoyed her stories. For those moments, she didn't feel quite as homesick. It didn't last long. A coffin! Tituba shivered.

The reverend often read to them the teachings from that popular minister, Cotton Mather. If that man's teachings were true, the egg coffin, the nightmares, and the girls' behavior, seemed to point to one thing, and one thing only.

The girls were-

"Bewitched!" She heard the reverend shout from upstairs. "In my house!" His heavy footsteps descended closer and he appeared in the keeping room.

"Tituba, has John Indian arrived home?" He didn't wait for a response, but rushed to the door and flung it open. "John!" He yelled for her husband to come in.

John's large frame filled the doorway. He briefly glanced at Tituba.

"You need me, sir?"

"Yes. Come into my study. I need to write a message for you to deliver. I also need to speak with you."

"Yes sir." Again, he glanced at Tituba. While his eyes only briefly met hers, she saw the same concern she felt. He followed Reverend Parris to his study and the door closed behind them. Her heart beat fast in her chest when the doctor came downstairs a moment later.

"Tituba, I need a word with you. I won't take you away from your duties for too long, but this is a matter of urgency."

Tituba sat down at the table where the doctor had motioned for her to sit.

Dr. Griggs stared at her intently for a moment. She noticed the dark, red marks on his throat and knew instantly who had put them there. He was an ugly man. His eyes reminded her of the tree frogs of Barbados. His cheeks were always red, even in the warmer months. His waistcoat fit tight over his bulging belly, and the fat extended to his neck.

"Do you have any cider, Tituba?"

"Oh, yes. I'm sorry. I should have asked, sir. Would you like me to warm it for you?"

"Yes, that would be fine." He watched her a moment as she dipped the cider from its barrel and poured it into a small pot over the fire, stirring it, and then pulling it off the hook, and pouring it into a mug she retrieved from above the hearth.

Dr. Griggs sipped the cider for a moment before speaking. "Tituba, the reverend tells me that Abigail hurt you."

Tituba didn't want to talk about that. It was dangerously close to what she wanted to hide. She had hoped to be kept out of this situation entirely. If she didn't answer, though, he'd be suspicious. Everyone in Salem was suspicious.

"We were here in this room. Reverend and Goody Parris were out, and I was here alone with the girls. I bent over the fire when Abigail pushed me. If I hadn't grabbed the hook, I would've fallen into the fire."

"Grabbed the hook? Did you burn your hands?"

"Yes, but John gave me some ointment. They are much better now." She held them out for him to see. He looked them over, then nodded.

"Did you say anything to her to provoke her to push you?"

"No sir. We were mending stockings and reciting the Psalms as Reverend Parris instructed. I got up to stoke the fire, and then it happened."

The doctor peered at her pensively. "Have the girls been associating with anyone unfamiliar lately, or someone you know the reverend wouldn't approve of?"

"They associate with who they always associate with, to my knowledge."

He sipped his cider again. His slurping noises unnerved her.

"Tituba, you're here with the girls more than anyone, is that right?"

"I suppose so, sir." She hid her shaky hands beneath the table.

"How long have the girls been demonstrating these bizarre symptoms?"

"A week or so, sir."

"What do you attribute it to?"

"I don't know, sir. I'm not a doctor." He narrowed his eyes at her comment.

Reverend Parris and John came out of the study. John had some parchment in his hand. He didn't look at his wife, but nodded to the doctor, and went straight to the door. Tituba wished he didn't have to go. She dreaded being in the room with the two men. She wanted to get up and do something, anything, but knew better. She remembered what happened the last time she disrespected the reverend in his home.

"Tituba, fix me some cider." He sat down with the doctor.

"Yes, sir." She rose, relieved. Maybe there would be no more questions for her. Maybe her part was over. If the girls didn't say anything, they would never know.

Reverend Parris spoke to the doctor. "I sent John Indian to Ingersoll's tavern to hire a messenger. I wrote some letters, beseeching the neighboring ministers to meet with me here for a prayer vigil. The gossip has already started. The girls have been seen carrying out their antics in public, I'm afraid, so we must move quickly to avoid any panic in the village. If a messenger starts out early in the morning, we should be able to meet the following day. I'll need your help, doctor, to convince them of what we believe."

"Reverend, one look at those girls, and trust me, they will believe."

"That's where you're wrong. We can't depend on them to perform at a moment's notice. There are times when they are perfectly normal, and there is no sign of the symptoms or actions you witnessed." Tituba handed him his cider and he welcomed it by immediately taking a sip. "I'll need you to relay what you've experienced here." Reverend Parris motioned to the doctor's neck.

"Aye. I'll be here, Reverend. I'd best be getting back before it gets too dark to see my way home." He took his coat from Tituba and muttered a farewell.

Tituba hated being alone with the reverend. She feared him more than she feared her father as a child. Goody Parris was ill again so she stayed in her bed upstairs. While she was aware of what was transpiring with the girls, she was too weak to concern herself other than asking Tituba about their welfare.

"Get yourself some cider, Tituba, and talk with me."

"Aye, sir." She didn't want any cider just then. She was tired of apple cider, even if it was better than the bitter water they had available in Salem. She longed for the rum she drank in Barbados.

Sometimes John could sneak her some ale from Ingersoll's, but it just wasn't the same. Not wanting to cause any unrest between her and her master, she poured up the remaining cider from the hanging pot, into the last clean mug, and sat down. She wouldn't be able to hide her shaky hands this time. He would expect her to drink the cider. He expected her to follow his every instruction without fail.

She often caught him staring at her figure. She didn't know why. His wife was the most beautiful woman Tituba had ever seen. She had been ill for some time, though, since shortly after Reverend Parris purchased her and John and brought them to America. Tituba thought it might have been the arduous journey here by ship that took its toll on Goody Parris. That, and the hard winters here. While still beautiful, Goody Parris had lost her energetic personality, and she spent less time with her husband and more time in bed. How Reverend Parris had convinced that lovely lady to marry him baffled Tituba. He was almost as ugly as the doctor, with his long, pointed nose and jutted chin. Tituba figured she had nothing to worry about in an intimate manner. The reverend was too pious to even consider adultery, even with a slave he owned. Yet, it still made her uncomfortable when he looked at her that way.

He spoke in his hard voice. "I know you know something about the girls, and it would be better for you to tell me before they do. What is your part in this?"

"I have no part, sir." He rose suddenly, reached across the table, and slapped her so hard, she lost her balance and fell to the floor. She cried out, covering her face.

"Liar! You are the devil's handmaiden! I see how you have been walking around here the past week. You have the devil's mark of guilt. I will ask you again. What is your part?"

"Please, sir. I don't know why the girls act that way." That much was the truth. She had never seen anything like it.

He sat down, and waved her away. "Finish preparing our evening meal. I'll deal with you later."

He looked weary, and Tituba almost felt sorry for him, but her stinging cheek prevented the emotion.

John came home just as she was clearing the table. She had brought up food for the girls and Goody Parris. There were no more incidents with the girls that evening. They allowed her to feed them, with the reverend standing by, watching. She was glad he was there, though, in case Abigail became violent again. She helped Betty with the bedpan, and changed Abigail's dressings since she wasn't allowed to be free from her ropes. Tituba pitied the girl, but she had to admit she felt much safer with her tied up. The reverend retired to his study, as he often did in the evenings, so Tituba greeted her husband with hushed tones.

He tipped her face and examined her swollen cheek. He looked sadly at her for a moment, then took her hand and patted it gently.

"Did you find a messenger?" she asked him.

"Yes. It wasn't easy, though. I sat for hours, waiting, and asking anyone that walked in. No one likes to roam alone too far with all of the Indian attacks. Even when I found a willing man, I'm afraid it took every penny the reverend gave me for bargaining."

"Are you hungry?"

"No. I ate at the tavern. Goodman Ingersoll took pity on me and gave me some ale and bread. I just want to rest, woman. I suggest you do the same. The next few days are going to be trying ones, if those girls continue with their ways."

Tituba didn't want to talk about the girls. She was terrified of what was happening. She just wanted to curl up with her husband on their pallet by the fire and pretend they were back in Barbados. Oh, how she wanted to be warm again.

CHAPTER FOUR

Sonneillon screamed curses at the sky. Rebecca Nurse still prayed.
He had placed his strong talons around her skull, and wreaked havoc
on her mind. He had reached through the core of her, and squeezed
her soul. He ordered every demon of discouragement at his disposal
to attack her. Still, she prayed. He used her aging, weakening body,
but she prayed for others who were ill. He used her sadness over the
apathy of the church members, but she prayed for their repentance.
He used her loneliness and reminded her that her children were too
busy for her, but she prayed for them and their families. He used her
discernment that Reverend Parris cared too much about rules and
not enough about hearts, but she prayed for him, too. Nothing
discouraged her from prayer. Her sisters were the same way. Mary
Easty and Sarah Cloyce couldn't be budged from their consistent
prayers any more than their sister, though he had tried every spiritual
weapon at his disposal. These faithful Christians and their prayers!
Why couldn't they be like the others? All it took to discourage them
was a few daily annoyances and they readily shirked their prayer
duties. He cursed again, and spread his wings, ready for flight. He'd
need to see Lucifer right away. He had an idea, but he'd need
permission before he pursued it. He hated to leave these warriors, for
he knew all too well that they had angels assigned to them. In fact,

one was standing guard nearby. Neither had acknowledged the other, but he knew the angel was just as aware of his presence as Sonneillon was of his. If his plan was carried out, it wouldn't matter how many angels were assigned to them. Dead Christians couldn't pray. He smirked as he lifted himself from the ground.

~⌒~

Uriel watched him fly away. He looked at the faithful warrior with her head bowed, tears flowing down her wrinkled face. He walked over to her and wrapped his wings around her, offering her comfort from the Most High.

Moments later, Rebecca walked the muddy road to her young friend's house. Lydia and her father lived on a small farm a couple of miles from Rebecca. Rebecca felt sorry for Goodman Knapp. That young man had loved his wife. He had adored Lydia, too. Lydia was a beautiful child, and had a delightful personality. After Goody Knapp passed away, Rebecca and her sister Mary had helped the grieving Goodman Knapp with his little girl. They took turns caring for her, and both grew to love her dearly, although Rebecca spent more time with her than Mary did. They had thought that he'd only need time to get over his loss. Lydia was now fourteen years old. Goodman Knapp still grieved. Lydia still needed the sisters to care for her. That was the reason Rebecca was making the journey to the Knapp home. Her old joints ached from the cold, but she knew she must speak to the girl.

She saw the woman and child before they saw her. Little Dorcas was picking up snow from the path and putting it in her mouth. Her mother Sarah pulled at her arm, hurrying her along. Rebecca's heart softened. Everyone in Salem village treated the Good family as though they were the slimy film on the top of the butter cream. Something to be scraped off and tossed away. Rebecca knew Sarah before hard times had hit her. She had always been abrasive in nature, speaking her mind boldly, but she had been a caring woman. She and Rebecca had even shared a friendship of sorts. Now, Rebecca dreaded passing her on the road.

"Well, well. Look who it be. The sainted Goody Nurse. Going to see that uppity girl again? Her pa let us sleep in their barn a few nights ago. Had to be out at sunrise, though. It wasn't her idea, mind you. She didn't want no part of us. Looks like ye be needing to bestow some of your Christian values upon that child, Goody Nurse. She's obviously not as saintly as you." Goody Good wiped her sleeve across her nose. Rebecca sighed. She remembered sitting down for tea with this woman. She had kept a tidy home. You wouldn't know it now, the poor soul. Not only had her appearance and manners deteriorated, but her bitterness took her joy as well. There was a time when Sarah had laughed. Rebecca decided to ignore the remarks directed at Lydia.

"Good morning, Goody Good. Where are you and little Dorcas headed today?"

"Here and there. And nowhere."

They exchanged stares for a moment. Rebecca thought she saw a flicker in Sarah's eyes. Was she remembering the old days, too?

"Here. Take these eggs. I was bringing them to Lydia, but you and the child need them more. Go to the edge of the woods and wait until my Francis is gone from the house, then go sit by the fire a while. You'll have to be gone, though, by the time he comes back."

"I'll take the eggs, but I won't be going near your place, Goody Nurse. Not after my last encounter with your man."

"Suit yourself." She handed Sarah the eggs from the basket. She knew better than to argue with Goody Good. Besides, she'd rather not risk Francis finding the pair in her house. He didn't like Sarah's constant begging for herself and her child. Rebecca figured it had a lot to do with how she spoke to everyone more than her neediness. Her husband was a kind man and wouldn't want anyone to be hungry, but Sarah made it hard to feel anything but indignation toward her. The village regarded her as a cast off, a pesky annoyance that they'd rather not acknowledge. As for the child, people tended to care more for pretty children. Not ones who looked like Dorcas. Dorcas had inherited her father's flattened nose and wide cheeks, and her mother's narrowed eyes. Rebecca knew she'd look better if she were cleaned up, but her knotted hair, and dirty cheeks and clothes added to her already unsightly appearance.

Sarah handed two of the eggs to Dorcas, and placed the others in her apron pockets. Rebecca didn't expect gratitude, so she just walked on in the direction of the Knapp place.

Paul Knapp was splitting wood when she arrived. He didn't look surprised to see her. He nodded at her and went back to his chore. Rebecca knocked on the door and smiled brightly when Lydia opened it. The girl looked delightfully surprised.

"Goody Nurse!" She reached out and assisted the older woman into the house. "Come sit by the fire. I'll heat you up some cider."

"No, child. No cider. Do you have any tea?"

"I'm sorry, but no."

"Just the fire will do then. My old bones aren't what they used to be." She sat down, welcoming the soothing warmth and the relief it brought.

"It's been such a time since I've seen you, Goody Nurse. How's Goody Easty? She was ill for a while, wasn't she? I wanted to get by to see her, but the cold was quite dreadful then."

Rebecca waved her excuse off. "Aye, child. She didn't expect a visit. I looked after her and she recovered nicely." The truth was not as lighthearted as Rebecca made it. Mary had been close to death, but Rebecca had sat by her bed and prayed for three days. She begged

God not to take her sister, her best friend. God had answered her prayer. She and Mary had always been the closest of the sisters. The baby, Sarah Cloyce, was much younger, so the older sisters had spoiled her. They were all close, but the older sisters had a strong bond that had never diminished, even after marriage and children.

"Do you have eggs in the basket, Goody Nurse? I have some salt meat I could give you for them."

"No, child. I had some, but I gave them to Goody Good and the child Dorcas. I'm sorry,"

Lydia frowned. "Goody Good. All she does is take and take. Why should we give up our winter goods for a beggar who doesn't care for herself?"

"The Good Book instructs us to take care of the poor, Lydia."

"The poor? She's not poor! She's lazy!"

"Aye. She is that now. She has given up, I'm afraid. There was a time when-"

"I know. You've told me about how she used to be, but right now is what matters. She walks around this village like she owns the place and expects us to provide for her like she's earned it." Rebecca saw anger in Lydia's voice and heard it in her tone. She had never seen Lydia act this way before. It didn't sit well with Rebecca. She decided to get right to the reason she decided to visit the girl.

"Lydia, there is talk in the village about the Parris household. Have you heard it?"

Lydia's face paled. "I've heard something about how they're acting in strange ways."

Rebecca reached forward and took Lydia's trembling hands. She had been right. The girl knew something. "Lydia, they have been diagnosed by the doctor and neighboring ministers as being bewitched."

Lydia jerked her hands away. "Bewitched!" She jumped out of her chair. "That's not possible!"

"I'm afraid it is. Or at least that is what's being said."

"Who is saying it? Did you hear that from the doctor himself?" Lydia's high-pitched voice revealed her anxiety.

"Mary talked to the doctor when he visited her house to make sure her lungs had healed from the infection. He told her that he witnessed the girls acting in a bewitched fashion." She went on to describe the details of Dr. Griggs' account.

Lydia sat down in the chair again and began to sob into her hands. Rebecca grabbed onto her shoulders. "Lydia, look at me, child."

She just sobbed harder.

"Lydia."

The girl raised her head and began swiping the tears from her cheeks.

"What do you know about this?"

"What do you mean?"

"I mean, what do you know about the girls' supposed bewitchment? I know you know something."

"I don't know anything, Goody Nurse."

"Those girls are part of your usual crowd, am I right? Goody Parris mentioned that you were visiting a few days before the first symptoms started."

"There were several of us there, Goody Nurse, including Ann Putnam."

Rebecca figured that girl's name would be included. She was a dominant leader like her mother.

"Reverend Parris wants to start an inquiry regarding the girls' condition. Your name was mentioned, along with the other girls. The reverend seems to think all of you were up to something the day you were at the parsonage." Rebecca watched as Lydia fought to keep a straight face.

"We were just talking, Goody Nurse."

"With Tituba?" Rebecca had been wary of the slave and her customs. Tituba came from a strange land with strange beliefs. She had a feeling Lydia had been exposed to those beliefs. She was a vulnerable and impressionable girl, and she had a weakness for pleasing others.

"Yes, Tituba was there, too." Lydia stared at the fire. Rebecca could see she would get nowhere with Lydia today. She would have to keep praying.

"If you don't want to tell me, that's fine. Just know I'm praying for you, child. The way those girls are acting isn't normal. Reverend Parris is not a happy man. He has everyone in the village riled up and looking for answers. You just be careful. He is looking for someone to blame."

Lydia jumped when her father entered the house. He looked between her and Rebecca curiously.

"Hello, Goody Nurse. I trust you are well." He stacked some kindling on the hearth.

"I'm as well as an old woman can be in these cold temperatures, Goodman Knapp. I just came for a short spell. I wanted to visit with your girl here to see how she's getting along."

He stopped stacking for a moment and looked up. "Am I to assume the gossip is true?"

Rebecca saw Lydia pleading with her through her eyes. Rebecca chose her words carefully. "If you're speaking of the reverend's girls, then, yes, I suppose it's true, Goodman Knapp. I decided to check on Lydia. I know it must be upsetting, her being friends with the girls."

Goodman Knapp nodded and went back to stacking wood. Lydia sighed relief. Rebecca stood up and pulled her coat tight, bid them goodbye, and started back home. She had hoped to spend more time with Lydia. She had also hoped Lydia would open up about what had gone on between all of the girls that day with Tituba. Rebecca shivered, but it was more than the cold that made her shiver. She had a bad feeling about all of this. She just couldn't shake the sense of dread since she had first heard of the girls' antics.

All the way home Rebecca whispered the twenty-third psalm, and all the way home, Uriel followed her. He was quite aware of the demons snarling and sniffling behind him. They cowered and kept their distance, but they watched and waited for any opportunity to attack the elderly saint who clung to her faith. He had greeted Semiel, who was assigned to the girl. They both had no reports of any new actions to take. They were simply ordered to guard. The angel felt strength as Rebecca quoted scripture and prayed. His job was easier. Guarding a praying saint was always easier. He looked back at the house they just left. That girl had great fear. Semiel had his work cut out for him.

"Now that she's gone, why don't you tell me what's going on? What do you know about those girls?"

Lydia didn't know how to answer her father. He could surely see her nervousness, and perhaps even hear the thunderous beat of her heart.

"It's that slave Tituba, Father. She is always telling strange tales and talking about strange rituals. She probably put a curse on them or something."

Her father said nothing. Did he believe her? She didn't want to get Tituba into trouble, but what she said was true. She just omitted the part about how she and the other girls readily agreed to participate in those stories and rituals.

"You stay away from the Parris house from now on. Don't

mention any of this to anyone, do you hear?"

"Yes, Father." The tone of his voice unsettled her. He sounded…afraid.

⌒

Semiel saw the large fear demon approaching the house. The smaller demon he had seen the other night was not present. He looked for Belias, too, but didn't see a sign of him anywhere. He must be wary. Belias could be hiding. This could be a trap.

"Stand aside, and let me pass!" The hideous creature demanded.

"You know I cannot do that."

"That's your choice. Don't say you weren't warned."

The nasty demon drew his sword and swiped at Semiel's head, missing by a few inches. Semiel felt the blackness surround him, and he longed for the prayer cover to lighten the darkness that deepened with each attempt to ward it off.

The fire singed him when the sword met his flesh. The blow weakened him, and the demon laughed. Semiel swung his own sword, but the large demon had speed as well as strength. Belias had chosen his warrior well. Why this girl? Why did he have to guard her so closely, and why did Satan want her so much? The answers didn't matter now, though. He flew up into the sky, then dived down and brought his sword onto the demon's head. The creature screamed as light split his spirit in half. He crawled to the door of the house, clearly attempting to reach the girl.

"Not today, devil." Semiel struck him again, clipping his wing. The demon howled and flew away, with his injured wing barely flapping in the wind.

Semiel leaned against the house, breathing in air. The light surrounded him again. He looked up to see Raphael grinning at him.

"Oh, now you show up. Now that all of the hard stuff is over."

"You handled it well."

"I'm not so sure about that. We need prayers, Raphael. Why don't we have more prayers? These Puritans pride themselves on their prayers."

"That's just it, Semiel. Pride has no place in prayers. It makes them useless."

Semiel shook his head. "That's the problem with outward obedience when the heart is dead." He didn't know how many more battles he could fight with just a few worthy prayers.

"A single, worthy prayer, from a sincere saint, is more powerful than you think."

"Would you quit reading my mind, Raphael? It' quite unsettling."

"I'm a captain in the angel army, Semiel. It's what I do." He laughed and flew back to his post high above Salem.

CHAPTER FIVE

Lydia gasped as Ann Putnam grabbed her arm and pulled her behind the barn.

"What are you doing? You're pinching my arm!"

"Where have you been? You haven't been to meeting the last two Sundays, and now everyone's starting to question why."

"My father wouldn't let me. He won't let me go anywhere, not even to see the sisters."

"Why?"

"You know why! Witchcra-"

Ann's hand stopped Lydia's mouth from completing the dreaded word. "Hush, you fool. If you know what's good for you, you won't say that word aloud. I refuse to be blamed for these absurd episodes that Abigail and Betty are so unashamedly displaying for all to see."

"You've witnessed them?"

"Indeed I have. You would've, too, had you been at the meeting last Sunday. They were so disruptive, Reverend Parris couldn't keep up with his sermon. I've never seen such folly. Anytime the reverend would say Jesus' name or talk about redemption, they'd scream out, as if in pain and agony. Oh, and what they screamed. I once sneaked inside the back of the tavern out of curiosity, and I heard strange words I'd not heard before. Abigail and Betty were screaming those same words and throwing their Bibles at the reverend. Then, they grabbed their throats and made choking sounds." Ann let go of Lydia's arm and sat down on a barrel, playing with bottom of her shoe. "It looks like nonsense to me. Their theatrical behavior is impressive, but I'm not convinced." She peered up at Lydia.

Lydia squirmed under Ann's stare. Why did she come to see her? What did she want? Ann never did anything unless it was to her advantage.

"What do you think is the matter with them?" Lydia asked.

"Nothing."

"What do you mean? The doctor said…"

"No matter what the doctor said. He doesn't know about their motive."

"What motive?"

"Do you remember what we did with Tituba, Lydia? If anyone found out what we did, we'd be accused of-"

She paused, then whispered, "Witchcraft."

Lydia shook her head. "No. No one would find out. We made a promise. Besides, what does that have to do with Abigail and Betty?"

Instead of answering, Ann asked another question. "Did you talk to Goody Good that night, Lydia?"

Lydia stilled. "Why do you ask?"

"Because Goody Good started wagging her tongue the next day, to anyone who would listen. She said she saw us and that we were up to something that day with Tituba at the Parris household. She named all of our names, including Betty and Abigail's. She said when she asked you about it, you acted nervous."

"Ann, Goody Good is always muttering about something. No one will pay her any mind."

"Are you certain of that? People in the village know how she gets around and watches everyone and everything. Remember how she disclosed the details of Goodman Hester's wife when she committed adultery? That woman ended up in the stocks for days, and then she had to move away."

Lydia looked around nervously. "I still do not understand how this has anything to do with Abigail and Betty possibly faking their symptoms."

"It's simple. Accuse or be accused."

"Are you saying they're going to start pointing fingers at...people?"

"Well, of course I can't say for certain, but I wouldn't put it past Abigail to convince her little cousin to cooperate in this nonsense. Or anyone else who was afraid." She tilted her head at Lydia and grabbed her hand. She smiled in that way that said she intended on getting something.

"You're not afraid, are you Lydia?"

"I...I...don't know."

"There's no reason to be afraid. As long as you stick to the agreement not to say anything about that day. They will soon be questioning all of us. You will stick to the agreement, won't you, Lydia?" Ann squeezed Lydia's hand so hard it hurt.

Lydia winced. "Yes." She hated being afraid of Ann, but she was even more afraid of being accused of witchcraft.

Ann released her grip. "Good. I'm glad we had this talk. I'd be most distressed to learn that you had joined Abigail in her little game."

Lydia hardly thought this could be considered a little game. Witchcraft was a serious offense and it terrified Lydia to think of what would happen if those girls named her as a witch. She shuddered.

"You'd better go now, Ann. My father would take the strap to me if he caught me talking to you right now."

"You'd better talk to your father and convince him to let you attend meeting. You don't want to give cause to any accusations or suspicions."

She looked around the barn, then darted away. Lydia wondered if she was headed to visit the other girls. Or maybe she had already discussed the matter with them. Was Lydia the only one who had stayed away? Her father seemed particularly afraid. Why was he so afraid? He couldn't possibly know what she and the other girls had done.

The two guardians who had stood at Lydia's side nodded to one another. Semiel had recruited Raguel when he saw Ann approaching. She had several snarling demons attached to her, and Semiel didn't want to take any chances. Raguel flew off as Lydia headed back to the house. Semiel decided to stay closer to her. He liked the roof for visibility, but Lydia's fear was strong, so he thought it better to stick as close to her as possible.

The Most High hadn't revealed Lucifer's plan, so he and the other warriors must obey orders and wait. He wondered why the demons were only harassing Ann. She was a strong candidate for possession. She had no prayer cover like Lydia. Ann had no protection against the Prince of Air. It was only a matter of time, unless, like so many, she didn't need to be possessed to do the devil's work. Semiel had seen her heart.

As Ann walked back to her homestead, her assigned demons lashed out at each other. The thirst for power surrounded her, and Ann's thoughts followed suit. She knew Lydia was afraid of her. It excited her. The other girls were afraid, too. Ann was the youngest, besides

Betty, but the older girls complied easily with her ideas and demands. Except Abigail. Ann fumed at the idea that she'd leave Ann out of such a brilliant plan. Ann hated to admit that it was brilliant. She should have thought of it herself. How dare Abigail not include her! After all, it was her idea to make the pact of secrecy to protect them all. Well, Ann wasn't about to let Abigail win. She'd talk to Mother. She'd help her. We'll see who accuses who, she thought. She hurriedly made her way to the Parris household. She'd see what Abigail was really up to first.

Ann raised her hand to knock on the door, but paused as she heard the voices on the other side.

"Who harms you child?" Ann didn't recognize the man's voice.

"You tell us, now, Betty. Tell us who torments you and Abigail." Ann heard Reverend Parris' voice this time.

"Tituba! It's Tituba, Father! She pinches us, and tells us we have to sign the devil's book."

"No sir! I am no witch, sir! I do not hurt these children!" Tituba's voice sounded frantic. Ann walked around to the side of the house. She stood on her tiptoes to look through the small window.

"Betty, Tituba wasn't even in the room when you cried out last. How could she hurt you?" This time it was Goody Parris who spoke to her daughter in a gentle tone.

"It's her specter, mother. She comes to me in the middle of the night, too. It's her! She chokes me and I can't breathe!"

Tituba stepped up to the girl. "Betty, you speak a lie!" Ann flinched as Reverend Parris knocked the slave to the floor. She cried out in pain, but did not get up. Instead, she covered her face with her arm and lay there, motionless.

Where was Abigail? She looked around the room as best she could from the tiny, darkened window, but only saw Betty, her parents, and three gentlemen Ann now recognized as neighboring ministers.

One stared at Tituba on the ground. He cleared his throat and spoke so softly Ann had to strain to hear.

"As the problem is contained to your household, Reverend, I advise you to sit still and wait. See what the Lord reveals in time."

"Reverend Hale, I will not have the devil's witchcraft destroying this village. Time is all he needs to win over the souls of these people so intent on indulging in their sins. This has already continued long enough. You've seen with your own eyes how these girls are tortured." He pointed at Tituba. "A tormentor has been named. I'm ready for legal recourse. Are you behind me on this or will you slumber in your apathy until this evil spreads far and wide, beyond this village?"

"Reverend Parris, this isn't a church meeting, and we don't need one of your sermons. I still say wait. If, as you say, Tituba was socializing with other girls, perhaps it's prudent to see if they exhibit similar symptoms. It could be the devil has decided to prey upon your children, and yours alone. Not every evil is witchcraft. Some evil is the devil acting on his own. If that's the case, prayer could resolve the issue."

Ann's toes burned at the pressure to stand tall enough to peer through the window, so she slowly backed away.

"Eavesdropping be the devil's pastime, girl." Ann jumped at the gravelly voice.

"Goody Good. I was just…"

"I know what you were just doing. Don't try to make up one of your stories to me, little Ann." Ann hated to be called 'Little Ann'. Sarah Good knew that. Ann's eyes squinted in anger.

"What are you doing here, Goody Good? Come to beg for a morsel of food to get you through another miserable day?" The demons laughed into her ear.

Goody Good resisted the urge to slap the girl. She didn't know a warrior stilled her hand. The demons snarled at Raguel. The demon of bitterness that had attached to Sarah Good shrunk back when Raguel arrived, but he noticed the warrior wasn't drawing his sword. He wasn't driving the demons away, only limiting their power. Bitterness claimed Sarah's mind again.

"You forget yourself, child. Mind how you speak to your elder, I saw you, you know. I saw how you talked to Tituba. I heard what Tituba said to you as you left this house that day."

"No one would believe you. You're a slanderous outcast, with a vulgar tongue. People grow weary of your begging, and your vile talk."

"They'll believe me. They're looking for someone to blame for those girls. They've already named Tituba. Who's next? You?" She laughed a cruel laugh, then spat on the ground in front of Ann. Ann jumped back in disgust.

"Watch yourself, Goody Good. My father-"

"Your father is a sniveling rat, feeding on the petticoat of your mother; and your mother is as uppity with pride as you are. You know what they say about pride, Little Ann?" Sarah reached out her foot, and swept across Ann's legs, knocking her to the ground.

"They fall." She cackled a laugh and disappeared into the woods nearby. Ann wanted to scream, but she didn't want to alert those inside the house of her presence. She no longer needed to talk to Abigail. She'd let Abigail and Betty play out their scheme, for their scheme now played right along with her new plan.

As she stood up and dusted off her dress, she looked toward the woods. "We'll see who falls, Goody Good."

Raguel watched as the demons clung to the girl when she left the Parris homestead. They were whispering in her ears, massaging her skull with their long talons. Unless someone intervened and prayed for the girl, she would belong to the Prince of Air. He looked at the direction where Goody Good had headed. She still had hope. The sisters prayed for her.

⌒

Reverend Nicholas Noyes left the Parris house with Reverend Hale. They walked a bit before Noyes spoke.

"I agree with Reverend Parris."

"Oh?"

"Yes. We need to move quickly to prevent a widespread infection of this evil."

"We're not talking about a physical disease, Reverend Noyes."

"Aren't we? Did you see that child? She clearly suffers."

"Yes, but that doesn't mean others will catch it."

"We do not know the extent of Tituba's influence. We must observe the other girls, and perhaps question the villagers. We may have a lair of witches in Salem."

"I fear we could cause a widespread infection of paranoia if we do not proceed cautiously."

"Witchcraft is contagious, Reverend Hale."

"As are ideas, Reverend Noyes."

The other man stopped walking and faced Reverend Hale. "Are you minimizing the effect of these evil forces?"

"Of course not. I can't, however, overlook the power of suggestion. Its influence is as strong as witchcraft. I've seen it at other times, in different situations. People readily latch on to suggested ideas, and then they can't be convinced otherwise once suggestion has its hold."

"Well, your opinion is certainly curious. Don't you agree with Cotton Mather's findings? His research and personal observances on witchcraft are notably the highest in the field."

"I'm well aware of Reverend Mather's writings and his oral

accounts of what he has seen and experienced, but even he might agree that our community would be better served if we didn't start a witch hunt at every door."

Reverend Noyes took off his hat and toyed with the rim. "He should be contacted then if we find the accusation against Tituba credible. As our next step is to observe the afflicted girls a bit more, and further question the slave, we'll soon arrive at a decision on whether or not to petition for arrest warrants. In the meantime, Reverend, I'd advise that you think seriously before discounting the idea that there are more witches out there. Usually where there's one, there are at least two." He placed his hat back on his head and mounted his horse. "Good day, Reverend Hale."

As Reverend Hale mounted his own horse, he didn't feel it was a good day. In fact, he felt it just might be the start of many bad days to come. He prayed all the way home.

As each man steered their horses in different directions, different forces accompanied them. Raguel the warrior guarded the faithful minister home, but Reverend Noyes had no idea that the very evil forces he feared had actually attached themselves to him, sneering and snarling over his mind and spirit.

CHAPTER SIX

Lydia sat with her father in the Salem Village meeting house. Paul Knapp had surprised his daughter when he announced to her on Friday that they would attend meeting. He had been to Ingersoll's and Lydia wondered what news he'd heard to prompt him to attend meeting again. He acted odd these days, even stranger than his usual demeanor. Lydia hated the meeting house. It wasn't just the hard seats. In the winter, the cold seeped through her clothing, bringing shivers that wouldn't leave her body until she stood in front of her fireplace, heating the afternoon meal. Chores on the Sabbath were forbidden, but her father had long ago abandoned the cold mush on Sunday in favor of warm bean porridge or stew. Summertime brought wet heat, and with the wet heat, the bugs swarmed. The men often smoked the meeting house to rid it of the loathsome insects, but there were so many of them, it only seemed to decrease them by a small margin. Gnats, mosquitos, and wasps swarmed, making it difficult for the minister to hold his congregation's attention. Lydia didn't know which was worse, as both winter and summer made for miserable Sabbath days. Spring and fall never seemed to last very long, while the treacherous seasons dragged on relentlessly.

Reverend Parris' eyes roamed the room as he spoke, and then stopped when he saw her. She sat very still as he stared and she stared back at him, trying to keep her face blank. She mustn't make her fear known. When he finally looked away, she scanned the room for the sisters. How she longed to speak with Goody Nurse or Goody Easty. She shook that thought away. She couldn't tell them. She remembered Ann's warning. She spotted the sisters with their husbands at the back of the room. Their younger sister, Goody Cloyce, sat near them, her husband also at her side.

"God's judgement be on those who do not adhere to the Law of Moses. Redemption draweth nigh to those who will seek it, but for those who deny the commandments of our Lord, eternity is lost to them. For it is Jesus Christ who said-"

"It burns! It burns!"

Lydia jumped in her seat at the horrible scream. She sought the source, and discovered Abigail Williams flopping in her seat a few rows back. The girl's body twisted and contorted in ways Lydia had never seen. It looked so odd. Everyone just stared. No one moved.

"Child, what burns?" The reverend yelled out. "Tell us who or what harms thee."

"Nooooooo. I'll not speak the name! The name harms me!" Abigail dropped to the floor, writhing in agony. Her eyes bulged, and she coughed a gurgling cough. Beside her, Betty started screaming, holding her ears.

"I repeat, who harms thee? Are they in this room?" Reverend Parris walked closer to the girls, but kept a safe distance.

"Pray over them, Reverend. Quote Scripture." Goody Nurse spoke quietly, but during a lull in the screams so that the entire room heard her.

"I believe I know how to deal with evil such as this, Goody Nurse." He dismissed her and turned back to the girls.

"Jesus, we commit these poor souls to your care…"

"No!" Betty screamed.

"It's burning! It's burning!" yelled Abigail, still twisting on the floor.

"She's pinching me! My arm! She's pinching my arm!" Heads turned to the new voice, screaming in pain. Lydia couldn't believe it. There, in the back, on the row across from the sisters, was Ann Putnam, holding her arm, and screaming louder than the other girls.

"Who's pinching you?" Her mother Alice asked.

"It's Goody Good! She's there! See? She hurts us!"

"Ann, Goody Good is not here! You know she doesn't attend meeting," her father said.

"It's her! That's her specter, floating in the air! Don't let her pinch me!" Ann screamed again, and clung to her mother. Her screams seemed to ignite louder screams in Abigail and Betty.

"Reverend, do something!" Thomas Putnam, Ann's father, yelled at the minister.

Rebecca Nurse stood and slapped her hand on her worn, leather Bible. "In the name of Jesus, I command thee to go! Evil spirits, leave now!"

Abigail and Betty stopped screaming, and looked around, dazed. Abigail rose from the floor and sat on the pew beside her cousin. Reverend Parris frowned at Goody Nurse, but he seemed relieved.

"She's still here!" Ann screamed from the back. Everyone, including Abigail and Betty, looked back at her. She pointed to the ceiling. "Goody Good is still here! She's holding the book. She wants me to sign it! There's Tituba, too! They want to hurt us!"

Rebecca Nurse shook her head at Ann. She looked at her sister Mary, who looked back at her. They seemed to know something. Was Ann faking it as Lydia suspected? Didn't Ann say, "accuse or be accused"? Abigail and Betty certainly were convincing in their agony. Lydia had never seen a body twist in ways like that before. It didn't even seem possible to get your limbs in those positions without breaking the bones. Lydia had never known Betty Parris to lie, either. She was a kind girl, and never wanted to harm anyone. Could her fear be prompting her to act out a plan with her cousin? Abigail was conniving, but when she sat back up, she had looked just as surprised as everyone else when Ann screamed. Of course, Ann could be planning something on her own, and Abigail had no idea she was going to join their bizarre behavior today.

Betty started screaming again, pointing at the ceiling, just as Ann had done. "It is Goody Good! And Tituba, too!" Abigail screamed with her.

"Sabbath meeting is adjourned!" The reverend grabbed his niece and his daughter by the arm, and headed out the door. The Putnams grabbed Ann and followed. The congregation started talking all at once. Lydia's father remained silent for a moment, then he stood. "Lydia, let's get home." Lydia wanted to run to the sisters, but she didn't dare disobey her father after all of the commotion. There was panic in the room. As they passed Goody Nurse and Goody Easty, her father nodded in their direction. They spoke a hello, then smiled at Lydia. Lydia wanted to cry. She longed to be little again, sitting on their laps and listening to the psalms they sang when she was sick or couldn't sleep. She longed to feel their hands stroke her hair. She just wanted to feel safe again. She didn't know if she'd ever feel safe again.

⁓

"That girl is terrified." Mary watched Lydia retreat with her father.

"As she should be, Mary. We witnessed something today. Satan's working in Salem."

"He's been working in Salem, Rebecca, for a long time now."

"Yes, but his presence is heightened now. We have a weak congregation, a Pharisee pastor, and children who are seeking what they ought not to seek. It's an invitation for demonic activity."

"Are you talking about the girls' outbursts? Do you believe it was demonic?" Her sister Sarah asked. Her eyes reflected fear.

"Yes, I do, sister, at least for Abigail and little Betty."

"What about the Putnam girl?"

"I have my doubts about that girl. Her outbursts were different somehow. Did you notice how her screams didn't match the times she grabbed her arm?"

"What do you make of her, then? Why would she pretend, and why name Goody Good as a tormentor?"

"I have my theories on that, too, but one thing is for certain, though."

Mary frowned. "What?"

"Regardless whether or not Ann is pretending or suffering as the other girls are, Satan is working either way. These Pharisee religion practices have played right into his hands."

"How so?" Sarah asked.

"If people are constantly concerned with what they do and don't do, in order to gain God's favor, then it promotes fear. Fear is the opposite of God's love."

"Right." Mary said. "His grace is about freedom, and those girls definitely aren't free, even if they are pretending."

"Yes. We need to pray, sisters. We need to pray unceasingly," Rebecca said. The other two knelt with her right then.

~⌒~

Sonneillon watch as his demons spat at the meeting house. They didn't like to be kicked out. The warriors stood guard at the door. They began to shine brighter, and the demons recoiled. Prayer! Those ladies were praying! Something had to be done about the sisters, especially the one that spoke His name as a commandment for them to leave.

Ann Putnam had sure helped their cause when she succumbed to her flesh and carried out her own plan. The demons laughed as they recalled how afraid the congregation looked when they thought Goody Good's evil spirit was going to swoop down on them and harm them. Verrier and Carreau had bowed as the other demons congratulated them on taking the forms of Tituba and Sarah Good for Betty to see. Abigail had just followed the suggestion.

The plan was working. Sonneillon smiled. He sat in a nearby tree where he had observed the meeting. He saw Uriel on top of the church, watching him. He shone bright as a star. For a fleeting moment, Sonneillon choked back a bit of fear, but then he remembered they were just getting started. Yes, death was coming to Salem village. It would be fast and furious and those prayer warriors wouldn't know what hit them. Who was going to pray then? With his small victory cry, he shot up from the tree limb and swooped over the meeting house, taunting Uriel.

The mighty winged warrior stood firm, gaining strength in the prayers rising up. If he had to fight, he'd be ready.

⌒

That night, Abigail settled into bed next to Betty. "Did you really see Goody Good and Tituba in the meetinghouse, Betty?"

"Yes. Don't you believe me?"

"Had you asked a few weeks ago, then no, I wouldn't, but now? Well, I think I'd believe anything."

"Are you scared, Abigail?"

"Yes."

The two girls hugged one another until they fell asleep. Sleep didn't last long for little Betty, though. She woke to see Abigail hovering over her.

"Abigail? What are you doing?" Her cousin floated in air right above her, her eyes glowed red. Betty screamed, but her cry strangled as Abigail wrapped her hands around her throat. "Surrender!" The deep voice sounded strange, as if it shouted inside her head, and not in front of her. Betty tried to free herself, but Abigail held tightly. I don't want to die, thought Betty.

"Then, surrender to me now! Do my bidding." She hadn't spoken aloud, yet Abigail acted as if she had. This isn't Abigail, she thought. Just when she felt she couldn't hold on any more, she felt Abigail's grip on her loosen. Her cousin's eyes rolled back into her head and she fell back on the bed in pain.

"Abigail! Abigail!" Betty screamed in terror. Footsteps sounded on the stairs.

⁓

The demon left Abigail's body, hissed at the winged warrior who had attacked him, and flung himself through the ceiling into the night sky. The angel stood by, ready to defend the Parris child again, if the need arose. That was a close one. He'd have to stick by this girl. Raphael ordered him to keep her safe, and to escort her until she had been completely freed from possession.

⁓

Reverend Parris entered the room, and ran to Betty's side. He held her as she cried. Abigail watched. What would it be like to be loved by her uncle? She wasn't sweet like Betty. She knew that. She just couldn't be like Betty. When a thought entered her mind, she just had to utter it. Was that so bad?

"Did I hurt you, Betty?" she asked.

"You choked me."

Abigail saw the marks on the girl's neck. "I didn't mean it. It wasn't me."

"That will be enough. We know what it was." Reverend Parris

tucked his daughter under her covers. He motioned for Abigail to climb in beside her.

Well, at least her uncle didn't blame her. She knew he had concern for her, but oh, how she wished he and her aunt would treasure her like they treasured her little cousin. Abigail was just an extra burden, a product of Christian charity, and a family obligation. They were obligated to care for her. What a horrible acknowledgement, Abigail thought. She'd always be an obligation to her family. They wouldn't love her, just care for her out of charity and responsibility.

"Is it safe for me to sleep here, Uncle?"

"Maybe you're right. We can make a bed for you downstairs."

"No!" Betty sat up. "I can't sleep alone. Please, Father, let her stay."

"If she stays, we'll need to tie her up again."

Abigail shook her head frantically. "No, please, Uncle. I'll go downstairs."

"Father, it will be fine. She won't hurt me. Please, let her stay with me. No ropes."

He sighed. "Of course, daughter. She can stay." He walked out, leaving them alone again.

"I'm sorry, Betty."

"'Tis not your fault, Abigail. You know that. But what made you stop? I thought you'd kill me."

"I don't know. I don't really remember anything."

"You looked as though something had hurt you, and whatever it was helped me. It stopped you from choking me."

Abigail didn't know what to say to that. "We'd better sleep now, Betty. I pray we do sleep for once."

The warrior watched over them that night. They both slept peacefully for the first time in weeks.

Tituba lay awake, terrified of what she'd heard. Reverend Parris entered the keeping room and kicked her husband's side.

"I need you up, John. I need you to start early on your chores so you can deliver a message to Thomas Putnam."

"Yes, sir." John immediately set about stoking the fire, and adding more wood. Tituba pretended to sleep. She couldn't face her husband yet. Her precious Betty had already named her, which hurt enough, but now that Ann Putnam had named her and Sarah Good. Tituba hated Ann Putnam. She was an evil child. Was this it? Was her own husband delivering a message that would start the course for her doom? She wished John would say something, but what could he say? He was a slave. His voice didn't count.

"Tituba?" He kneeled and whispered above her head.

She rolled over and looked up into his face. He reached down and wiped her tears as he had done so often since they had come to Salem with the reverend.

"We could run away, Tituba."

"Where would we go, husband? It's winter. We wouldn't last a week. The ports wouldn't let us on a boat. Our skin color would give us away immediately."

"We could find a way. At least we'd be together."

"It's me that's accused, not you. I won't ask you to risk your life."

"Wife, you know I'd die for you, don't you?"

"Yes, but I don't want you to."

"John!" Reverend Parris summoned him. He kissed her lips and then walked into the study. Moments later, he whispered goodbye as he stepped outside and closed the door.

Tituba buried her face into her blanket and sobbed.

CHAPTER SEVEN

March 1692
Salem Town

The wind howled and the rains flooded the rivers. The roads, already wet from melted snow, became so muddy that walking anywhere became a dreaded, tiresome chore. Thomas Putnam and his brother Edward, along with two other men, traveled on horseback to Salem Town. Every few minutes, they stopped to scrape the mud from the horses' hooves or the mud would become too heavy for the horses to pick up their feet to walk.

"Do you think they will believe us?" Edward asked Thomas, once they were back on the horses. The wind blew hard into his face so he almost shouted to be heard. Thomas rode beside Edward, with the other pair of riders taking up the rear.

"We'll make them believe us."

"But it's your daughter making the accusations. They could question the motive, and wonder at the possibility of a vendetta against the three women."

"My daughter is not alone in these accusations or afflictions, Edward. You saw the other girls in the meeting house. And now there has been news that Dr. Griggs' niece is afflicted as well. She has named the Osbourne woman as her tormentor, along with Sarah Good."

"Another girl?"

"By God, man, haven't you been keeping up with it all? She was chased by a wolf, which she discovered to be Goody Osbourne who had transformed herself into the creature to terrorize the poor girl. It's quite an ordeal. Why do you think we're taking legal action? Witchcraft in Salem! We can't have it! And I won't have these women terrorizing my Ann. These witches need to be extinguished."

Edward nodded, but wasn't confident of what he was hearing. His niece had a tendency to want her way, and she'd go far with her antics just to get it. She was much like her mother. Thomas was often blind to it. Was this one of those times? Surely even she wouldn't resort to accusing someone of witchcraft. And what of the other girls? They just couldn't be faking their torment. He saw it with his own eyes. Oh, it was real all right. His brother and his wife were all too eager to jump in and suggest that the women be arrested immediately to prevent any more children from being afflicted. Edward was happy to comply, considering witchcraft terrified him. Edward stopped as Thomas raised his hand and the traveling companions dismounted to remove the mud from the horses' hooves again. As Edward scraped, he sure wished it was going to be as easy to rid Salem village of this new evil that had befallen them.

Magistrate Hathorne and Judge Corwin looked none too pleased to see men from Salem Village. Edward assumed it was because of the many petitions for separation of the village from the town. Their desire to be independent from the town had been denied once again only days prior. The men of Salem Village were tiring of the delays to grant their petition to be an established town of their own. They knew it was a matter of discord between the village and the town that had been playing out for years. They had not only brought the matter before the town's meeting, but they were also petitioning the General Court, over which judges Corwin and Hathorne resided. Thomas was at the head of the pursuit for autonomy. He and John Proctor had publicly disputed the issue several times. Goodman Proctor felt it wasn't a smart move economically to be independent. Edward didn't know what to think. On the one hand, it'd be nice to establish their own laws and methods of handling official matters, but what if Goodman Proctor was right? The villagers struggled enough without increasing their problems due to misplaced ambitions. Thomas spoke to the judges, so Edward decided to pay attention.

"Good day, Your Honors. We're here to swear out official complaints on three women in our village."

Magistrate Hathorne dipped his quill and started writing on parchment paper. "What is your complaint?"

"Witchcraft, sir."

Magistrate Hathorne stopped writing.

"Did you say witchcraft?"

"That I did, sir."

He looked at Judge Corwin who shared his surprise. "What cause have you to complain?"

"We have children afflicted by some unseen evil. They have named three women as their tormentors."

"Have procedures been followed?"

"Aye, sir. They have been observed by ministers Samuel Parris, Nicholas Noyes, and Jonathan Hale, among others. Their afflictions have been upon them for two months now."

Judge Corwin joined the interrogation. "How many others have witnessed their afflictions?"

"Quite a few, Your Honor. Their last public display was yesterday in the meetinghouse. My daughter-"

"Your daughter?" Magistrate Hathorne asked.

"Yes, sir. She had her first episode yesterday. Reverend Parris asked who her tormentor was and she named Sarah Good. The other girls confirmed Sarah Good's identity, along with Tituba, and yesterday Sarah Osborne was named as a witch."

"Tituba? The reverend's slave?"

"Aye, sir, that is correct."

"You are aware that the punishment for witchcraft is hanging." It wasn't a question, but a statement of warning.

"We are aware of that, sir, but our children are suffering. The evil must be punished and that punishment expedited, if possible."

"There will have to be pre-trial examinations if they are arrested. Then we will determine if a trial is necessary."

"Aye, sir. We understand."

Magistrate Hathorne looked at Judge Corwin and he nodded. Both judges began writing on parchment paper, then folded and stamped a seal to hold them in place. "Give these to the sheriff, and Constable Herrick and Constable Locker. I remind you that you must have Sheriff Corwin and the constables arrest the women and let them follow the legal procedures. There will be a formal interrogation at Ingersoll's Tavern tomorrow morning."

Thomas accepted the papers, and bid the judges farewell. Edward noticed Thomas' mood lifted as he walked out. Maybe he was relieved because of the concern for his daughter's plight, but Edward thought it strange that anyone could whistle after suggesting three women should hang.

～ع

When Magistrate Hathorne was sure they'd gone, he looked at Judge Corwin. "If what they say is true, and we are part of eradicating this devil's curse from Salem Village, our names will be known. Perhaps we'll earn a seat in Boston."

Judge Corwin said nothing.

～ع

Sarah Good stared at her husband with contempt. "What do you mean, I'm on my own with this baby? What's changed? I've already been on my own with this child." She pointed at little Dorcas, who was sleeping on the floor of the little tool shed where her father had been sleeping for a month now. He had been working at the Jones' farm for food and lodging. For himself.

"You haven't cared for me or our child for some time now."

"You are the one who had the debt before we married."

"My dead husband had the debt, not I. You knew about the debt before you agreed to take me as your wife. Or have you forgotten that little vow you made before the Reverend Burroughs and the fine folks of Salem Village? The same folks who were our friends, and now turn your wife and daughter away when they need food and a warm place to sleep."

"Do you think I have a warm place to sleep, woman? These temperatures aren't likely to keep a man warm at night, much like a wife with a bag of cold bitterness wrapped about her." Before she could respond to that, he added, "Besides, you have yourself to blame for the folks of this village holding contempt for ye. All your complaining and fussing aloud, blaming everyone for your own faults, and cursing them when they don't want to help ye. Who would want to help a woman with your vile tongue?"

Sarah's temper boiled hot and she was vaguely aware of her hand picking up an ax and swinging it at him. He screamed, and ducked, then shoved her backwards. Pain seared her head and she heard Dorcas cry.

"Mama!"

She came to her senses at that moment, remembering she not only had Dorcas to care for, but a new baby was on the way. Their father was not worth going to jail, no matter how pathetic he might be. Sure, maybe she was pathetic, too. Had been for quite some time now, but she still cared for her daughter. She looked at her husband who was putting the ax back on the hook on the wall. She must have dropped it when he pushed her. She remembered how smitten she was when she met him. She thought she loved him, but now Sarah knew she had just wanted someone to care for her. Her deceased husband had left her destitute. He had cared only for himself, and now she discovered that William was no different. Oh, he had pretended to care for her for a while. Since he had willingly taken on her debts when he married her, she had just thought he loved her. Perhaps he did love her, at first. The debt had taken its toll on both of them. She didn't know why she had continued to let him touch her. He disgusted her now. She shivered. Still, she must say it.

"I'm sorry, William. I don't know why I did that."

"You got the devil in you, woman."

She sighed. "Aye, I suppose I do." She walked over and grabbed Dorcas by the hand. "Say goodbye to your father, Dorcas."

"Bye, Papa."

"Where ye be headed now?" he asked her.

"I suppose I'll be leaving Salem Village, William. There's nothing for me here. Little Dorcas needs more than this, and so does this new child. I'm finished begging." She was tired of this life she lived, with the bitterness and anger, and the shame she felt when she faced old friends who begrudgingly gave her charity. Her pride had been wounded long enough. So had her spirit.

"Where will you go?"

"Boston, or Groton. I'll hire little Dorcas and me out as servants. The baby will have to be adopted." She could hardly bear to say that. How would she give up her own child?" She felt sick. Her husband didn't even flinch.

She turned around and walked out of the little shed, thinking she'd never see that man again, but also knowing it didn't bother her as much as it should.

Outside the shed stood Constable Herrick, along with the sheriff and Thomas Putnam. Oh, how she loathed Thomas Putnam and his wife Alice. The feeling was mutual. His eyes gleamed with boastfulness. Sarah had heard about their daughter's foolishness at the Sabbath meeting. She had shrugged it off, thinking it wasn't possible for anyone to believe such nonsense. As the constable stepped up to read her the official arrest warrant, Thomas Putnam yelled at her husband to take hold of Dorcas.

"What is this?" William asked.

"Your wife is under arrest for witchcraft. She will be held until questioning tomorrow morning at Ingersoll's Tavern, at the hour of ten. You can attend if you want, but it's not a trial." Sarah thought he wanted to add "yet" to that statement. It was there, on the tip of his arrogant tongue.

Constable Herrick grabbed her arm. "Come along, Goody Good. It won't do you any good to fight."

Sarah supposed it wouldn't. She looked at Dorcas, who was crying. "It's alright, child. Stay with Papa." She looked at William. "You have to take care of her, William." He nodded. She ignored Goodman Putnam's stare, and allowed the constable to help her onto the horse. Her head pounded now from the fall minutes ago, and nausea swept through her empty stomach. A hopeful thought entered her mind as the constable led her horse away from the Jones farm.

At least she might get a decent meal from this, and once this ridiculous episode was over, she'd carry out her plan to move to Boston and start a new life. She felt a leap in her stomach. Sadness accompanied the bile in her throat as she felt her little one move. If only she didn't have to start a new life without the baby.

⌒⌒

Tituba's husband John brought a chicken home that day to clean the chimney. "Thank your husband, for I've spared you the tedious chore of sweeping the thick soot out of that chimney. When you finish, we can use her to lay eggs. It's about time we started replacing the hens we lost. She's a good layer. A fellow at the tavern brought her in to trade for some small labor at his place. I'll go first thing in the morning before my work at Ingersoll's."

"Oh, John. You work so hard already." She was touched. He knew she loved eggs, and how much she dreaded cleaning the chimney. Goody Sibley had told her about using a chicken to clean the chimney. Tituba had never heard of such a thing, and was quite shocked, but Goody Sibley said it didn't harm the chicken. Tituba still hated to frighten the bird in such a way.

"Do you think it's alright, John? To throw the chicken down the chimney?"

"Aye, it's fine, wife. She'll be frantic, for sure, and her wings will do the work for ye, but her fate is better than some."

Tituba consented. John helped her put out the fires and remove the ashes. When they cooled, he dumped the ashes away from the house, then came back and climbed on top of the roof. Only seconds later, she heard the horrific squawking. The reverend and his wife had taken the girls out for an afternoon drive, so they weren't home to hear the commotion. Tituba wished she couldn't hear it. The poor chicken was so distressed Tituba wanted to climb in there and get it out. It was growing colder, too, without a fire to heat the room. Black dust and soot filled the house. Tituba opened the door and started waving the floating ash outside with her apron. John came down to retrieve the chicken. He pulled the fluttering chicken out of the chimney and they both laughed at the soot covered bird. No longer golden, the now black bird suddenly stilled and looked at Tituba. She instantly felt sad for the chicken. She didn't know why, but it reminded her of herself somehow. Tituba had never felt more lost than she had the last few days. She had been through her share of heartache and fear, but this was different. The last few nights, she'd had nightmares, but when she woke, the creatures she dreamed about were there, in the keeping room. She didn't dare scream out. There had been enough screaming at the parsonage lately. Then, last night, a tall dark shadow appeared before her, telling her to kill Ann Putnam. He told her if she didn't, he'd kill her. She couldn't determine if she'd been dreaming or not. He sure felt real. When he had appeared to her, she hadn't been able to move. She didn't tell anyone, not even John. She was in enough trouble. What would they think if the devil himself communicated to her? She looked at the chicken again. He stared back at her.

"Don't put it in the chimney again, John."

"I have to, Tituba. There's still thick soot in the fireplace. She needs to go down again."

"Please don't." Tears filled her eyes.

John's face softened and he nodded. "I'll clean her up, then sweep out the remaining soot."

"No, John. It's my duty. You have to chop wood before the reverend returns. I'll clean the chicken and the chimney, then put the fire on again for supper." She stroked the blackened chicken, which started squawking and trying to flap its wings again, so she took it to the barn. She heard her husband chopping wood as she dusted the chicken off with some bound straw. She gave it some dry corn and water. It seemed happy enough to run around outside, despite the cold, so she went back to the house to finish the chimney.

That's when she saw them. Constable Herrick and Goodman Putnam were riding alongside Goody Good on horseback. Fear struck Tituba in the gut. She had hoped the message John had delivered had nothing to do with her. Tituba wondered if that was why the Reverend came home and suddenly announced that they'd be going for an afternoon ride. It'd be getting dark soon. She had thought it strange that he'd choose to be away when he didn't like being out after dark, but figured he was doing all he could to help the children, not to mention his ailing wife. Constable Herrick dismounted and grabbed a document from his coat pocket as he walked toward her. John stopped chopping wood, and looked up with a frown on his face. She watched understanding dawn in his eyes. He dropped his ax and ran to her. Now it made sense. Reverend Parris did not want to be here when his slave was arrested for witchcraft. The slave that had tenderly cared for his wife every day that she was sick, and then his daughter and niece as they became mad from the devil. His slave that changed bedpans, prepared meals, and cleaned and spun thread for them.

Only shame could drive a man away from his own home in the dark when he was afraid of it.

"Tituba, we have a warrant for your arrest."

"What is the complaint against her?" John asked.

"Witchcraft."

"I guess you'll be cleaning that chimney after all, my husband." She embraced him quickly before Constable Herrick drug her to the horse that Goody Good sat on. The other woman didn't speak to her as Tituba climbed on the horse behind Sarah. Tituba wasn't surprised. Even a homeless beggar who was arrested for witchcraft ranked higher than a slave in the same predicament.

CHAPTER EIGHT

John Proctor stood at the back of the almost crowded room. He looked around at those who greedily anticipated the morning's events. He wasn't surprised at the crowd that had assembled at Ingersoll's. News traveled fast in Salem Village. Thomas Putnam didn't look happy to see him. That was fine with John, for he had no desire to converse with Goodman Putnam or any of the committee members who disregarded his advice not to break away from the town. The ignorance of their logic astounded him. He and other progressive thinkers in the village had tried to discuss the benefits of staying politically connected to the town. Economically speaking, Salem village would fare well remaining a part of the growing commerce from the port, not to mention Salem Town already had an established government, although they were about to reorganize it according to Crown standards, but reorganizing was quite the head start on establishing. John sighed in disgust when he thought of their last meeting to discuss autonomy. Set in his strict puritan ways, Putnam, along with his outspoken and obnoxious wife Alice, led the crusade on the village becoming its own community. They were thrilled when Samuel Parris became minister of their congregation. He held to the strict Puritan customs and laws, ones which John doubted were actually following what Jesus taught in the Scriptures.

He had missed the meeting Sunday because his wife Elizabeth had been ill and he didn't want to leave her. She had wanted to attend the questioning today, but he had urged her to stay in bed. Besides, this was probably just formality and would be resolved after today. The judges would see how ridiculous these accusations were and life in Salem Village would resume its dull routine.

"Goodman Proctor, I'm a bit surprised to see you here." He turned and looked into the lined, gentle face of Rebecca Nurse. Goody Nurse and her husband Francis were dear friends of his and Elizabeth's. They, too, opposed the break from Salem Town. Goody Nurse was getting on in years, and Elizabeth had mentioned concern for her just days ago. He had shrugged it off, but now as he looked at her, her advanced frailty was obvious. A godly woman, she had counseled and encouraged him through the years when he needed it most. When he and Elizabeth lost their child, Rebecca was there, caring for Elizabeth, and preparing their meals, despite having to care for her own household. For that, he would be forever grateful. She had also been a surrogate mother to the Knapp girl. She and Goody Easty really stepped up when Goody Knapp passed away, leaving that poor baby alone with her grieving father. Many villagers had reasons to love this woman, despite how they felt about the issue of separation from the town. She had nurtured and cared for many of them in time of need.

"Goody Nurse, sit here." He took her arm and guided her to the wooden seat at the back against the wall. Her hands shook as she sat and placed her Bible on the table in front of her. That was just like Rebecca, he thought. She never went anywhere without her Bible.

"So what do you make of all of this, Goody Nurse?" He was curious about what she thought.

"I suppose the Lord will reveal His purpose in His own time, John." She spoke quietly. She only called him by his surname when she was serious, and she never did so when others could hear. It wasn't considered proper for a woman to call a man who wasn't her husband by his surname. He frowned. She looked concerned. Surely she wasn't worried that these women would be put on trial for this. He knew the three women weren't the most popular in the village, but to be placed on trial for witchcraft? Based on what? Three girls acting out in hysteria? No matter how the people felt about one another, he couldn't imagine anyone wanting an innocent person to hang for witchcraft.

The judges walked in, and the murmuring hushed. Magistrate Hathorne raised his brows when he noticed the crowd, but said nothing as he followed Corwin to the table at the front of the room. Thomas Putnam whispered something to him, to which he waved his hand in dismissal. Putnam frowned and took a seat next to his wife and Ann. Reverend Parris sat nearby, with his niece and his daughter. For girls rumored to be hysterical, they were certainly calm now. Too calm. The reverend wrote something in His Bible. He, too, carried his Bible everywhere, but somehow he didn't hold it the same way Goody Nurse held hers. John had never cared for the minister, though he suspected there were worse men of the faith. He did seem sincere in wanting to serve his ministerial duties well. His eyes drifted to Reverend Noyes. Now that was a man that made John's skin crawl. Noyes had always been self-serving and ambitious. The other minister present, Reverend Hale, had always been kind. He spoke with a humbleness the other ministers didn't possess.

The constables brought the women in, bound in chains. All three looked solemn and quiet, including Goody Good who was known for her outbursts and harsh language. John noticed John Indian in the crowd. He stared at his wife, but the slave wouldn't look his way. He didn't see Goody Good's husband, nor Goody Osborne's. Just as well. Neither of those men supported their wives in the best of times.

In minutes, more people poured in the already crowded tavern. John recognized some of them, but others he didn't know. He did know that he couldn't stay in this room with all of these people pressed into each other. He started to make his way out, when he heard Magistrate Hathorne's voice over all of the murmurs.

"This session will now adjourn and reopen at the meeting house. If you wish to witness the questioning, you should begin making your way over post-haste." He gathered his papers and stood, with Judge Corwin following suit. John decided to wait until the crowd cleared a bit, so he could assist Goody Nurse. The roads were treacherous from all of the rain so she'd probably need the help, whether she wanted to admit it or not.

"Where's Goodman Nurse, Goody?" he asked Rebecca as he helped her out of her chair.

"The rain has washed away some of our fencing on the east side. He's out repairing it today. He thinks this witch business will blow over soon." She let him lead her out the door onto the muddy road.

"I expect he's right, Goody Nurse. This is pure nonsense, and I wager a guess that after today, we will hear no more of it."

She remained silent. John had to ask. "Goody Nurse, is there something you know that I don't?"

"I hope not, John. I pray not."

⌒‿

Sarah Good's wrists and ankles burned raw from the chains. She had worn them since the moment they put her up at the watch house the night before. She couldn't even take them off to relieve herself and had to squat over the spread of straw that Tituba and Goody Osborne used for the same purpose. The stench filled the room through the night. That, coupled with the burning pain from the chains made any sleep impossible, other than dozing, and she figured her misery was equally felt by her fellow prisoners, though they didn't speak of it. She didn't wish to speak to them, and obviously, the feeling was mutual. She wished the Constable Herrick wouldn't rush her, for it made the chains brush her already chaffed skin on her ankles, and she winced with each step. The wet mud from the road seeped into her shoes, her feet sticking. She lost her shoe, but the constable urged her on, so she finished the walk with her bare foot sinking into the cold, wet mud. It reached her raw ankle, burning her skin even more. None of this was a bad as the humiliating body search in the back of Ingersoll's tavern by Goody Ingersoll that morning. She had been instructed by the constables and the Reverend Parris to search the women for any moles, warts, or birthmarks. These marks were signs of the devil and if found, they proved their service to Satan. Goody Good endured the search over her limbs, but when Goody Ingersoll moved her hands over her naked breasts, she slapped her. Goody Ingersoll screamed, and the constables ran in, grabbing her by the arms, forcing her to sit still for the remainder of the search. That was when William burst in, telling them he had seen a mark on her thigh and thought they should know about it. Sarah had been humiliated many ways in this community, but never had she felt so low in all of her life. She wanted to fight them off, but the thought of the growing child in her womb caused her to give in to their demands, so the men held her fast as Goody Ingersoll searched her most private parts. Now, as she sank in the mud with every step, she wondered just how far she'd sink before the day was over.

⌒‿

Tituba watched Goody Good walk in front of her. When her shoe came off, Tituba tried to reach for it, but the constable jerked her up, and pushed her on. Tituba had never liked Sarah Good, but now she felt sorry for her. Her man had betrayed her this morning, when she needed him most, and probably to make himself look good in the community. No one deserved that.

No one deserved this, either. She hurt. The chains burned, but she also ached in her stomach. Nerves had caused the pains, which had made her visit the hay spread several times in the night, shaming her in front of the other women, but it couldn't be helped. Her head ached from wanting water. They had given them little water before locking them up with a guard outside. She saw her husband, walking a short distance from her, but she just couldn't look at him. If she looked at him, she'd break down and cry. She didn't want to cry or they might perceive it as guilt. She had no guilt. Those girls had to be acting! Especially that Ann Putnam. She looked at Sarah Osborne. Poor woman. She had bruises on her eye and her cheek. Everyone had talked about how her husband beat her. Now, Tituba suspected it was true. She decided then to look at her own husband John. He was already watching her. She held back the tears as she thought about how good she had it. Her man was there, silent, but supportive. Somehow, her feet felt lighter as she finished the last steps to the meetinghouse.

Inside, the women were escorted to the front. The judges were already seated at the table. It was cold. Reverend Parris instructed John Indian to start a fire in the stove.

"The wood is wet, sir. Looks like the wind knocked the shelter down."

"Then go to the nearest house and take from their covered stack. Once you make this fire, you'll need to get right on repairing that shelter, but get some of the men to help you. We're going to need this stove going for the examination." Her husband didn't flinch at the reverend's insensitivity. As a slave, he'd become accustomed to being treated as a lesser being. Besides, Tituba hoped they'd question one of the other women first, so maybe he'd still have time to listen to her examination.

CHAPTER NINE

Lydia couldn't believe she had managed to sneak into the meetinghouse without her father seeing her. He told her to stay home. She had followed him from a distance after he left to go to Ingersoll's that morning. Then, just as she was about to sneak up to peak in and listen, everyone started pouring out of the tavern. She had ducked behind the watch house, until she was sure the crowd had gotten far enough down the road so there was no risk of her father seeing her.

She just had to see the examinations for herself. This couldn't be real. Could it? Didn't Ann say that Abigail and Betty were faking their symptoms? Then, on Sabbath, she acted out in the same way. Although, it didn't seem to Lydia that Abigail and Betty were acting. How were they so powerful, and how did they make their voices sound like that? So deep, and so frightening.

Ann was a different story. She had been surprised to see Ann afflicted, and crying out that Sarah Good tormented her. Lydia had wanted to talk to her after the meeting, but her father had whisked her away right after Thomas Putnam had demanded the reverend intervene. Her father shocked her with his firm, painful grasp on her arm all the way home. He ordered her to stay on the homestead unless he accompanied her. Remembering his harsh warning that he'd whip her with the strap, she slipped into the back of the room, ensuring her petite stature was hidden behind a tall gentleman. There were so many people crowded into the meetinghouse that she doubted anyone would notice her, including her father.

~

She was wrong. There was one that noticed her. Belias watched as Semiel walked in with Lydia. The prayer cover was strong with that girl. He looked over at Rebecca Nurse. Even now, her lips were moving to match her silent prayers. He was assigned to Sarah Good for now, but he wanted that prayer warrior. Sonneillon had his hands full, overseeing all the demons working on the minds of Salem village. Perhaps if he proved himself with this woman, he'd get a better assignment. His plan to make Goody Good pave her own way to her demise worked. He smiled with pride. Semiel watched him, but he didn't care. He was mainly here to guard, along with all of the angels in this village. Lucifer's power must be strong here to make these valiant warriors so weak. He looked around. Where was Sonneillon? Where was Verrier and Carreau? There were many demons in the room. It was enough to accomplish what needed to be done here today, but Belias wanted to know why he and he alone was overseeing the lesser demons. Then, he saw them. Sonneillon was there, with the girl Ann Putnam. Verrier had hold of little Betty, and Carreau was capturing the mind of Abigail Williams.

Belias decided to focus on Sarah Good. She was standing with the two constables. He looked around, and through the outer wall, he could see Tituba and Goody Osborne chained outside in the cold, awaiting their time to be questioned. Someone else noticed them, too.

John Proctor looked out the window and spoke up. "Why are the other women standing in the cold? Can this not be as humane a procedure as it is legal?"

Magistrate Hathorne searched the crowd to see who dared speak up before the examination even started. "Only one of the accused may be in the room at once, Goodman Putnam." He knew John Proctor well. They were on the same side on the autonomy issue, but Belias figured that sure wouldn't be the case here.

"So we just let them shiver in the cold for an undetermined amount of time?"

Hathorne's chest rose in a deep sigh of annoyance. Then, he spoke quietly to the constables. Constable Locker stood up and walked outside. John Proctor watched as he led the women away.

"Where are they going?"

"Back to the watch house. Now there will be no more spoken on it."

"The watch house isn't much warmer." John said.

"I said there will be no more spoken on this matter, Goodman Proctor." John sat down, scowling at the judge. Magistrate Hathorne ignored him. He picked up his feather quill and began dipping it into his ink, writing on his parchment paper. He looked up at Sarah Good, then at the afflicted children. "We will begin the proceedings now." He motioned for Constable Herrick to nudge Goody Good forward. Belias prepared to help her speak.

⌒⌣

Sarah Good controlled the bile that threatened to erupt just as she stumbled forward with the constable's pull. The sickness was violent with this child. She hoped the questioning wouldn't take long, and she could be released to get Dorcas and go lie down somewhere. William better be taking care of their daughter.

"Mama!" As if she conjured her little girl by the thought of her, there stood little Dorcas, on a bench, her father sitting down near her. He hushed her, and pulled her back to sit. Tears filled Sarah's eyes. She wanted to run to Dorcas. They hadn't spent a night apart since the child was born.

A scream sounded throughout the building. Sarah jumped in surprise with everyone else. Abigail Williams waved her arms in front of her, swatting and screaming as if bees swarmed over her, stinging her. Betty jumped up, screamed and pointed in the air around Abigail. "It's her! It's Goody Good!" Then, she grabbed her arm and screamed again.

Gasping and murmurings ensued all over the room, and the judges tapped on the table to quiet the crowd.

"Children, what has you afflicted in this manner?"

Ann spoke up. "It's Goody Good! Her spirit is lunging at us! Don't you see her?"

Sarah didn't move. The girls shocked her. Something hurt them, but it certainly wasn't her. What did they mean when they said it was her spirit?

"Sarah Good, what evil spirit have you familiarity with?"

"None" She answered. She almost emptied what little was in her stomach. She worked to hold it down.

"Why do you hurt these children?"

"I do not hurt them. I scorn it."

Who did you employ to hurt them?"

"I employ nobody. I am falsely accused, sir."

Magistrate Hathorne stared at her, then back at the girls, who were writhing in their seats, mumbling in distress. He looked back at some papers on the table.

"I have reports here stating that you have cursed the Parris household. Witnesses claim you muttered as you left their house not long before the girls became afflicted. What did you mutter? Is it true you were angry that they turned you away for charity so you cursed them?"

"I did not mutter. I thanked him for what he gave to my little Dorcas." That was a lie, but she was afraid to admit she had cursed them in anger.

"If it is not you who hurts these children, who is it?"

"I do not know."

The questioning went around and around while the girls continued their intermittent screams and cries and twisting around in their seats, or on the floor. Sarah soon became so sick, her head ached and spun and she wanted desperately to lie down. She longed to scream at the judges to stop.

"Why do you not attend meeting on the Sabbath?"

"I lack proper clothing."

"What do you mutter when you walk away from people?"

"Why do I have to tell you what I say to myself? It was for my own ears, and the Good Lord's, if He listens."

"Why don't you want us to know what it is you are saying?"

"If you really must know, I will tell you." She could barely stand up. She might as well do what they say.

"Tell us now."

"It's the commandments. Can a woman not say the commandments anymore without suspicion?"

"If that is indeed what you were muttering. What exactly were you reciting?"

She sighed. What was he asking her? Oh how her head ached, and her stomach.

"Goody Good!"

"It was…it was…a Psalm. It was a Psalm."

The judge narrowed his eyes. "Let's hear this Psalm."

Sarah's anger grew. Why was she letting this man harass her so? She was no witch. These people hated her. That's why she was standing here, answering these ridiculous questions. She looked

Magistrate Hathorne right in the eyes. "Deliver me from my enemies, O my God: defend me from them that rise up against me."

The room grew silent.

This time Judge Corwin spoke to her. "Who do you serve?"

"I serve God."

Magistrate Hathorne countered, "What god do you serve?"

"I serve the God that made Heaven and Earth. Who do you serve?" She couldn't help herself.

A voice sounded from the crowd. "Just answer his questions, Sarah." She recognized the soft voice immediately. Rebecca Nurse. Sarah wanted to be angry, but the gentle voice soothed her. Her moment of peace didn't last long, though.

"Silence! William Good, are you present?" Magistrate Hathorne called out.

"Aye, sir. I'm here."

"Have you ever noticed any suspicious behavior from your wife?"

"No witchcraft, if that's what you mean, sir, but she has been a bitter wife."

"Bitter?"

"Aye. Why, the other day, she swung an ax at me, and even admitted that she had the devil in her. In fact, it sorrows me to say she has been an enemy to all good in the time I've known her." Voices all over the room shouted their agreement. Some began telling their own stories of encounters with her.

Hathorne stood up. "I said, 'Silence'!" His voice boomed over the room and the people immediately hushed.

If Sarah could ever hate anyone more, she didn't imagine that person, for her husband brought such a rage to the surface of her heart that it scared her. She might not be tormenting the children, but she could certainly torment him at this moment. It was that same rage that overtook her at the Jones' shed when she had swung the ax at him. She didn't know what held her still, for she could well imagine her spirit choking the father of her children. William, the coward that he was, would not look in her direction. Dorcas cried next to him and he did nothing to comfort her. Yes, she could kill William with her bare hands if they weren't chained.

When the judges finished questioning her, she still had to remain and listen to account after account from villagers, testifying to times where she had practiced witchcraft upon them. If she hadn't felt so miserable, she'd have laughed at how insane the accusations sounded, especially the one where she laughed and it brought boils upon a neighbor's pig. If she had that power, William would be covered in them now.

"Sarah Good, we hereby declare that the evidence presented here today supports the necessity to try you for witchcraft in a court of law. Constable Herrick, escort Goody Good to the watch house for now. She can be transported to the jail once these examinations are completed. We will hear Goody Osborne's case next so bring her here expediently."

A shrill hackle rang out from the back of the room. All eyes searched for the source of the loud laugh. There, a couple of rows behind Goodman Proctor, stood Bridget Bishop. She wore her brazen red petticoat as she so often did. Sarah knew she rarely attended meetings and most of the women despised her for her boldness with their men, and her improper humor when she served them at her tavern. She had been kind to Sarah so many times, letting her clean the floors of the tavern for a meal, and had even given Dorcas milk and sweet bread. The people could say what they wanted to about Goody Bishop, but most of them weren't fit to hold her candle. So many spoke of charity, but mocked this woman who had helped Sarah and her daughter more than they ever had, just because she didn't follow their rules.

"Goody Bishop, sit down!" Goody Putnam stood now, her face showing fury at the woman.

"Why? So I can listen to more of this ridiculous questioning?"

"You will respect your official judges!" Reverend Parris said.

"Respect? She doesn't know anything of respect! Look how she dresses!" Another woman spoke. Sarah couldn't see who it was.

"I'll give respect to whom it's due. As for my dress, it's happy. That's something all of you could do with. Happy. Instead of chasing witches in folks who are just trying to get along in life, same as you. If they do it differently, that doesn't make them a witch."

"Are you claiming these girls are liars?" asked Magistrate Hathorne.

"I didn't say that." She looked at Sarah. "All I know is that woman is no more a witch than I am."

"Perhaps you are with her!" said Goody Putnam.

She cackled loudly again. "I know of only one witch in this church, Goody Putnam."

Alice gasped.

"Silence! I mean to have silence in this procedure!" Magistrate Hathorne brought his fist down on the table. The thud echoed in the now silent room.

Bridget lifted her chin and looked around. "If any of you men tire of this nonsense, I'll be waiting with some ale to quench ye thirst." She flipped around and walked briskly out the door, her red skirt rustling around her petite frame.

Magistrate Hathorne said nothing for a moment. Then, he nodded to Constable Locker.

Sarah numbly allowed the constable to escort her out of the meetinghouse. Children began spitting on her. Their parents warned them not to anger her or they might be tormented as well. They had a combination of hate and fear on their faces. She looked up and saw the Knapp girl as she neared the door. Was that pity in the girl's eyes? And fear? Sarah was afraid, too. Evidence? What evidence? How could they call what transpired here today evidence? Goody Bishop was right. It was pure nonsense. Yet, here she was, being tried for witchcraft. As she walked outside into the frosty air, her baby turned in her womb. What would happen to her baby? What about Dorcas? For the first time in years, Sarah allowed herself to cry.

～

Alice Putnam hated that Goody Bishop. Now, here she was, speaking against her Ann and threatening to turn people's minds against the accusations. How dare she come into this meetinghouse. She never attended meetings, but she came to the questioning. Why? Her haughty spirit astounded Alice. What made her haughty? She wasn't a gospel woman, but a brazen, crass, and improper woman. The way she walked in public. A woman ought not to swing her hips in such a manner, and wear her bodice so tight against her chest. She just wanted to show off, and gain the wrong sort of attention. Well, she'd better watch out. Right now, it wouldn't be hard to convince anyone that she belonged to the lair of Salem witches. After all, she certainly wasn't popular, except with men. She looked at her husband Thomas. She knew he had frequented Goody Bishop's tavern, and she knew why. Oh, she never thought he had committed adultery. He had too much to lose, and he was too weak to handle a status loss. However, she knew he fancied Goody Bishop's boisterous ways, and of course, the way she dressed delighted him and the other men. Although she was an older woman, Bridget had an attractive way about her. She had aged well. Too well. Goody Bishop invited sinful lust, and Goody Putnam had long wanted to put a stop to it. Now Providence had brought her a way. She wouldn't rush it, though. She'd wait for just the right time.

Alice didn't see the demon attached to her. Sonneillon smiled. He had Alice Putnam right where he wanted her. Providence, or God, had brought her nothing. No, he had sown the idea in her head and heart, and she lunged at it. She may think her husband was weak. She had no idea. Her weakness played right into the devil's hands. Lucifer would be pleased. The plan moved along nicely.

CHAPTER TEN

Lydia didn't like Sarah Good, but she didn't want her in jail. She had to do something. The girls were lying, weren't they? She heard John Proctor say this whole thing was about the girls wanting attention, but Lydia was afraid it was just as Ann had said. They were accusing before they could be accused. If only Sarah Good hadn't started talking about that dreadful day. Lydia was just as much a part of this as Ann and the other girls. Little Dorcas was crying for her mama because Lydia had wanted to participate in a forbidden activity. She was so weak. Following after Ann like a baby calf follows its mother, begging for approval like it begged for milk.

Her guilt intensified when Sarah Osborne was escorted into the meetinghouse in chains with her head down. Lydia had heard of her troubles. She had been ill for some time, or at least that was what she claimed. The bruises on her face offered credibility to the rumors that her husband beat her. Whatever the cause, Goody Osborne did not look well at all. Come to think of it, neither did Goody Good. Could they really be witches? Perhaps they looked that way because they had the mark of the devil upon them. Lydia didn't know what to believe anymore. Her friends appeared genuinely afflicted. Even now, when Sarah Osborne walked into the room, their hysterics escalated again. The questions started again, too.

"Why did you stalk one of these girls as a wolf?"

"I have never stalked anyone, especially as a wolf. I cannot be something I'm not."

"You didn't make a contract with the devil and receive his power to harm the children?"

"I have never made a contract with the devil. I wish to harm no one." Her voice shook as she spoke.

"Eleanor Hubbard said it was you who stalked her as a wolf. What do you say to that accusation?"

"I say that I have no knowledge that the devil would use my likeness to harm anyone."

"She's lying! She has the lying spirit in her!" someone shouted from the crowd. Lydia couldn't look to see who it was, or she'd risk being seen by her father.

"Silence!" Magistrate Hathorne shouted again. "What lying spirit is speaking through you right now?"

"I have no lying spirit."

"Why did you say you were more likely a victim than a tormentor? We have several witnesses that claim you said as much."

"Because of my dreams. I was pinched by an Indian in one dream, and in another, I was told by a voice not to go to meeting."

"So you obeyed the voice?"

"No. I went to meeting anyway."

"My records show you haven't been to meeting in some weeks."

"Aye. I have been ill. My husband will confirm this as truth."

He looked at her a moment then turned to Judge Corwin. "We may not have enough evidence, here."

A scream erupted from Eleanor Hubbard. She bent over, holding her stomach. "She's striking me in my middle! Please make her stop!"

Magistrate Hathorne looked at the girl, then back at Goody Osborne.

"Why do you hurt this girl?"

"I do not, sir. I do not know what or who hurts her, but I do not."
She clasped her hands nervously. Eleanor cried out louder this time,
holding her wrist. Reverend Parris walked over to her, followed by
Reverend Hale. They both gasped.

Reverend Parris held up her wrist. "See her wrist marks! Just there!"

Lydia couldn't believe it. Even from where she stood, she saw
deep red abrasions like rope burns on Eleanor's wrists. The crowd
roared in disbelief.

Magistrate Hathorne quieted them once again. He looked down
and wrote something on paper, then he spoke quietly to Judge
Corwin, who whispered something back. Lydia wished she could
hear what he was saying. She wanted them to let Goody Osborne go,
but what if she did hurt Eleanor? How else did she get those marks?
Her stomach swam with nerves. The magistrate finally spoke aloud.

"The evidence presented here today warrants a trial for Sarah
Osborne." He motioned to the constable to accompany her to the
watch house.

～

Belias looked to Sonneillon for approval. He didn't get it. Sonneillon
ignored him, despite the fact that he just ordered the little violent
demon to inflict harm upon that girl, which solidified that pathetic
woman's guilt in everyone's mind. What would it take to please
Sonneillon? He had to find a way to rise up the ranks. This mission
offered him the chance, and he wouldn't blow it. He had to do
something big. Determined, he flew out of the meetinghouse, ready
to attach himself to Sarah Good.

Uriel motioned to an angel to follow him.

～

Moments later, Tituba walked in. She searched the crowd and somehow, she knew Lydia was there. She held Lydia's gaze for what seemed an eternity before focusing on the judges at the table. Her expression didn't hold the pride and animosity of Goody Good, but it didn't hold the humility of Goody Osborne, either. Her expression was more of a mixture of fear and confusion. She must have exchanged brief words with the other two women and so she felt little hope in answering their questions honestly. Her confused expression grew when the girls started writhing on the floor when she walked in. Lydia's heart sank. Beautiful, exotic Tituba was in chains, being questioned for witchcraft, all because the girls begged her to play forbidden games with them. Tituba was strange, but she had always been kind to Lydia, and Lydia didn't want her to be in trouble. The series of questions began again.

"Tituba, what evil spirit have you familiarity with?"

"None, sir."

"Why do you hurt these children?"

"I do not hurt them."

"Tell me now. Why have you done it?"

"I have done nothing. I know not how the devil works."

"So you have not spoken with the devil?"

"No. He tells me nothing."

"Tell the truth!"

"I do. I speak the truth!"

The judges badgered her for an hour. Lydia's head pounded from holding her neck in an awkward position so she could see.

For what seemed like the hundredth time, the magistrate asked, "Who is it that hurts them if it's not you?"

"The devil, for aught I know."

"What shape does he take when he hurts them?"

Tituba brought her chained hand up to her head to rub it.

Ann Putnam screamed. "She burning my head! See? She's touching her head so mine will burn!"

"Tituba! Why do you hurt these children? Tell me now!"

Tituba shook her head, clearly distressed. "I-don't hurt them."

"Then who is making them scream so?" someone yelled.

"I will have silence during the examination or you will be removed!" Hathorne yelled out. He continued, "Tell me Tituba! Why do you hurt them?"

"It was the devil! He made me!" she yelled.

Lydia listened as Tituba began telling the most bizarre stories. She looked around, everyone listened intently, some gasping while some laughed. Others yelled, "Hang her!"

Amazingly, after Tituba started admitting guilt, the girls ceased their fits. They sat calmly while Tituba relayed how she had served the devil.

The magistrate continued to question her, nevertheless. "Have you seen the devil take any shapes while you served him?"

"No. No shapes."

"How does he appear to you?"

"Uh…like a man. Yes, like a man."

The magistrate wasn't satisfied with that. "How else does he appear?"

"Like a black dog? Or a hog, I think."

Goodman Proctor stood up. "Can't you see she's making it all up? Gather your wits about you."

Magistrate Hathorne banged his gavel again. Goodman Proctor sat down.

"Who else does his bidding with you?"

She didn't speak. She bit her lower lip and looked down.

"Who, Tituba? Who else serves the devil?"

She looked up at him, then at the girls, who started writhing in their seats again.

"Sarah Good, and Sarah Osborne, I think. Or maybe—"

She suddenly screamed and dropped to the floor. The constables struggled to pick her up. Ann, Abigail and Betty screamed, too. The room grew louder and louder as people murmured in panic.

"What's the meaning of this, Tituba?" Reverend Parris spoke up.

Tituba's eyes rolled in the back of her head.

"She's having a seizure!" someone yelled. Lydia tried hard to see, but her father glanced back so she ducked behind Goodman Corey.

Tituba yelled, "The devil! He has me!"

"Someone pray over her!" Rebecca Nurse stood up.

Reverend Parris walked over and jerked his slave by the arm to stand her up. "Stop this nonsense and answer the questions!"

"Reverend Parris! Unhand her and take your seat." Judge Corwin said.

Samuel Paris didn't like to be told what to do, especially with his own slave, but he let go and reluctantly took his seat.

Tituba's tortured expression transformed in an instant. She stilled, and she gazed to the ceiling.

"Tituba, what did the devil do to you?" asked Judge Corwin.

"He told me I must kill her." She pointed to Ann. Ann's mother screamed. Ann started holding her throat and making choking sounds. Her eyes bulged and her face resembled beets.

"Stop it, Tituba! You mustn't harm the child." Magistrate Hathorne said.

"It is not I." She stated in a monotone voice.

"Not you? We just saw you point to her while admitting the devil told you to kill her."

"It is the others. Good and Osborne. They hurt her. I am innocent."

John Proctor yelled out, "This is ridiculous. The other women are in the watch house!"

"Silence in my court!" Magistrate Hathorne yelled. "One more outburst, Goodman Proctor, and I will ban you from these proceedings. Tituba! How do these women hurt them?"

"It's their images. They are here, floating around the girls. "

The demons laughed, taunting the angels who stood nearby, just watching. They had transformed themselves into the images of Goody Good and Goody Osborne.

Magistrate Hathorne and Judge Corwin were dumbfounded. They looked around, with fear, as if they, too, would see the women floating around the room. Tituba spooked Lydia, too. She wanted to get out of there, but she had to see the end of Tituba's questioning.

"Constable!" the magistrate yelled. "Take her to the watch house. Eat your evening meal, then transport these women to the Salem jail. They must be guarded at all times. He looked at the crowd. "This examination is officially adjourned. Further notice of trials will be announced." He and Judge Corwin stood up, and the meeting house cleared while the judges mulled over the events with the ministers. Goodman and Goody Putnam escorted their daughter out. Alice Putnam smiled as she left.

No one noticed Lydia who was the first to dart out the back, running to the cover of the woods, all the way home to await her father and feign an interest in a meeting she herself had attended.

⌒‿

"Raphael, what is the meaning of all of this? What is Lucifer doing?" Uriel asked. Semiel leaned in to hear their captain's response.

"I just learned his plan and came to tell you and the others."

The other angels present at the meetinghouse joined the conversation.

Raphael continued, "This is much bigger than I anticipated. This goes beyond persecuting the faithful warriors of Salem Village."

"So Lucifer isn't here to hang saints?"

"He's here to hang them, but oh so much more, I'm afraid. What he has planned will affect this land for years and years to come. The seed planted here from this turmoil will continue to grow, long after these trials are over."

Semiel frowned. "How is that possible?"

"Think about it. Why does Lucifer hate this new land?"

Understanding dawned in Uriel's eyes. "He's after the court system."

Raphael crossed his arms. "Exactly."

"Will he win?" asked Semiel.

"Only time will tell. If he does, just remember, he still loses. Now, we'd better get back to our posts." The angels saluted their captain with their swords, and floated up and over the trees, each making their way to their assignments.

Raphael sure hoped the faithful were praying.

CHAPTER ELEVEN

Paul Knapp grabbed Rebecca Nurse gently by the arm. "I need to speak with you, Goody Nurse."

He led her away from listening ears as everyone filed out of the meetinghouse. Most didn't linger. They had spent enough time away from their duties.

"Goodman Knapp, I must say I was quite surprised that you attended these proceedings."

"Yes, well, I have my reasons."

"Yes, I suppose you do." She linked her arm in his, not just for her support, but for his own.

"I need you to tell me about Lydia. The truth, Rebecca."

"What is it you want to know, and since when have I lied to you, Paul?"

"My apologies, of course. You haven't. My concern for Lydia is not unreasonable, given the circumstances. I'm sure you agree."

She looked around before answering. "I do, but keeping her away from what is happening might not be the answer. It is natural that she'd have a curiosity about such things."

"There is nothing natural about what went on in there today, Goody Nurse."

"Goodman Knapp, most of Salem Village crowded into that

church today, along with some from Salem Town. Did you hear the fear in there? People mumbling about what Goody Good had done in the past, and how Goody Osborne had isolated herself from the village, including Sabbath meeting. Trust me. It's best Lydia makes an appearance."

He sighed, and rubbed his chin. "What do you know, Goody Nurse? I need you to tell me."

"I only know your child, Paul."

"What does that mean?"

"It means it's time you started knowing her, too." She unhooked her arm, and grabbed his hands. She patted them between her own. "Before it's too late."

Paul watched her walk away. He realized he still didn't know any more than what he knew when he first approached her. He looked back at the meeting house. Reverend Noyes stood at the door, watching him. His cold, hard stare unnerved Paul. He shivered, nodded at the reverend, and walked home, feeling more anxiety with every step.

When he opened the door at home, Lydia knelt at the hearth of the fireplace, sweeping the ash to the side to cool so she could store it for making lye soap in the warmer months. Paul watched his daughter for a moment, aware that she had not noticed his arrival. She worked hard, and never complained. He wanted to say something nice to her, but couldn't find the words.

"Did you remember to store the fat from the morning breakfast?" His voice came out gruffer than he'd intended.

Startled, Lydia jumped, then fell slightly over the fire, her palm just touching the flames. She cried out. He was at her side in minutes.

Taking her hand, he looked it over, then led her to the table. He retrieved the lard and rubbed it on her burn.

"Thank you, Father. I'm sorry, I didn't know you had come in."

"It was my error. I should have announced my presence better." He blew on the reddened skin.

She drew back her arm. "I'm fine, Papa."

He looked up in surprise. She didn't seem to realize she'd called him that. The last time she'd called him Papa, she had been a small child, climbing onto his lap. Her mama had been alive and well, his life as it should be. He didn't know if he wanted her to call him that again. When did they become so formal? He wasn't sure, but he didn't know if he could go back, either.

He stood up, grabbed the leather pouch he'd fashioned to gather wood, and headed outside. He might not know how to talk with his daughter, but he knew how to keep her warm.

⌒‿

Lydia stared at the door for several minutes after he shut it. Her palm stung, but his abrupt leaving stung more. What did she do now? Was it because she had pulled away when he was comforting her? Had he been comforting her? Lydia didn't know what to think. He'd always cared for her needs, albeit in a stoic manner, but there was something gentle in his touch this time and instead of thrilling her, it scared her. He had been acting strangely lately. Since the witchcraft accusations, nothing had been the same.

He didn't come back until she had prepared the evening meal. "I had to split some of the wood from the barn. The rains have soaked the outside stacks." Lydia was glad he had thought to store some wood in the barn. Wet wood only put off smoke, not heat.

"How much dry wood do we have?"

"We have enough for a couple of days, but I will be moving some into the house so the fire can dry them out."

"I was going to clean the chimney tomorrow, Father."

"It will have to wait. We have to have dry wood. We don't know when the warmer days will arrive."

She nodded, and dipped some stew onto his plate, along with some bread. There wasn't much meat in the stew. She had cut up the rabbit her father had brought home the day before, and separated it for three meals. Lydia didn't mind the sparse meat. It was nice to eat something besides beans and salt meat. She had some canned vegetables left from their summer garden. Using them for stew was prudent, because a pot of stew would last about three days.

"You haven't asked about the examinations."

"Oh, yes. I was curious. How did it go? Is it over?"

"No. There will be a trial."

"Why?"

"They decided the evidence was too great. Frankly, I wouldn't exactly call it evidence."

"You wouldn't? Why not?"

"Never mind. You'd better eat. I need your help bringing in the wood to dry out." Lydia knew the subject was closed as far as he was concerned, but she just couldn't take it anymore. She was tired of being dismissed from any conversation or encounter they had.

"I was at the meeting, Father." She looked down at her plate.

"What did you say?"

"I was at the questioning today. I snuck in the back. I'm sorry, Father, but I had to know if-"

He stood up and slapped her across the face. She fell into the floor, shocked and holding her pained cheek.

"I ordered you to stay home!"

"Papa, I…"

"Don't call me 'Papa'!"

He walked over to her and pulled her up. He grabbed her by the chin. "What were you thinking? I told you to stay away from all of this! Do you understand? I don't want you ever to disobey my orders again!" He was yelling into her face. She had never seen him like this before. He had whipped her with the strap, but he had never struck her, and she had never witnessed such frightening anger in his voice. She backed away from him slowly. He stood staring at her, like he wanted to say something else, but then he grabbed his coat and walked outside. Lydia didn't wait for him to come back. She grabbed her own coat, and ran outside into the cold. Looking around, she didn't see him, so she ran. Semiel flew beside her, alert. The girl had a traumatic experience, so she was vulnerable to attack.

After what seemed like hours, she arrived at Rebecca Nurse's homestead. Once she saw the familiar house, she allowed herself to cry. That is how Francis Nurse found her. On her knees, sobbing in the cold, right outside the house. Sonneillon sat on top of the roof of the Nurse home. He scowled down at Semiel as he joined Uriel at the door.

Once inside, Rebecca insisted Lydia drink some hot tea. While she sipped the tea, Rebecca took off her shoes and wet stockings and rubbed her near frostbitten feet. Then, she rubbed some salve on her chapped cheeks. When Lydia's shivering finally ceased, Rebecca pulled a chair up close to her, and looked her directly in the eyes.

"What happened, child? Why are you here at this hour, and why are you crying?"

Sobs threatened to erupt again. She swallowed her tears, and tried to explain.

"I snuck into the questioning today, Goody Nurse, and decided to tell Father. It was a mistake. I've never seen him so angry. He struck me on the face and yelled. He's never been the most nurturing of fathers, but he's never hit me before. I was frightened, so I ran here. I'm sorry for bothering you at this late hour. I'll go." She stood to leave.

"Sit down, Lydia." Francis Nurse spoke firmly. He had been

standing silently by since he had brought her inside. Growing up, he'd always been firm, but kind. Lydia had always obeyed him. She sat down again.

Rebecca winked at her husband, then patted Lydia's hands. "Go on, child. Tell us the rest."

"The rest?"

"Aye, child. Tell me what you've been hiding, and I'll tell you what your father is hiding."

"My father is hiding something?"

"Yes, and while I think he should be the one to tell you, it doesn't look like he will, so it's up to me. But first, you tell me what you have to do with this whole witchcraft dilemma. Don't try to deny it. I know guilt in your eyes when I see it."

"Oh, Goody Nurse! It's all my fault!" She started crying again, and covered her face with her hands. Rebecca pulled her hands away from her eyes, then wiped her tears from her cheeks. "Tell me", she said.

"It was weeks ago."

"The day you were at Reverend Parris' house?"

She folded her hands in her lap and looked down at them. "Yes. Abigail had told Ann about this game Tituba had shown Goody Sibley once, where you could tell what your future is. It was with an egg. Ann begged her to do it with us, so we could know who our husbands were, but then it was-."

"It was what, Lydia?"

"It was a coffin! The shape was a coffin! And then she told us death was coming to Salem!"

"Oh, Lydia. Those are the devil's games. You should know better than to play those kinds of games."

"I know, Goody Nurse, and I'm sorry now, but Ann is quite persuasive, and she and Abigail together are impossible to deny. Even

Tituba obliges their requests. And now she's in jail! I even told Father that she had probably cursed the girls because I was scared. He still doesn't know I had anything to do with it."

Rebecca sighed. "He knows, child. He knows."

"How? How does he know?"

"He might not know the details of your involvement, but he knows something is amiss. Which brings us to this." She indicated the mark on her cheek. "Has your father ever told you where he's from?"

"He's not from here?"

"No, child. He's from Groton. Have you ever heard of Elizabeth Knapp?"

"The Elizabeth Knapp? Who hasn't, Goody Nurse? Wait…she's from Groton…we're not related to her, are we? The girl who was bewitched and caused a whole stir? She's in Cotton Mather's book!"

"She's your aunt, Lydia."

"What?" She jumped up, almost spilling her tea. "I thought she was a servant in that minister's house."

"She was. Your father and aunt were left destitute when your grandparents died of smallpox. Your father and sister split up, each trading servitude for room and board. Your sister worked for the minister, and your father went to work for a blacksmith. That blacksmith had a daughter, your mother." She smiled momentarily at Lydia's surprise, then continued, "Your aunt was only sixteen, and your father wasn't quite eighteen. Months after they were settled, your aunt started exhibiting symptoms similar to what Ann and the others are exhibiting. She accused people of witchcraft, and caused an outbreak of fear in the community. The minister was careful to examine each accusation, and only one of the accused was brought in for questioning."

"Only one?"

"Yes. Lydia, it was your mother."

"What?"

"It was when your father and mother were already betrothed to marry. It caused quite a rift between your father and his sister, who were very close before the accusations."

"What happened?"

"Some people were convinced of your mother's guilt, much like some are convinced of these women's guilt. They were calling for her to be hanged."

"Hanged? My mother? But she wasn't! I mean, they married, and had me. So-"

"You're right. There were some who were adamant about her innocence. Also, your aunt changed her story often, not to mention the only 'evidence' was spectral evidence, where your aunt testified to seeing your mother's apparition."

"But that's what was presented at the questioning today! That's the evidence that sent them to jail!"

"Exactly, and it almost sent your mother to jail, and it almost had her executed. Your father risked his relationship with his sister to save her, and thankfully, the men in power there listened to the minister, and didn't follow through."

"The minister believed my father?"

"Yes, and others who supported your mother. He also said spectral evidence wasn't enough to convict."

"Poor father."

"Yes. Now you understand why he's so afraid of this."

Lydia nodded, thinking. "But Goody Nurse, what happened to his sister, my aunt?"

"She repented later, and she claimed she accepted Christ. At least that is what your mother told me when she told me this story."

"My father didn't tell you?"

"No. But he knows I know, and I believe the Proctors know. Your mother and Goody Proctor were close friends. He didn't want anyone else to know, and neither did your mother. They believed it was safer that no one knew she was an accused witch. Now I know why."

"Has he seen my aunt since?"

"Not that I know of. Your mother said she married and moved to Boston. She had tried to ask your father's forgiveness, but he refused. Your mother wanted him to reconcile with your aunt, but as soon as they married, they moved here to start over, away from the gossip and scandal in Groton. According to your mother, the aftermath was harder to bear than the actual accusations."

"Was my aunt the only afflicted girl?"

"Yes."

"Was any of it real or was she lying?"

"Your mother said she claimed it was real, but that her eyes were opened later. The minister believed she was in fact afflicted, but that her accusations were unfounded and brought on by the hysteria that came from being demon possessed."

"Do you think that's what happening to the others? Because we played the games?"

"I'm not sure, Lydia. Have you experienced anything since that day?"

"Not really. Sometimes I have great fear, Goody Nurse."

"Fear isn't of God, Lydia."

"So am I serving Satan? Am I going to Hell now because of what I did?"

"Lydia, we all deserve Hell for what we do, but there's no way we're not going to do wrong."

"What are you saying? We're all doomed for Hell? Even you?"

"Yes, initially, but we don't have to be, child. Why else would Jesus come to die?"

"He died for our sins."

"Yes, exactly. Don't you see? He took the punishment so we wouldn't have to."

"But we can't just keep sinning and go to Heaven. Reverend Parris preaches about God's wrath and punishment. He says-"

"I know what he says, child, but look to what God's Word says. God is more concerned about our hearts than our actions. We can never be good enough to earn Heaven. Salvation is a gift."

"But God hates sin. He punishes those who sin."

"Aye. He does hate sin, and there are certainly consequences, but He loves the sinner, and offers mercy."

"What about sickness? Did God punish my mother for something when she was sick?"

"No, Lydia. Not everything bad is a punishment. I know that's what you've been taught, but it isn't right."

"Goody Nurse, you're contradicting our minister?"

"I'm only speaking the truth, Lydia. The truth I've found in His Word."

Goody Nurse was scaring Lydia with her blasphemous talk. One couldn't be a Christian and not act like a Christian. It just didn't make sense. "I'd better get home, Goody Nurse. My father will worry."

Francis finally spoke after silently listening to their conversation. "I'll get a horse and take you home." He walked out and left them alone.

"Lydia, I wish we could talk more about this."

"No offense intended, Goody Nurse, but we'd better not. I've gone against the rules enough." She stood to button her coat. Rebecca grabbed her arm.

"Lydia, be careful. Satan is working here like he worked in Groton."

"But it worked out in Groton and my mother was set free. I'm sure it will work out that way here, too, Goody Nurse. In fact, I feel much better now that you told me my family's story."

"Lydia-"

"Good night." She bent and kissed Rebecca's cheek, before heading out to meet Francis at the barn.

Rebecca shook her head. "Your family's story is not over yet, child."

CHAPTER TWELVE

Paul met Lydia and Francis on the road. He figured she'd go to their homestead. Relieved, he thanked Francis and lifted his daughter onto his horse. They headed home. The wind slapped their faces, making it nearly impossible for them to speak, so he figured they'd talk when they got home. He was so ashamed of himself for striking his daughter. His father had hit him and his sister often, and Paul had sworn he'd never do that to his children. It was understood that fathers had the right to hit their children, but Paul didn't believe in it, at least not in the way he had struck Lydia earlier.

Once inside the house, Lydia heated the stew since neither of them had eaten. Paul came in after taking care of the horse, and sat down to eat. "I owe you apologies, girl."

"It's fine, Father."

"Papa."

"Sir?"

"Call me Papa, Lydia."

Her eyes wide, she nodded.

"Now, I must apologize for striking you. That was abominable on my part, and I wish you to forgive me."

"Of course, Fa-Papa."

"So you had a talk with Rebecca?"

"Yes." She put down her spoon. "She told me about your sister."

"She what?"

"Please don't be angry with her. She wanted me to know why you're so afraid of these accusations."

"Aye, I am at that. I guess it's time you knew." He was relieved it finally came out after all of these years. Secrets had a way of wearing on a man. "You understand that it would be dangerous to reveal this to anyone else, especially now."

"Of course, Papa, but there's something you should know about me."

"Oh?"

"It's about the day I was at the parsonage. Tituba-well-Ann-"

He didn't press her, just waited.

"Well, we had Tituba tell our fortunes."

He said nothing, but picked up his bread and dipped it in his stew, and finished it while Lydia sat quietly, waiting.

Finally, when he thought he wouldn't say something he'd regret, he spoke.

"Was it worth it?"

"Sir?"

"The fortune? Was it worth all of this trouble it has caused?"

"We don't know that this is why the girls are acting this way, Papa."

"Be truthful, girl. Was it not after this recreational afternoon with those girls that Abigail and Betty began acting out?"

"Yes, Papa."

"What about Ann?"

"What about her, Papa?"

"You know her well enough, I presume. Are her accusations authentic?"

"I'm not sure." She proceeded to tell him of Ann's visit and her threat to Lydia.

"Ah. Cunning, that one. Does she have anything against the slave, or Goody Good and Goody Osborne?"

"She has never cared for Tituba, and no one likes Goody Good, Papa. I don't know about Goody Osborne."

"I hear that the Hubbard girl is the only one who accused Sarah Osborne."

"I heard that, too."

"So the question is, who is telling the truth, and who is lying? Who else knows about that day at the parsonage?"

"Just Rebecca and Francis Nurse, and the other girls. Goody Good suspected, but now that she's accused-"

"Yes. Sadly, she won't be an issue. You may go to the trial, but you stay clear of the afflicted girls, and anyone who is cheering them on."

"Yes, sir." She cleared the plates while he read from his Bible by candlelight.

"Papa?"

He looked up over his Bible.

"Do you believe Mama's in Heaven?"

"Of course I do. Why would you ask such a thing?"

"I heard some ladies say that she must have sinned in order to get so sick, and then die."

"Don't ever say that again." He stood up to put another log on the fire.

"I'm sorry. It's just that-"

He turned around. "Lydia, your mother was a saint. Now that is enough said on the subject."

"Could I ask another question?"

He sighed. He was growing weary of this new business of exchanging information when he hadn't been accustomed to it. "What is it?"

"Do you know where my aunt is?"

"Do not mention her to me again, Lydia."

"But Father, she is your sister."

"Your mother was my wife. She was never the same physically after all she went through in Groton. That is why the fever hit her so hard. Not because she was a sinner. You can thank my sister for your mother's departure from this earth. And I'll thank you never to mention her again."

With that, he stormed out into the cold, slamming the door behind him, and on any emotional progress he had made with his daughter.

⌒〜

Just a few miles away, in the Salem jail, Sarah Good hurt all over. The sickness had been unbearable with this baby, and had not subsided even during these later months. She emptied her stomach so much that soon she was projecting bile. She preferred that to beans, which was all they were giving her and the other women. The only place she had to empty her stomach was the same corner where they had to defecate and relieve themselves. The stench increased her nausea so much that she begged God to let her die. Then, she'd remember her baby and little Dorcas. They needed their mother, such as she was. In spite of what she'd become, she would take better care of them than their no good father. How she longed to see Dorcas. The ache from her absence was worse than all she endured since her arrest. Was William seeing to her daughter's needs? Or was he trying to hoist her off to a neighbor? Perhaps he didn't care for her at all. Maybe little Dorcas was by herself, taking up where her mother left off, going door-to-door, and begging for a morsel to stay alive for one more day. Another wave of nausea overtook her, and she crawled over to the straw stack, which needed to be swept out and changed, and proceeded to heave. Her head pounded while her slick, stringy hair fell forward. Sarah's arms felt so heavy that to move that simple strand of hair seemed unbearable.

A brown hand appeared in front of her face and pulled the hair out of her way. Tituba. She and the slave had never gotten along. Tituba had never welcomed her at the parsonage when she begged, although she was kind to Dorcas. She always gave them a little something, but Sarah thought her to be haughty, especially for a mere slave. In turn, Sarah had wielded her nasty insults at the slave, which didn't help her reception at the reverend's house. Yet, here she was, showing a small kindness to Sarah. No, not small. A big kindness, for at that moment, Sarah felt like embracing the woman. She hadn't embraced anyone but Dorcas for a very long time. Instead, she heaved once more, then laid back down, slipping into unconsciousness.

Tituba shook her, then helped her get back to her spot as far away from the putrid stench as possible. Nearby, Goody Osborne slept. Sarah did not know how she could sleep as much as she did in these wretched conditions, but she knew the woman had been ill so maybe it was best she slept. She wished she could sleep. Then maybe she wouldn't feel the nausea. Maybe she wouldn't feel the headache and the body aches. Maybe, just maybe, she wouldn't feel the heartache. And the fear.

Was Tituba scared? She had heard the crowd yelling "Hang 'em!" No doubt Tituba heard it, too. What did she say when she was questioned? Did she accuse Sarah as Sarah had accused Goody Osborne? She felt a measure of guilt for that one, but only a measure. She had to find a way out of this and take care of her children. If that meant accusing others so as not to be convicted, then so be it. Tituba had no children, and Goody Osborne's children were grown. Sarah knew it was a horrible thought, but if anyone was going to hang for witchcraft, it shouldn't be a mother with two small children.

She needed water. If she could crawl over to that hole in the wall, and reach her hand out and scoop some water from that puddle, she could sip it. It would be a while before they'd bring water, and when they did, it wasn't much. Again, a brown hand appeared, and this time it was cupped. Tituba poured the water from her hand into Sarah's mouth. She drank greedily, but weakly, so she choked. Tituba went back to the hole in the wall, and brought back more of the mud-tainted water for her fellow prisoner. She did this until Sarah seemed satisfied. Sarah wondered if the reason the slave was so tenderly caring for the woman who called her names came from a place of guilt. It didn't matter. For now, Sarah survived. That was all that mattered. She must survive. Her baby kicked at that moment. She tried to smile at Tituba, but her eyes fell shut and for the first time since her arrest, she slept deeply.

❧

Tituba watched her prison mates suffer. Were these the same women she saw strangling Ann in the meetinghouse? If it was, they certainly weren't hurting anyone now. They were the ones hurting. Tituba had never been so frightened in her life. At first, the questions scared her. Then, what she saw scared her more. The devil had floated in front of her face. At least he looked like what she thought the devil should look. His hot breath had suffocated her in the meetinghouse. She could hear people screaming in the background, but his voice was loudest. *Accuse or be accused.*

The loud and horrible voice sounded like it came from inside her, rather than from the hideous creature in front of her. What if it came back? Oh how she missed her husband. If she could just talk to him. They were allowed no visitors at this time because they didn't want anyone else to be afflicted. Tituba hadn't afflicted anyone. She herself had been afflicted, but those girls were claiming to see her form attacking them. How was that possible? Did the devil control her and somehow she wasn't conscious of it? Did the devil control the others, too? If so, were they even guilty? She had called out these women's names. Shame flooded her soul, and she wanted to lie down and weep. Only, she was too weak to do so. Meager amounts of food, along with meager amounts of water left her in a pitiful state. Crying seemed too great a task, even for her grieving heart. Did she endure all of this for nothing? Leaving her home in Barbados, coming to this new land, only to die from false accusations? Were they false?

If Sarah Good was possessed by the devil, was the child in her womb also possessed? She wondered if it would look like the devil when it was born. Tituba had heard stories about babies being possessed when they were born. They usually had some kind of hideous mark upon them, or a deformity of some kind, and if anyone suspected they belonged to the devil, they'd be killed instantly, despite the mother's cries for her baby's life. What would happen to this baby? If it even was a baby. She rubbed the sides of her arms.

Tituba had never had a child. Once when she was young, she had been hurt badly by a man who had visited her master at the time. He thought it was his right to take her. Tituba would never forget the shame of that day, and the disgust she felt when he violated her innocence. Later, when she discovered the absence of her woman's curse, and her swelling belly, she went to her master and told him what his friend had done to her. He was angry, but knew that a slave's word meant nothing; so in secret, he took her to a physician and had the baby "taken care of". He paid a hefty sum to persuade the physician to do as he asked. Tituba pleaded that she keep the baby, but her master wouldn't hear it. She screamed and fought, and the pain was so unbearable she passed out. For days, she bled and bled, until her master took her back to the physician. He hurt her again, but this time it was more than physical pain, for he told her she could never bear children. Tituba wasn't the same after that. The resentment for her master grew every day, and she wanted to end her life rather than look at him. He apologized later, and seemed genuinely remorseful, but she just couldn't get past it. Then one day, he bought John Indian. John was a beautiful, tall, strong man. His kindness toward Tituba scared her. She had never been treated with such tenderness and respect. Day after day, they grew closer and closer, until their master allowed them to marry. Tituba had never been so happy, but she knew she had to tell John the truth. She could never give him children. He had surprised her with his gentle response.

"I love you, Tituba. I'd rather be with you and no children for the rest of my days, than have a house full of children with a woman I could never love the way I love you."

Her heart warmed at the memory. They had been so happy, although she thought of her unborn child often. Then, their master decided to become a ship's captain and bought a ship. He sold his property, including Tituba and John Indian. That was when they met Reverend Parris. When he bought them, they were convinced that it didn't matter where they went, as long as they were together. She never imagined they'd be separated. Yet, here she was, alone and accused.

That night, she finally dozed. In her ears, the demon whispered over and over, "Accuse or be accused."

⌒〜

The warrior Uriel watched the demon with disgust. He turned to the one beside him. "Is there nothing we can do?"

"We have our orders." Raphael answered.

"This is a dismal and dark place, with no light."

"There is always light, Uriel."

"Why can't we shine it?

"In due time. All in due time."

"They suffer so. Why can't we fight?"

"We need the prayer cover. Too many are either fascinated or fearful about these accusations. They do not seek God's will. They seek their own."

"We can't interfere with man's will."

"Right. Let's not forget, though, that the Most High always offers hope to those that seek it."

Uriel pointed at the women on the dank prison floor. "Will they seek it?"

"Only time will tell. In the meantime, we'll be ready."

CHAPTER THIRTEEN

John Proctor's servant girl, Molly Warren, acted skittish these days. His wife, Elizabeth, grew impatient with her more every day. Running a tavern meant that John had to depend on his wife to help serve drinks and other refreshments to travelers on the road while he and his sons ran the farm. His two sons were barely men themselves, but John didn't know how he could run the farm without them. Since Elizabeth worked in the tavern, Molly was supposed to take up the slack to keep the household running properly, and help Elizabeth when needed. The tavern was in the front of the house. A large room, it had small tables and chairs along the perimeter. Larger tables sat at the center, with equally long benches flanking the sides. In one corner of the room, there was a structure, halfway enclosed, where ale mugs lined the walls inside, visible to customers. A large fireplace covered the back wall, and served to meet the needs of meals for weary travelers, as well as the household. There were a couple of smaller rooms on the bottom floor with beds for lodging, but upstairs was strictly for the family.

Located on Ipswich road, it was where strangers met up. Local customers weren't encouraged by the village officials. John knew it was more about politics than geography. He wasn't well liked by those who wished to separate from the town. He had spoken publicly about his feelings on the subject. It didn't matter. He had plenty of business with strangers traveling by and stopping in for rest and refreshment, and there were a few locals who didn't take part in the area's political and social matters.

He watched as Molly fumbled while she served today's patrons. Elizabeth yelled for her to get the soup from the fire, but she spilled the ale and had to pause to clean it up. Elizabeth stopped her cleaning and ran to get the soup. She began ladling it into bowls. She looked over at Molly, who dawdled, and set the soup pot onto the end of the table. She walked over and grabbed Molly by the arm, pushing her to the water bucket to rinse out her cloth.

"Finish this, girl!"

Molly cringed and scurried to the bucket. John felt his wife's frustration. Since the trials, Molly had been slacking in her work, and acting bizarre. Not like the afflicted children, but her actions were odd. Apparently, the girl feared that a witch was everywhere she looked, and she entertained paranoia. This problem wasn't confined to the Proctor residence. All over the village, and into surrounding areas, fear had begun to spread like fire about witches. If those women at the jail were witches, who's to say they were acting alone? John couldn't believe that at the last meeting, people were guessing who else could be witches. They threw out anecdote after anecdote about the three women who were already in jail, considering their imaginings about their past behavior were proof enough that substantiated their guilt. It was all rubbish as far as he was concerned.

John walked over to his wife and whispered, "You need to rest. I'll take over."

Her eyes shined with fatigue. "John, what are you doing here? I thought you were helping Goodman Nurse fix his fence."

"We finished early. You go lie down in the back. I'll serve. When the boys arrive, they can help close up. Molly, fetch her some warm water so she can wash up, and help her change for bed."

Molly scurried to the fireplace. "I wish she'd rush like that when I give her an order." Elizabeth said.

John looked at her and smiled. "She just needs a firm hand." His face suddenly turned serious. "Like many of the girls in this village."

"Now, John, you'd best keep out of all that nonsense."

"Elizabeth, I can't sit by and watch innocent people be hanged. Someone needs to speak up."

"Do you really think it will come to that, John?"

He sighed. "I don't know. I've never seen such crazy talk. People are speculating about how many witches there are in the village. Makes a man wonder who will be accused next."

"Do you believe those girls are pretending?"

"I don't know what I believe. The little Parris girl and her cousin seemed real enough, but that Ann—well, we know her and her mother. I have my doubts. Who can say? All I know is I don't think the slave and the others are doing them any harm." He looked down into his wife's gentle, green eyes. "Enough of this talk, wife. You go rest, and when I finish tonight, I'll come join you." He winked, and pressed his lips to her forehead. Elizabeth still excited him, though they'd been married eighteen years. He pulled her to him, but briefly. There was time for that later. For now, there was work to be done, and she needed to rest. She gave him a knowing smile, then walked to the stairs, with the nervous Molly on her heels.

As John went about his work, he thought of the woman upstairs, and how much he loved her. He hadn't believed it possible to love again after losing his second wife too soon. Elizabeth had come into his life like a ray of sunshine, eliminating the darkness that had threatened to engulf him. He couldn't bear the thought of losing her, not after losing two wives already. Surely God wasn't so cruel.

He shook the thought from his head. Now why were his thoughts heading there again? He had been with his precious Elizabeth for almost two decades. She was in fairly good health, other than the occasional illness. He had no cause to fret. Besides, he had too much else to fret over, and letting his fear and imagination take over his mind proved dangerous these days.

Molly rushed back into the tavern room. He put her in charge of serving the soup and bread, while he served the ale, and kept the fire going. His sons sauntered in wearily a couple of hours later, after the last of the patrons moved on, and immediately retired to their room upstairs. Some of the patrons paid for lodging so Molly got busy readying their rooms while they tended to their horses in the barn.

Just when John was about to put out the fire for the night, the door opened. Paul Knapp stepped inside, and shook off the mix of snow and rain on his coat.

"Goodman Proctor, I'm sorry to be arriving so late, but there's a matter of extreme importance I need to discuss with you, and the late hour is necessary to ensure privacy."

"Certainly. Come in. Would you like some ale?"

"No, man. I've never favored it. If we could just sit by the fire a spell, I'd be grateful."

John led the way to the fireplace. He decided to put a log on it in case his lodgers would want to warm themselves when they came in from the barn. "You should know we might only have a few minutes. I have visitors staying the night."

Paul nodded. "I saw them at the barn. This will only take a minute." John watched him struggle. What could be so important that Paul Knapp would bother to visit at such a late hour? Paul didn't visit much, at least not since Goody Knapp had passed on.

"John, if you recall, your wife and mine had a close friendship of sorts. I know that she-" He hesitated, holding his hands palms out, warming them, but John sensed that he only stalled the conversation.

"I know Emily confided in Elizabeth about our troubles in Groton, before we came to Salem. I know she told her about my sister's accusations against her.

John cleared his throat. "Yes, she did. Your troubles there sound all too familiar, I'm afraid."

"Exactly. That is why I came. I must ask that you and Elizabeth keep this knowledge of what happened in Groton to yourselves, for Lydia's sake. I'm sure all of this will be over soon, but after what I witnessed in Groton, concerning my sister and my wife, I don't want to leave it to chance."

"Of course not. But if I may, why do you think your sister accused your wife?"

"It certainly wasn't due to any guilt on her part, Goodman Proctor!" Paul stood with clenched fists.

"Please, sit. I didn't mean any offense. I guess I'm just trying to make sense of what's happening here."

"There's no way to make sense of it. Just like before."

"I know this is a sensitive topic, Goodman Knapp, but I'd like to know if there were any similarities between your sister and these afflicted girls."

"Aye, there are a few. My sister acted peculiar, that's for certain. She'd roll her eyes back, and yell out obscenities, and then she'd even scratch and bite herself."

"Was there any strife between her and your wife?"

"None that I had ever witnessed. Emily seemed shocked that she had named her as her tormentor. We were all shocked when people started believing her. We were grateful for our minister's good sense. He convinced everyone of Emily's innocence, and that she wasn't the cause of Eliza's affliction."

"Did you believe your sister was truthfully tormented?"

"To tell you the truth, I don't know what I believed. I only knew Emily was innocent. That's all that mattered to me at the time."

"And now?"

Paul's thoughts had drifted. He looked back at John as if he just registered the question. "Now I just want Lydia safe."

John nodded.

"I'd better get back to my daughter. Thank you for hearing me out."

"Of course. I'll speak to Elizabeth, though I doubt she'd utter a word otherwise."

"I had to be sure." With that, he left. John walked out behind him to see if he could help the visitors in the barn. Neither man had noticed the small shadow on the stairway.

Molly Warren couldn't believe what she'd just heard. Lydia was the daughter of an accused witch! And that could only mean one thing. Perhaps not all of the witches in Salem village were locked up in jail. Yet.

The small demon hungrily lapped at Molly's heels as she prepared for bed. Her mind was easy to manipulate as she settled down to sleep. The fearful ones were always easy. He filled her dreams with images that fed her fear. The next morning, Molly had made up her mind. She had to tell someone what she'd heard.

⌒⌒

The next morning, at another tavern, in Salem town, Bridget Bishop set about making breakfast. At this time, she had no traveling lodgers and she was glad for the quiet. Sometimes a few drifters would pour in for breakfast, but she hoped she'd get a respite this morning. Minutes later, the door opened, enveloping Bridget with the cold and the unwelcome guest.

"A mite early, aren't you? Mind you close that door promptly, and let the fire have a chance." She looked up at the newcomer, only to freeze in place. An unwelcome guest for sure.

"My, my. Look who dares to enter my scandalous abode."

Alice Putnam looked around the room. Bridget thought she should drown from all of the air she sniffed so haughtily. One could hope.

Alice finally settled her eyes upon Bridget, taking in her apron looped with red and yellow threads. "Interesting wardrobe choice as usual, Goody Bishop. Is there any color you won't wear?"

"Gray. I'm not too fond of drab." She roamed her eyes down Alice's gray bodice.

"I wear the colors of humility and prudence."

"Colors can't lie that well, Goody Putnam."

Alice's lips thinned. She fought for control. Bridget had witnessed Alice's temper more than once when she didn't get her way.

"Is there a purpose for your visit? Because I know you didn't come for the company."

Alice walked over to the fireplace and stoked it. "Do you like fire, Goody Bishop?"

Bridget sighed. "Why do ye ask?" She wished this dreaded woman would leave her in peace, though she was curious about what she wanted from her.

"You like to stoke fires, don't you?" She prodded at the large log, igniting sparks. Some flew up the chimney. Others landed on the large hearth.

"What are you playing at?"

Alice lifted the poker, then swung it around, its end dropping ash onto the floor. She pointed it right at Bridget. She stepped closer. Bridget backed away, watching.

"My Ann is a tortured girl. She and her friends aren't well. The court sees that. I don't think it would bode well for anyone to slander their testimony."

"Are you threatening me, Goody Putnam?" Bridget felt the heat on her chin. The poker was a bit too close. She backed up more.

"Everyone knows about your previous accusation, Goody Bishop."

"That was years ago. My case was dismissed because there wasn't any evidence. Just some youths getting spooked over a few wild horses."

"Everyone remembers. People thought you had bewitched those horses. There has always been talk about you, Goody Bishop. The way you dress, the way you flaunt your wiles around men."

"Humph. My wiles. I'm sixty years old. I don't have any wiles left. Or are you worried your man would prefer my old wiles to your cold ones?"

Alice's face reddened three shades darker than the fire poker, which she pushed toward Bridget with force. Bridget grabbed it with her hand and jerked it away. She refused to scream from the burning pain. She shook it at Alice. "Go home, Goody Putnam. You've stoked all the fires you're going to here."

"You witch!" Alice yelled as she rushed to the door.

Bridget stood at the door and laughed as the woman started down the road. "Guess you spook better than horses!" She cackled and shut the door.

She put the poker back in its place, then opened her cupboard to find the ointment she needed. Her hand burned, but the ointment soothed it momentarily. She had dealt with worse.

She thought of her late husband Thomas and the bruises she often carried after a blow with him. Oh, she had dealt him a few bruises of his own. How they had fought. Both of them had the tempers of a wild boar, but they had such passion for one another. Bridget sure missed that man. She snickered as she remembered the humiliation they endured, having to stand in the public market, holding a sign which displayed their offense of public name calling on the Sabbath. Bridget supposed they deserved it. Served them right, acting like fools. She still had what Thomas had called a "fiery tongue." She just often said what she thought. Sometimes she said things just to shock people, like she had just done with Goody Putnam. She didn't know why. She tired of all of the hypocrisy around this village, and Salem Town, too. All these folks with their prayers and their Bibles, going to Sunday meeting like they didn't just curse their neighbor for crossing over on their property. Or these women folk going on about piety when they couldn't wait to get out of that meeting house and gossip about the ones in the pews next to them. Rules, rules, rules. Nothing about hearts. That reverend spoke like God was this great big magistrate judge, holding his gavel, and waiting to slam it down upon their heads for every sin they committed. Her Bible talked about Jesus' great mercy and love. Oh, she knew mercy hadn't come free. For appreciation, she really needed to repent of some of her ways. She needed to mind her tongue, but it sure seemed better to speak outright than to speak in secret and pretend you didn't say it. She also didn't see how wearing a few colorful garments made her a harlot, just because it wasn't tradition. She didn't attend meeting like she should, but listening to that Reverend Parris was pure torture. She didn't know how those church members did it every Sunday. Worship shouldn't be about pretense. Worship should never be practice over purpose.

Rebecca Nurse and her sisters weren't pretenders. Elizabeth Proctor was saintly enough, too, she supposed. Perhaps if things were different, she could be friends with those ladies. Sarah Good was more like Bridget. Frowned upon in righteous circles. She was a beggar, but she didn't deserve to be strung up for this nonsense going about. Witchcraft indeed. Most folks would find the devil in a morsel of scorched bread if they'd be so inclined. She looked down at her apron. Or in colored thread. Maybe she should listen to that Goody Putnam and keep her mouth shut. It might take great effort, but she could do it. In her mind, she heard Thomas laughing at that thought. "Yes, Thomas. I suppose that is humorous." She shook her head and went back to her now cold breakfast.

CHAPTER FOURTEEN

Martha Corey watched as Ann Putnam and Molly Warren whispered to one another. Why was Molly on the bottom floor of the meetinghouse? She belonged in the galley upstairs along with the other servants. Martha didn't trust that Putnam girl. She'd wager her whole stock of butter that Ann's recent outbursts were a farce, if it wasn't a sin to wager. Martha had been at the hearing of the so called "witches". There had been a sinister nature in how Ann had reacted to the women when they were in the courtroom. She wasn't sure about the other girls. Betty Parris was a sweet little thing. Martha couldn't imagine that child going against Tituba. They had seemed quite close. Abigail was a bit precocious, maybe even slightly rebellious, but even she didn't seem maliciously vindictive. No, Martha would swear on the Lord's book that Ann was the vindictive one in all of this. She couldn't believe how much talk circulated the village, with people questioning who else could be a witch in their midst.

Giles nudged her. She looked sideways at him in surprise. "Ye best be paying attention and stop looking at that afflicted girl, Martha. It won't do ye any good to be involved in it," he whispered.

She nodded. She looked over and saw Rebecca Nurse smile at her. She smiled back. She'd like to talk to Goody Nurse. Maybe she'd pay

122

her a visit soon. She looked around the room again. The meeting house wasn't as full as she expected it to be. Perhaps the village folk's fear was greater than their curiosity. All this talk of witches. It was insanity, as far as Martha was concerned. She had never cared for Goody Good, but Martha knew she wasn't a witch, just an embittered old hag with a sharp tongue. She didn't know Tituba well, but she just seemed odd, with strange customs. Perhaps she had dealt in witchcraft. She had confessed, but did that really mean anything? She had also called out the other two women, and Martha was convinced they were no witches. Poor Sarah Osborne. She had looked so weak and sickly. She should be home in bed, not chained in shackles, in horrid prison conditions.

When the sermon was over, Martha realized she had not heard it at all. She had spent the whole service ruminating over those girls and the witch scare.

Giles merged outside with the men while Martha stayed inside the meetinghouse. The March temperatures were brisk, and the wood stove provided a measure of comfort for the women as they talked around it.

Martha sidled up to Rebecca and greeted her in a low tone. They spoke a moment about their farms, and a bit about their health. It wasn't long until they could hear the murmurs about the three accused witches.

Martha spoke up. "It's all rubbish if you ask me."

"No one asked you, Martha Corey." Goody Anderson said.

"Well, I'm saying it whether ye asked or not."

"Martha-" Rebecca started, but was interrupted by Elizabeth Proctor.

"I quite agree. This whole thing seems to be the work of girls having idle hands." She didn't notice that Goody Putnam was listening nearby.

"Yes, and you know what they say about idle hands. They do the devil's handiwork," Martha answered.

"Are you implying that my Ann is serving the devil?" Goody Putnam stepped in front of Martha, her eyes glaring.

"Thou sayest." Martha met her stare, calmly.

"Goody Putnam, all we're implying is that perhaps Ann and the other girls are just bored, and are in need of some entertainment. Maybe they do not understand the seriousness of what they have started." Elizabeth said.

"Goody Proctor, you and Goody Corey are quite ready to jump to those witches' defense. Be careful that you aren't questioned for doing so."

"Questioned by who, pray tell?" Martha asked.

Goody Putnam said nothing, just stared into Martha's eyes.

"Take your threats elsewhere, Alice Putnam. You do not frighten me."

"If you're not frightened, then maybe it is you who does the devil's handiwork." Goody Putnam said.

"Alice, mind your tongue. We are in the Lord's house, on the Sabbath. Threats aren't the Christian way." Rebecca took Martha's arm to guide her outside. "Come along, Martha. There is a better way to fight."

Martha hesitated. She wanted to say more, but Rebecca's calm demeanor soothed her anger, and she relented. Before she stepped outside, she looked back. Alice Putnam still stared at her as she whispered to her daughter next to her. It struck Martha how very alike the two were. It was more than the likeness in their appearances, with their light hair and pale skin. It was their eyes. Martha would swear on the Lord's book that she had seen glimmers of fiery red in both pairs of eyes as they watched her leave the meetinghouse. She picked up her step to follow Goody Nurse and Elizabeth Proctor. She had no desire to linger.

Lydia stood back, watching the exchange. Her father talked to the men outside about farming conditions. He told her he'd fetch her when he was ready to leave. He had consented to allowing them to attend meeting. He thought it best to carry on as usual, and not to draw attention to themselves in any way. He asked that she stay out of the conversations regarding the witch accusations as much as possible. So she just stood silently by as Goody Putnam spoke to the women still huddled around the wood stove.

"If you ask me," Alice Putnam started in her mocking tone, "Anyone who defends those who harm my daughter is a servant of the devil. Why else would they defend proven witches?"

"Proven? But there's no trial yet. Are they really proven to be witches?" Goody Sibley asked.

"How can you doubt my word?" Ann said. "Those women tortured me!"

"And me!" Abigail exclaimed.

"Where's your cousin, Abigail?" Goody Anderson asked.

"My uncle sent her to stay in Salem Town. He hopes to protect her." Her voice resonated sadness. Lydia knew Abigail longed for Reverend Parris to care for her as he cared for Betty, even if his care for Betty was distant compared to other father's affections for their daughters. Until lately, Lydia's father hadn't been much different.

"Well, let's just hope he can protect her from the witches not yet arrested." Goody Putnam said.

"There are more witches?" Abigail asked.

"Like I said, the only reason you'd defend someone so vehemently is if you're one of them."

"But Goody Nurse has defended them. She is a saintly woman. Surely you aren't suggesting she could be a witch," Susannah Martin said.

"I suggest nothing. You heard her. She mocks my Ann and the

other afflicted girls. Maybe she uses her saintly appearance as a cover for her wicked deeds. Why would anyone defend a spiteful beggar and a slave accused of witchcraft?"

"Goody Putnam, we all know you have had harsh words with Goody Nurse. Your families have never gotten along," said Susannah.

"That has nothing to do with this. Think about it. Why would a true saintly woman defend a foreign slave and two outcasts of the church? Why, she'd probably defend Goody Bishop as well."

"What does Bridget Bishop have to do with this?"

"You saw her at the examination. The way she stood up and mocked the proceedings, and mocked my Ann. She insulted me, and laughed at all of us. She's probably a witch, too. Why else would she wear those ungodly colors?"

"This is ridiculous!" Susannah Martin stormed out of the meetinghouse.

Alice didn't acknowledge her departure.

"Alice, if this is true, what do we do?" Goody Sibley asked.

"We'll tell Reverend Parris. He's our spiritual leader, after all. We'll let him handle it." With that, Ann followed her, and the women walked out behind her. No one seemed to notice Lydia who stayed behind. Fear prevented her legs from following them.

"Are you afraid, Lydia?"

The voice startled Lydia into motion. She whirled around to face Molly Warren. Where did she come from?

"What? Why do you ask?"

"I know how close you are to Goody Nurse. I just wondered if you're afraid about what Goody Putnam said."

"What about you? They were talking about Goody Proctor, also. Are you afraid for her?"

"Not so much. If she is a witch, she should be arrested. Don't you agree witches should be arrested?"

"If they're truly witches, then yes, of course."

"You doubt Ann and the others?"

Lydia feared answering. She saw how the other's motives were twisted.

"I just mean that all of the evidence hasn't been heard."

"Would you defend Goody Nurse if she were a witch?"

"I-she isn't-"

"Like you said, all of the evidence hasn't been heard."

"No one could possibly think Goody Nurse is a witch!"

"I don't know. Once when I walked past her on the road, she stared at me. Then, I discovered a rash on my face when I arrived home."

"That's not evidence, Molly." It couldn't be.

"No? I've heard other things about her and Goody Corey as well. As for Goody Proctor, well, I live with her. I have plenty to present before the court. What about you? Can anyone present anything about you, Lydia?" She walked around Lydia, like a cat circling a mouse.

"What are you saying? If you're talking about the day at the parsonage, you were there, too, Molly. And so was Ann."

"Shhh! Be careful, Lydia. I know things. Things about your mother. You don't want to make enemies."

"Molly! Make haste. We're heading home." John Proctor stood in the doorway, eyeing his servant girl suspiciously.

Molly instantly transformed into a subdued person, rushing to the door like a scared rabbit, and looking nothing like the girl who had just been taunting Lydia.

What did all of this mean? What was happening? Lydia walked out of the meetinghouse, and made her way to her father. Feeling eyes on her, she turned and saw Ann staring at her. Lydia shivered. She had never seen anyone look that way before. Only one word came to mind. Evil.

That night, she spoke to her father over their dinner of rabbit stew. "Papa, something alarmed me today. At meeting."

"Oh?" He looked up from his plate.

She relayed the women's conversation she heard, and the one she had later with Molly.

Her father jumped up. "This is why I don't want you around those viperous females! If you really want to know who the devil's servants are, look no further than the Putnams, and that Molly Warren has spent plenty of time with them. Rebecca Nurse is no more a witch than I am!" He grabbed his coat from the peg by the door.

"Where are you going, Papa?"

"I'm going down the road to the Proctor tavern. Don't worry about the fire. I'll tend to it when I return."

"But Papa, do you think it wise to anger Molly?"

He pointed his finger at her. "I won't let it happen again."

∽

The banging on the downstairs door woke John. He and Elizabeth had retired early for the evening. It had been a hard week, with all of the additional guests coming in to see the women being questioned. He was thankful for the Sabbath day of rest.

"John, whoever that is, they sound angry. Be careful."

He patted Elizabeth's hand and walked downstairs. The chill hit him as he opened the door to Paul Knapp, who shoved his way inside, and didn't bother with any formal greeting. Instead, he blurted out, "Where is she?"

"What? Where's who? What are you doing, man? Barging into my home? Are you mad?"

"Yes, I am. Mad with anger." He grabbed John. "Now, I'll ask again. Where is that wicked girl you have living here?"

"Take your hands from me, Paul. I might have a few years on you, but you don't have the experience."

Paul let go and curled his fists at his side. "I thought I could trust you, John. Of all the men in this village."

"What has gotten you so riled up, Paul, and what do you want with my servant? What does she have to do with trusting me?

"How did she know about Groton?"

"What?"

"Groton! I know it was you who told her. She lives in your house!"

"Why don't you calm yourself, and give me the full account of why you're here, and why you're so fighting mad."

Paul sighed, and John pitied him. The stress of the trials were getting to everyone. If there wasn't a fear of actual witches, there was a fear of being accused.

Paul started talking, and John's anger grew. He called his servant girl.

Molly Warren walked in with frightened eyes. She had always feared John, not because he was cruel, but because he didn't put up with any nonsense, and the girl was prone to nonsense. He often had to remind her of her duties, and keep her on task. John wanted to be rid of her, but his wife had mercy on the girl. She had no family, and needed a place to live until she could marry. That was another reason John loved his Elizabeth. Her heart was as pretty as her face.

"You wanted to see me Goodman?"

"Molly, I hear you are threatening Lydia Knapp. What do you have to say on the matter?"

Mary shook her head vigorously. She looked nervously at Paul, who stared back with thunder in his eyes.

"No, that is untrue. I'd never-"

"Are you saying my Lydia is a liar?" Paul stepped toward her, but John stopped him with a hand on his chest.

"Molly, explain yourself. Now."

"I only meant to warn her. Since her family has a history of witchcraft."

Paul shoved John away and slapped Mary across the cheek. She cried out and shrunk to the floor.

"Paul, control yourself!"

"You know what's she doing, John. You just heard it come out of her mouth. She means to accuse my Lydia."

"Paul, go on home. I'll handle it." Paul started to say something else. He looked down at Molly who was now sobbing on the floor. He nodded. After he left, Elizabeth appeared. "What was all that about, John? I heard Goodman Knapp yelling." She looked from Molly to John.

"It seems the girl here is up to mischief again. I'll explain later. Molly, go on to bed. We'll discuss this in the morning."

She just looked at him.

"Go to bed, girl." She turned to go, then stopped.

"Molly, what is it you want to say?" Elizabeth asked her.

"Shouldn't you have defended your ward? I live in your house and an outsider attacked me. Yet, you didn't defend me."

"Molly!" Elisabeth gasped that the girl would speak to her husband with such insolence.

"I defend truth. I defend what's right. You'd do best to remember that," John said. Mary stared back defiantly, but she knew she'd better say no more. She turned and walked to the stairs.

"Did Goodman Knapp hit her, John?"

"Yes, he slapped her. He acted no different than I would have, I'm afraid. After what happened to his wife, I can only imagine what these events are doing to him." He took her hand in his and kissed her palm. "I don't know what I'd do if I lost you."

"John, don't talk like that. We're going to grow old together."

John smirked. "I'm already old, dear. Not sure what you ever saw in an old man like me, but I'm forever grateful you saw it." His wife was only forty-two years old to his sixty years. He'd never understand how he caught her eye, and her heart, but he often thanked the good Lord above for that miracle.

Elizabeth grinned. "I still see what I saw then. I see a strong man who stands up for good. I see a Christian man who wants to please God. I see a man who doesn't let others strong arm him, but he's gentle to those who need him." She wrapped her arms around his waist. "And I see the same handsome man I married eighteen years ago, who can still make my heart leap when he walks in the door."

John kissed her and held her close. "I'll protect you 'till I die, sweet woman."

"Are you tired?" she asked him, a soft smile in her eyes.

"Not at all."

CHAPTER FIFTEEN

Sarah Good's labor came fast and furiously. The pain sliced through her lower back and even into her upper legs. It hurt so much she almost begged God to take her life. Then, little Dorcas' face came to mind. She had to hold on. Her daughter needed her. She'd get out of here. These ridiculous accusations would cease and she'd be set free. Surely she wouldn't be convicted of witchcraft. God couldn't be so cruel. Hadn't he done enough to her?

Now that she'd been moved to Ipswich jail, to be near a midwife, she was alone. Sarah didn't know why she missed the slave and Goody Osbourne. It's not as if the three of them held many conversations in the watch house. The other two were now in the Salem jail, awaiting trial. Sarah feared the trial. So many disliked her. Now Sarah regretted making so many enemies. She thought of Rebecca Nurse. Just maybe she still held some compassion for Sarah. Of course, Sarah hadn't given her a reason to. Pain brought her back to the moment. The sheriff still hadn't returned with the midwife.

She didn't want to have her baby in jail, under these circumstances. It would have been bad enough to have a baby in someone's barn. At least here it was a bit warmer than the watch house, though, and now she only had to contend with her own stench.

Belias watched the woman double over in agony, and reveled in her pain. Part of his plan had been to delay the midwife's arrival, so she'd have the baby alone. He had a nasty little demon with him, and the creature struck Sarah hard in the middle, intensifying her contractions. Sarah cried out, and the demon sneered, eager for more.

"Enough." Belias ordered. It was his turn. He spoke to Sarah's mind, creating confusion and doubt, but mostly fear. Her pain made her a ready recipient of his mental torment.

No one cares if you live or die, Sarah Good. Your children would be better off without you. Your life is hopeless. No one will help you. Your own husband betrayed you. God has never loved you. Your whole life has been a disaster. You have never been important to anyone. You're better off dead. Just do it. Kill yourself and end your misery.

Sarah screamed and the guard ran in. "Shut ye mouth, witch. Ye'd better hope that babe of yours isn't born with horns. He'll die before he can catch his first cry." He walked out, leaving her to her despair.

Sarah cried over and over, "God, please give me mercy! For once, Jesus, please give me mercy!" The demons recoiled in horror. Her pain immediately decreased.

Hours later, she delivered a tiny little girl. She looked down into her beautiful baby's face, and wept.

"Little Mercy. I won't call you Mercy Good. What a joke for your father to own that last name. He's a no good father and he has no right to ye. You'll just be Mercy. God did give me mercy after all, and I plan on thanking Him for it." She kissed her newborn's sweet head, and prayed for the first time in years.

Belias cursed and slung the small demon against the wall. He scampered off in defeat. The angels beside Sarah continued to speak words of life and comfort to her soul. Sarah drifted to sleep with little Mercy at her breast, no longer feeling any pain or fear.

Rebecca Nurse finally climbed into bed beside Francis. She had awoken with a sense of urgency to pray for Sarah Good.

"What ye up to at this hour, my love?" Francis rolled over and peered at her in the moonlight streaming through the window.

"I needed to pray, Francis. For Sarah Good."

"Don't waste your prayers on that woman, Rebecca. She don't want them, nor does she deserve them."

"None of us deserve them. You know that."

He sighed. "I suppose you're right. I do know she can't be a witch."

"Why do you say that?"

"Because the woman hates me. I'd be turned into some kind of creature by now if she was truly a witch."

Rebecca smiled, though he likely couldn't see it in the shadows.

"Too bad the others can't see it that way."

"Do you think there's any danger to Martha and Elizabeth, or even you, after meeting yesterday?"

"I don't know. It all seems like a dream. One day we're all carrying on with our lives, and the next we're all afraid of witches, or being called one."

"Mighty peculiar. Rebecca, maybe we should pack up and leave Salem."

"Francis, I'm an old woman, and you're an old man. We're too old to move again. If the Lord wants to take me, I have no say in it. I refuse to live by fear. Fear is what started this mess."

He said nothing, but pulled her close. Minutes later, they breathed evenly together. It had been a long time since they had fallen asleep in each other's arms.

Outside their window, Sonneillon snatched Belias up by the head. His strength didn't surprise Belias. This wasn't the first time he had been the target of Sonneillon's wrath. He brought Belias' head to his. The larger demon's hot breath singed his nose and it burned.

"Why are you here? This is not your post!"

"I just wanted to-"

"I know what you want. You want power. You have none. Let me remind you of what little power you have." Sonneillon thrust Belias on the ground and placed his foot on his back. Pain seared through his body and he couldn't breathe. He tried to beg for mercy, but Sonneillon's laugh covered his broken whimpers.

He lifted his foot and pulled Belias up. Weak, he could barely stand, but he didn't dare allow himself to fall. Sonneillon would see it as an invitation to more torture.

"Now. Be a good little demon and do as you're told. You have no place with the prayer warriors. I told you to stay with Sarah Good for now."

He towered over Belias to stress his point. He was in charge.

Belias nodded, and started to crawl away.

"Belias!" He stopped and turned in fear.

"No more suicide attempts. Your little pathetic attempt at that failed, and you'd better be glad. Lucifer wants her to hang with the others."

"But Sonneillon, it was a brilliant plan. If she had killed herself, they'd be convinced she's a witch. They'd all be convinced!"

"Don't you see, you fool! They don't all have to be convinced. This isn't about scaring a bunch of pitiful little Puritans. This is about destroying their system. This goes well beyond the here and now. Oh, forget it. This is why you need to stick with your little job, and let us bigger demons handle the important stuff. If you slip up again, you will have a new job, but it won't be a higher position. It will be the lowest of low. Is that clear?"

"Yes, Sonneillon. It's clear." He crawled away, pondering what he just heard. What was that about? Why were they really here?

CHAPTER SIXTEEN

In Salem prison, Magistrate Hathorne stood beside Judge Corwin as they questioned the two women in the jail. Reverend Noyes acted as attending minister. Sarah Osborne looked weaker, and Magistrate Hathorne wondered if she should be let go. Then again, the devil had ways of deception, including using physical appearances to confuse the innocent. He'd have to be careful not to get sucked in.

"Goody Osborne, what association have ye with the devil? Why did you turn from your faith and go the wicked way?"

"I did not, sir. I would never turn from my faith."

"Then why did you miss Sabbath meetings? Only the wicked skip Sabbath meetings." Judge Corwin asked.

"I've been ill, sir."

Magistrate Hathorne had heard the rumors. Perhaps her husband beat her because he sensed the wicked in her. He had heard tell that she had cross words with a neighbor, and when she left, she turned around and looked at the woman, and then the neighbor's cow died less than an hour later. That was only one rumor he had heard concerning Goody Osbourne.

"Goody Osborne, what say you on the charges against you? Tituba named you, Sarah Good named you, and those girls named you. They stated that you hurt them."

"I did not, sir. I wouldn't hurt children."

"Guard!"

The guard came in, knowing what he had to do. Goody Osbourne visibly braced herself, and Judge Corwin winced as the constable brought the whip down upon her. "Confess witch! Confess your evil ways!" the guard shouted with each blow.

"Enough, man. Goody Osbourne, it is in your best interest to confess. Do so, and you will receive mercy." Judge Corwin said.

"By mercy you mean I stay in prison until I die. I see no difference in that and hanging. At least with a trial I'll have a chance."

Magistrate Hathorne shook his head. "It is, of course, your path to choose."

Judge Corwin began the questioning of Tituba, who appeared to be in a trance. Judge Corwin looked nervous. Magistrate Hathorne didn't blame him. He, too, looked around the jail. What's to stop Satan from bewitching them in this very place? Were the chains enough to stop these witches from hypnotizing them with their evil magic? He shook his head. Nonsense. Witches had no power over God's ordained officials.

"Tituba, answer the question. Do you confess to your evil?" Reverend Noyes demanded.

Tituba rolled her eyes back. The guard raised his whip.

Corwin grabbed his arm to stop the strike. "Tituba!" He yelled.

"He wants to cut my head off."

"Who?"

"The devil. He aims to have my head if I confess."

"If you confess, you will be absolved. Your soul can be free of him," Reverend Noyes said.

"No. He doesn't want me to confess." She started moving her chains all around, and rolling back and forth on the prison floor. "NO! Get away! Leave me be!"

"Tituba! Who harms you?" asked Judge Corwin.

"It's Goody Osborne and Goody Good! They torment me so! Make them stop!" She cried out in pain.

Sarah Osborne spoke. "I do not harm her. I'm right here. You see I have not moved."

Magistrate Hathorne spoke. "Clearly it's your spirit. Someone is hurting her, and she claims it's you."

Judge Corwin called the guard again. "Search her."

The guard looked over Tituba's arms and legs.

Magistrate Hathorne's stern voice stopped him. "No. Search her everywhere." The guard looked at him in surprise. He stripped Tituba until she was bare and searched her naked body right in front of the men. Tituba wailed as the guard's hands roamed her body, looking for marks.

"There!" Reverend Noyes yelled out. The guard stopped and pulled back. Apparently, he didn't see anything yet. Magistrate Hathorne moved closer. Sure enough, there were claw marks on Tituba's skin. Fresh, bloody, claw marks. The guard picked up his whip and started beating Sarah Osborne. She cried out weakly, then fell silent. Magistrate Hathorne ordered the guard to leave, and he, Noyes, and Corwin mulled over what had just transpired. When they left minutes later, they had made their decision. There would definitely be a trial.

～～

Tituba cried long after they left. Sarah Osbourne crawled over to her. The two women held each other, but did not speak for a long time. Finally, Tituba whispered to the other woman, "I'm sorry."

"I know." Goody Osbourne rocked Tituba like a mother rocked her baby. Somehow, that was the most comfort she had experienced in years.

～～

They moved Sarah Good back to Salem jail since the trials would be held there. When Mercy was a couple of days old, the guard came in and grabbed little Mercy, searching her over for marks or deformities. He didn't bother handling the baby gently, which caused Mercy to scream pitiful, weak cries. When he handed the baby back, Sarah spat in his face. He then slammed his club into her head so hard she almost dropped Mercy. She decided then and there she'd better behave.

Since she needed to be nursed, they didn't take Mercy, but allowed Sarah to keep her with her in prison. It wasn't the best conditions for a newborn, but Mercy needed her mother. Sarah still hurt from the delivery, and her breasts burned raw from nursing, but as she snuggled the tiny bundle to her chest, she thanked God for this small measure of comfort in an otherwise dark place. She looked at the other women. Goody Osborne didn't look too well. Sarah wondered if she'd make it until her trial. She wanted to help her, but she barely had strength to care for her baby. She had to care for Mercy first. Tituba didn't look at her. Sarah saw her clothes, torn from her body, her nakedness uncovered. She knew what had happened. They had searched for the marks again. Why was this happening to them? If Sarah was stronger, she'd try to escape, and she'd take her baby, and Dorcas, and these two women, and they'd escape where no one would find them. For now, she'd do what she could. Providence had given her Mercy, so she figured it was about time she offered some.

"Tituba."

Tituba jerked her head up when Sarah spoke her name.

"I don't blame you, Tituba. This is not your doing."

Tituba dropped her head into her hands and sobbed.

◦───◦

Tituba had been shocked that Sarah had spoken to her. Even though she wasn't a respectable woman, she was still free, and had always held an attitude of snobbery with Tituba. Perhaps these circumstances gave one pause to reflect on just how much they had in common. She didn't know, but it felt so good to have someone speak to her, and excuse her from suffering such guilt. How could she tell these women what she had seen? She didn't mean to name them as her tormentors, but she had seen their faces. It had been their faces, twisted into evil snarls, and pinching and clawing at her skin. She had screamed out in fear, at what she saw in that moment. But once she had named them, the faces had turned into hideous creatures that looked nothing like the women that shared the jail cell with her. She couldn't tell the judges. She just couldn't. They'd accuse her of changing her story, and protecting her fellow witches. Tituba had been afraid. Then, when that guard touched her naked flesh, she remembered another man touching her violently. Tituba shivered in horror. The only comfort in this whole nightmare was that the Reverend Parris would have to pay her jail fees since he was responsible for her. Tituba almost managed to smile at that thought. Almost. She didn't know if she'd ever smile again.

⌒‿

Thomas Putnam arrived at Judge Corwin's house just before noon. His servant ushered Thomas into the room where the judge so often did his official business. The fireplace to the left did little to knock the chill out of Thomas, but maybe that was because his chill was not of a physical nature. Thomas hated what he had to do today. He had always liked Goody Nurse. While he had definitely had words with her husband over political matters, he had always appreciated her kind nature, and sweet smile. She had never given him cause to dislike her. His wife had a different opinion. She usually did.

Judge Corwin sat at his long table, dipping his quill into his ink bottle, and then transcribing notes onto parchment. He didn't look up until he finished writing whatever he wrote. His nephew, Sheriff Corwin stood to the side, eying Thomas with curiosity, but he said nothing. He held a piece of bread, which he tore with his teeth, and chewed noisily, grating on Thomas' nerves.

Goodman Putnam, what business have you here?" Judge Corwin addressed him now, seemingly impatient.

Thomas cleared his throat. "I have news of more tormentors, sir."

"Oh? How reliable is the source?"

"Well, sir, it is my daughter, Ann, and my wife who witnessed it."

"I see. And who are they accusing?"

"Goody Nurse, sir, to start."

The sheriff dropped his bread, then immediately bent down to pick it up. Judge Corwin narrowed his eyes.

"What name did you say?"

"Goody Nurse, sir, and there's Martha Corey, and also Elizabeth Proctor and Goodman Knapp. She saw their specters when they started tormenting her."

"When did they make this claim?"

Yesterday. My wife saw the marks herself, Your Honor. Someone definitely hurt my daughter."

"You're sure she named Rebecca Nurse? And Elizabeth Proctor?"

"Yes. I was quite surprised myself. Had it been Goodman Proctor-"

"Are there any other accusations against these people?"

Thomas didn't get offended. It was procedure to have as many accounts of the accused before an arrest.

"Yes, Your Honor. Molly Warren claims she has witnessed suspicious behavior from Goody Nurse, and also that Goody Proctor has harmed her as well. She claims that Goodman Knapp came to her a fortnight ago, trying to force her to sign the devil's book. She has a large mark upon her face where he struck her."

"Did anyone else see this occur?"

"I'm not sure, sir. I only came to report what I know."

The judge stared at him a moment, then bent down and wrote on a fresh piece of parchment paper. He folded the paper, and heated his seal before pressing it to the folded paper. He handed it to his nephew.

"It's a good thing you're here, then, Sheriff. You have some arrests to make. Follow procedures. We will have a hearing first thing, with the afflicted children present."

Thomas swallowed hard. As much as he wanted the witches punished, he didn't like reporting Goody Nurse as a possible witch. It just didn't feel right.

~

John Proctor walked in from the fields just in time to see Sheriff Corwin and Constable Herrick arrive. His chest burned with indignation. Were they here to arrest him? He wouldn't be surprised a bit. He wasn't liked by everyone since he was on a different political side these days. The fools. Imagine if he went to jail for being a witch, simply because he wanted progress. And simply because he didn't abide by the Reverend's rules for righteousness. Just let them try to arrest him.

"Goodman Proctor, is your wife on the property?"

"My wife? What do you want with my wife?" He wouldn't let them question her. It'd only frighten her.

"I'm sorry, Goodman, but your wife is hereby accused of witchcraft, and is to be arrested and taken to Salem jail for questioning."

John Proctor laughed. Then he saw their faces. They were serious. He stepped up to Sheriff Corwin and stared him in the eyes.

"You must be mad if you think I'm going to let you take my wife."

"Not mad, Goodman. I'm under the authority of Judge Corwin.

See for yourself." He handed John the sealed warrant.

John took it, then ripped it apart. "I don't care whose authority you're under. You will not take my wife!"

The constable raised his musket and brought it down on John's head. He fell, but stood up and started swinging his fists. He hit the sheriff, who stumbled into the constable, knocking him down. Both men recovered quickly, and overpowered John. He was strong, but he was no match for the larger, younger men. He fought to release their grasp, but then the sheriff knocked him out. When he woke, the men were gone. So was his Elizabeth.

Molly Warren was inside the house, going about her duties as if nothing had happened. John pulled out the strap and whipped the girl until she admitted her part in Elizabeth's arrest. He made her tell everything she knew about it, and she told him that the sheriff and constable were going to the Knapp farm first, then to the Nurse homestead. He whipped her again until he felt ashamed of himself. He didn't feel bad enough, though, to apologize. His Elizabeth was headed to that stinky, rotten filth of a jail because of her. He detested the sight of her, and knew he might kill her if he didn't get away from her, so he threw down the whip and ran to Rebecca Nurse's house.

When Rebecca opened her home to him, he was surprised to see Lydia Knapp sitting at the fireplace. Her father Paul stood with Francis nearby.

"John, what a surprise. Come in and warm yourself. Must be a day for visitors. Oh, my John, what happened to your head?"

"This isn't a pleasant visit, I'm afraid. My Elizabeth's been arrested for witchcraft." He told them about his row with the sheriff and the constable. "And I'm afraid they were headed to your house, Goodman Knapp. Goody Nurse, they're heading here next."

Rebecca sighed, and Lydia covered her mouth in horror.

"You're not surprised, Goody Nurse?" John asked her.

"I'm sorry, John, but no, I'm not. I was afraid this was going to happen."

"That's it. Lydia, you and I have to leave now," Paul said. "Goodman Proctor, I have to ask that you keep it quiet that we left. Maybe we can get quite a distance away before anyone knows we're gone."

"Papa, where will we go? What about Goody Nurse?"

"Enough, Lydia! You heard what I said." He looked hard at her. "I told you it would not happen again." He picked up his hat off the peg by the door and started putting on his coat. "Thank you for the supper, Goody Nurse. I'm sorry to be leaving at a time like this, but we'll be saying our goodbyes now."

Rebecca started to speak, but horses neighed outside. John looked out the window. "Run. All of you. I'll try to distract them."

"What? Who is it?" Paul asked.

"It's the sheriff and the constable. I guess I was knocked out longer than I thought. Paul, Francis, take Lydia and Rebecca to my place, and hide until we can figure something out. Saddle up the fastest horses and get out of here."

"No, John. If they're here for me, I'll go with them. There's no use running at my age."

Francis protested. "Rebecca-"

"Francis, we talked about this."

Before they could discuss it further, the door opened.

"I would have knocked, but as this isn't a social call, I figured it'd be a bit hypocritical." The sheriff had papers in his hand, just like the paper John had seen when they came to arrest his wife.

"Why are you here, Sheriff?" He asked. His temper flared. He balled his fists at his side. "And what did you do with my wife?"

"Well, Goodman Proctor, you get around, don't you? Constable Locker has escorted your wife to jail, along with Goody Corey. And they're about to have some company."

145

John raised his fist, but Rebecca reached out and gently touched his arm. He brought it down to his side.

"Ye must have learned ye lesson, old man. You don't want to be knocked out again. Now, be still. We've got a job to do." He turned to Paul.

"You know," said the sheriff, "It's convenient finding you here, Goodman Knapp."

Paul stepped forward. "You'll not take her."

Sheriff Corwin ignored him. "It seems here we have two warrants in hand, one is for Goody Nurse, and one is for you."

"Me?" Paul stood shocked, but relieved that the sheriff didn't mention his daughter.

"No!" Lydia ran to her father.

"Be careful, girl. It'll be you next." Sheriff Corwin said.

"Leave her alone, Sheriff. She's only a child." Rebecca said.

"Witches can be anybody, Goody Nurse, you know that, being as saintly as you are." His sarcasm enraged John.

"Who has charged them?" he asked.

"I don't have to tell you that, Proctor, but it be your servant girl, Molly Warren, and that Putnam girl, Ann. We've already arrested your wife and Martha Corey, and these two are the others they have accused."

"Poor Martha," Rebecca said, her eyes filling with tears. The constable took her arm.

"Wait," Rebecca said, "Let me get my Bible. Please, just let me take it with me."

"Witches don't read Bibles."

John wanted to slug the sheriff for that, but he didn't dare fight this time. He was afraid that Francis would join him, and the older man couldn't afford to get into a tussle. Sheriff Corwin grabbed for Paul, but Lydia stepped in front of him.

"No, please, you can't take him!"

Paul pushed her back. "Stay with Goodman Nurse, Lydia."

"But, Papa."

"I mean it. Stay. This will all be over soon."

Francis stepped up. "You're not taking my Rebecca!" He shook his small, frail fist at the constable, who held her arms.

"Am I going to have to knock you out, too, Goodman Nurse?"

"I'll not let you take my girl, Sheriff." Francis' voice shook with emotion.

"You have no choice." He held up the warrant. "It's the law."

John placed his hand on Francis' shoulder. "Let her go, man. Now is not the time."

They started out the door. Paul looked back at his daughter while Rebecca just kept her head down.

"No! Wait!" Lydia ran to her father and slammed into his chest. She wrapped her arms around him. John tried to pull her away, but she held tight to her father.

Paul bent his head down to hers, and whispered, "You're safe. That's all that matters." Sheriff Corwin jerked him away from Lydia. He and the constable led the two prisoners to the horses. Paul and Rebecca didn't look back as they rode away.

Francis just stared down the road after his wife while Lydia sat on the ground and wept.

John decided to do something he didn't do enough. He prayed.

CHAPTER SEVENTEEN

The constable tied ropes around Rebecca's ankles and feet. He stretched them so tight that she cried out. He looked at her warily, as if he expected her to cast a spell on him. She wasn't so sure she wouldn't if she could, after the way he had spoken to her husband and Lydia.

The odors burned her nostrils and threatened her stomach. She had been placed in the watch house with Goody Corey and Goody Proctor.

"Rebecca, drink some water." Martha held out a ladle for her to take, but Rebecca had no desire to drink, especially the rank water, which always left a bitter taste on her tongue. She never favored cider, but it did cover the taste of the water, so she longed for some now.

"You must drink. Just swallow it fast, and it's not so bad." Rebecca took the ladle and drank swiftly, wincing as the vile substance washed down her throat. She didn't say anything, but Martha was wrong. The water tasted so bad, Rebecca almost gagged.

"I couldn't believe it when I saw Goody Proctor here, but you, Rebecca. Of all people accused, I'm certainly shocked to see you here. I am convinced this is all nonsense."

"Perhaps." Rebecca said.

"Aren't you frightened, Rebecca?" Elizabeth spoke for the first time.

"Yes, I am. I'm afraid there's something bigger happening here. I don't think all of the afflicted are lying. Someone or something is hurting those girls, or at least most of them." She still wasn't so sure of Ann's sincerity. "I just know it's not any of us in this room."

"Do you think it's the others, then, Goody Nurse?"

"No. I do not."

"Not even Sarah Good or Tituba?"

"Not even them."

"Then who do you suppose hurts them?"

She paused and looked up to the ceiling.

"Goody Nurse?" Elizabeth prodded again.

"I don't want to frighten you, but I believe what we have here is definitely the devil's handiwork, as the ministers and judges suggest, but it's not our doing."

"But how do you explain what is happening to everyone? All of the fits, and even the girls seeing our shapes? They don't act like they're faking, and they even have marks on them."

Martha spoke up. "If you're saying what I think you're saying, then there may be no fighting this."

"We don't have to fight, Martha. You know what the Word says about that."

"He fights for us."

She nodded and smiled.

Elizabeth didn't understand. She shook her head.

"Goodness, girl. Think. Don't you know your Bible?" Martha had never sweetened her words.

Rebecca spoke softly. "It's demons, Elizabeth. Satan is using his demons to torment the girls. They can take the form of anything or anyone if allowed."

"You can't be serious!"

"Oh, I'm quite serious."

Elizabeth shivered. She looked around the small, watch house space, and wondered if a demon hovered over them now.

◠◡

Sonneillon wanted to tie that rope around the Nurse woman's neck and pull until she had no more life in her. That would shut her up. She just couldn't stop talking about God's Word, and prayer. The same with that Corey woman. Well, maybe he couldn't kill them, but he could torment them until their own people did it for him. He called for the demon of anxiety and depression. The demon had great strength, and Sonneillon knew he'd revel in using his powers on these women. He sneered at the Nurse woman, though she could not see him.

"Try holding to your faith now, prayer warrior. Your God won't heed your prayers this time." He flew off, taunting the angels who watched the other demon enter the watch house. He wanted to fight. Why were they avoiding battle? Sonneillon laughed. This time the Prince of Darkness had the upper hand. It felt good to be on the winning side.

◠◡

Martha did not sleep well that night. The demon enjoyed filling her dreams with the tortuous memories.

Martha looked at her vegetables. She'd have to be careful and water them more with this dry spell. It wore her out to carry the water back and forth, but they needed the stores for the winter. The sun beat down on her, and she stripped off her apron. If Ben wouldn't whip her, she'd just strip down to nothing. She smiled at that thought. She'd cause some talk then. She heard something behind her and turned around. Shocked, she stumbled backwards over her garden, and tried to crawl away from the large half- naked man. An Indian! On her homestead. Ben was too far away. He'd never hear her scream. She saw his hatchet hanging on his side, and the scalps around his neck. Was she going to die today? He reached down and grabbed her by the hair. He dragged her to the woods, and proceeded to pull up her bodice. She screamed, but she knew no one heard her. He didn't seem to mind her screaming. She felt him press down onto her and she went numb. Could this be happening? As he violated her, she decided to fight. She brought her teeth down onto his arm, and he picked up a nearby rock and slammed it into her head. Blinding pain stopped her from fighting him anymore. When he finished, she thought for sure he'd kill her. Instead, he just stood and stared at her. Then, he turned and walked away.

Martha bolted upright. For a moment she forgot where she was. The smells brought realization.

"Martha, are you alright?" Elizabeth Proctor asked. It was dark, and Martha couldn't see her face. She hoped she didn't wake Rebecca.

"Aye. Just a bad dream."

Elizabeth didn't say anything. It made sense, having bad dreams in this place, under these circumstances. Martha wondered how they'd sleep at all. Fear and discomfort didn't promote rest.

"Martha, you screamed." She heard Rebecca's tired voice.

"Oh? Did I? I'm sorry." The two women fell silent again.

She wondered what they heard. What they now knew.

Martha hadn't dreamed of that day in a long time, although there wasn't a day that went by when she didn't think of it, if only briefly. That man destroyed her marriage. Ben had come home, right as she walked out of the woods. She had stayed there, in that very spot where the Indian left her, for maybe an hour. Numb with shock, she had wrapped her arms around herself and rocked, willing what had just happened to go away. Then, when she finally chose to get up and go back to the house, Ben saw her, and he ran to her. He had never looked at her the same after that day. He had never touched her the same, either. Martha had felt so dirty, and didn't think she'd ever feel clean again. Then, when she found out she was expecting a child, she knew. It was his. She didn't know how she knew, she just did. Ben had suspected, too. He wouldn't talk of the baby, and when it was born, everyone knew. Having a mulatto child disgraced her, and Ben. The shame didn't stop her from loving the babe, though. As soon as she held him, she knew she'd love him forever. Ben treated him well, but never embraced the role of father. He held him at a distance. Martha understood, but it hurt. It wasn't the baby's fault. It wasn't her fault, either. That's when she started clinging to her faith. She started searching Scripture to fill the emptiness and shame she felt every day. She hoped to erase that man from her memories. While she couldn't forget, she did find peace in Jesus. Because her boy looked so much like an Indian, most figured out what had happened to her, but they still treated her like she should be ashamed. Why? She had not asked for what happened to her. Some said she had angered God and He brought his wrath upon her, and cursed her with a mulatto child. How could anyone look at her sweet boy as a curse? No, Martha knew better. He was a blessing that God gave her to ease the pain of that horrid day.

After Ben had died, and she married Giles, he had made it clear he didn't want Thomas in the house with them. So Thomas hired out and worked and lived at a farm in a neighboring community. Martha saw him occasionally, but not enough. She missed her boy. She hoped no one told him that his mother had been arrested for witchcraft. She hoped no one would convince him she practiced witchcraft. He had lived with enough undeserved shame.

Martha heard the even breathing of Elizabeth next to her. She wondered if Rebecca slept now, too. Martha didn't want to sleep and see him again. How she hated that face. Suddenly, she heard the weak voice of her older friend, singing a familiar psalm. Her voice crackled with her raspy throat, but Martha thought it to be the sweetest sound she had ever heard. She closed her eyes, and let the words wash over her.

> *Shine thy light in the darkness, Oh God*
> *Let not the enemy harm me*
> *Reveal thy plan in the trial, Oh Lord*
> *Thy glory the world to see*

The next morning, John arrived at the meeting house for the examinations. The room had a chill that remained long after everyone piled into the seats. Those who couldn't find seats stood at the back of the room. In the balcony, eyes peered down on top of him. He knew they watched him. Some thinking he could be a witch, and others feeling sorry for him because his wife was a witch. He had heard the talk as they waited for the questioning to begin. With many, the accused already had a guilty verdict.

John had hoped to see Elizabeth, but Martha Corey had been examined first, and now Rebecca Nurse would go before the judges. He hoped Rebecca fared better than Goody Corey. She had answered the questions with abrasive responses. Over and over she stated she was a "gospel woman", which seemed to anger Nicholas Noyes and Magistrate Hathorne. John had never liked Reverend Noyes. From the look on his face, he seemed to bask in the proceedings. Sick, John thought. The whole thing was sick. Neighbors hungrily piled in, eager to see the accused witches. Others believed in the innocence of Rebecca and came to support her. Rebecca had many friends. She had always been praying for villagers, and ministering to any needs they had. In fact, if there was anyone needing godly counsel, people directed them to Rebecca more than Reverend Parris. He looked around and saw Lydia. He walked up to her and spoke in a low tone. "What are you doing here? Your father told you to stay with Goodman Nurse."

"I won't abandon my father, Goodman Proctor. Would you stay away if Goody Proctor asked you to?"

John had never heard the girl speak in such a strong fashion. She had always reminded him of one of the little rabbits on his property, ready to bolt at the slightest noise. He had to admit she was right. He wouldn't leave Elizabeth even if she asked him to, and no one could expect Lydia to leave her father. He patted her and led her to a seat beside him.

"Where's Goodman Nurse?" he asked her once they were seated.

"He couldn't bear to come. He has been ill with grief."

Anger surged through John's chest. Indignation for his friends and for his wife consumed him and he controlled his urge to wrap his hands around the throats of all presiding over the questioning, and the so called afflicted children as well. The idea that Goody Nurse practiced witchcraft was laughable. And his Elizabeth. She wouldn't hurt anyone. He looked up as they escorted Rebecca in. The room of muffled voices instantly quieted. He looked over at the afflicted girls. There were more now. He recognized Mavis Walcott, Eleanor Hubbard, and Mercy Lewis in the group, and of course, his own servant girl, Molly. He'd see to her later. As soon as Rebecca entered the room, Abigail and Ann starting twitching and whimpering like small children being forced to sit for sermon.

Magistrate Hathorne wasted no time and jumped right to his first question. "Goody Nurse, here are two afflicted children who complain that you hurt them. What do you say to this?"

Rebecca's quiet dignity expressed itself by the set of her shoulders and the lift of her chin. She did not falter when she spoke.

"I can say before my Father in Heaven I am innocent and I know God will clear me."

"If you be guilty I pray God discovers you, and makes it known. These children and now others claim you are not only harming them, but imploring them to do iniquity. Is this true?"

"I am innocent and clear." Her tone possessed a calm and steady note, and John saw the magistrate struggle with her answers.

"So you're saying you're innocent of these charges of witchcraft which have been brought against you?"

Ann Putnam stood up, shouting at Goody Nurse, "You know you aid the devil! You brought the black man and his evil book and tempted me to sign it!" Murmurs grew louder and louder until Magistrate Hathorne silenced the crowd.

Then he looked at Rebecca. "What do you say to this?"

"Oh, Lord, please help me." Rebecca looked up at the ceiling. She spread her hands out, and that's when the afflicted girls moaned and flinched, matching each movement of her hands with their every motion. John couldn't believe what he was seeing. They couldn't have rehearsed this. There's no way they could know how Rebecca would move her hands while she prayed.

"When your hands are loose, they are afflicted. Do you not see?"

Mavis Walcott and Eleanor Hubbard cried out, "It's her! Cant' you see? It's her!" They screamed in pain, and held their arms.

The constable walked over and examined Mavis' arm. There, on her flesh, was a fresh bite in the shape of a crescent. The room's volume grew with the excited voices. John wanted to run and get out of there. He couldn't process what he saw. Elizabeth would be next. He had to stay for Elizabeth. Next to him, Lydia shook. He wanted to pull her close for comfort, but didn't dare. There were too many suspicious minds in this place.

"What say you?" The judge shouted at Rebecca. He stood and

pointed at Mavis. "Why do you harm her?"

"The Lord knows I have not hurt them. I am an innocent person." Her voice wavered, and John wondered if her faith wavered, too. This bizarre set of circumstances would do it.

"You have long professed to be a Christian woman. These agonies are disturbing. You stand there with dry eyes, while these weep with suffering."

"You do not know my heart." She stared at him, calm in her voice now. This sudden change soothed John. Lydia stopped shaking next to him.

The magistrate would not relent. "If you are guilty, you'd do well to confess it. Confess and bring glory to God."

"I am as clear as the unborn child, and truth brings glory to God."

"Do you have any familiarity with spirits?"

"No, sir. I have familiarity with my God alone." She shook her head with this answer. The afflicted started screaming while holding their heads, writhing in agony.

John jumped up. "This is insanity! Those girls are having little fits, and I'll tell you the solution to this whole thing! They need the devil beat out of them at the whipping post!"

"Sit down, Goodman Proctor, or leave this courtroom now!"

John challenged Hathorne with his eyes.

Judge Corwin said calmly, "Goodman, sit. You do no one any favors causing a stir." John clenched his fists at his side, but gave in, knowing Elizabeth would be next and he didn't dare miss her questioning. He looked at Rebecca, but she wouldn't look at him.

"Do you agree with Goodman Proctor, Goody Nurse? Do you doubt the sincerity of the afflicted?" Magistrate Hathorne questioned.

"I cannot tell, sir,"

"That's strange. Everyone has an opinion on the matter."

"I must be silent on my opinion."

"Oh? Does this mean you think them pretending? If so, you accuse them of murder. Witchcraft is a hanging crime. If they knowingly accuse you falsely, isn't that murder?"

"I cannot tell what to think of it."

"If they see your shape, and it is that which hurts them, are you not guilty?"

"I cannot help how the devil uses my shape. He may appear in my shape to do me harm, also."

"You answer as an innocent woman, but the afflicted children reflect your guilt. I have no choice but to order you to Salem jail to await your trial."

John couldn't believe it. Many in the crowd began protesting in her favor until the judges silenced them once again. John experienced great fear. If they would send Goody Nurse to jail based on these pathetic outbursts, then his Elizabeth wouldn't stand a chance.

An hour later, John watched helplessly as they led his love out of the meetinghouse in shackles, knowing she wouldn't be home tonight. Paul had been questioned before her, and he, too, was sent to the Salem prison. Lydia had not stopped weeping since she first laid eyes on him, but she did so quietly. She didn't alert her father to her presence in the meetinghouse. Each time an accused would enter the room, the afflicted would start to twist and contort their bodies and cry out in pain. The judges saw it as evidence and nothing the accused could say would convince them otherwise.

He moved to leave when Lydia gasped. He followed her gaze and shock held him to his seat.

Little Dorcas Good walked into the meetinghouse, with shackles on her small hands and tiny feet.

CHAPTER EIGHTEEN

Sarah Good looked at her two children with a deep ache in her spirit. How could she have let this happen? Her Dorcas shouldn't be in jail. Her baby shouldn't be in jail. And, although she felt tremendous guilt, Sarah didn't belong here, either. They had already brought others in, the same day they brought in her Dorcas. Of all people to accuse, how could they accuse a four-year-old child, and an old, pious woman like Rebeca Nurse? Sarah knew Rebecca was no witch. She knew Dorcas was no witch. She knew she was no witch. So perhaps they had it wrong on all counts. None of the jailed were witches. What did this mean? How could something like this happen? Rage at her husband surfaced again. She embraced the anger. It helped her cope with the cruel conditions. That man had helped to put her and Dorcas, and their newborn child in this cell.

Dorcas clawed at her skin. Sarah stilled her hand.

"Stop scratching, Dorcas."

"It itches so, Mother." Dorcas pulled her hand away, and ran her nails along the baseline of her neck.

"You'll only make it worse." Sarah found it hard to persuade her daughter not to scratch when she clawed at her own skin. The lice were unbearable. Sarah had felt the first sign of them a couple of days ago. First, they invaded her sleep as they nested in her hair. Then, they assaulted her private area, which made any level of comfort impossible. She tried to scrape the little pests from her daughter's scalp, but there were just too many in the cell, and each inhabitant of the jail endured their misery. She worried about little Mercy. The sweet little babe had stopped feeding, except for a tiny session here and there. Sarah was certain she had lost weight. It was always damp in the cell and had been getting warmer in the middle part of the day. There were no windows to circulate air. The stone walls blew heat at them. Sarah tried to cool her daughters with some of the water in the pail, but it was warm and stale, and did little to soothe them, inside or out. At night, it was cold, and they shivered. There were no blankets, but even if there were, they'd be damp by the morning.

Sarah knew she shouldn't keep the baby in the jail. The conditions were horrid for her. She couldn't just watch her weaken. She had told the guard the babe needed care that she couldn't offer in prison, and asked if he'd find her a wet nurse. He had laughed and said, "No one wants to care for a witch's babe."

Sarah supposed that was true. Little Mercy squeaked and whimpered in her sleep, stretching her small arms out. Sarah kissed her tiny hand, and prayed that God would spare her child this wretched torment. She went to sleep, dreaming of a field of flowers, where her baby slept in the soft grass, with the warm sunlight on her face.

The next morning, little Mercy was dead.

⌒⌒

Lydia hated being home now. She didn't know why it was so different. It wasn't as if her father talked to her much through the years. Maybe it was because things were different now, but she missed him greatly. She had refused to stay with Francis, and he didn't push her. He seemed to understand her desire to be home. She didn't figure on how lonely it would be without her father.

Things in the village were different now. People only talked of the accusations and upcoming trials. Lydia hated it. She had tried to see her father. They had moved him to Salem jail. She wanted to bring him food, and cider, but they forbade her to see him because he was being questioned. She had ridden all the way there, but had been turned away. She asked to see Goody Nurse, but they denied her that as well. She had sobbed all the way home.

A knock at the door surprised her. Ann stood smiling at her when she opened it. What did she want?

"How dare you show your face here? After what you did?" Lydia surprised herself with her bold talk. She surprised Ann, too.

"What did I do, Lydia? I only told the truth about what happened to me. You should be angry with Molly Warren, not me. She reported your father, not I."

"You accused Goody Nurse."

"I had to, Lydia. She does the devil's bidding. You should be glad to know it now."

Lydia couldn't believe she had ever been friends with this girl. "I want you to leave, Ann."

"There's a reason why I came, Lydia. I wanted to warn you."

"Warn me about what? What else can you do? My father and Goody Nurse are in jail! What did they ever do to you, or Molly Warren?"

"I'll show you what Goody Nurse did! Look at my arms!" She pulled up her sleeves and Lydia saw the whelps below her elbows, and the bite marks on her arms.

"Goody Nurse did not do that to you!"

"Goody Nurse hurt me and my mother. She has fooled you and many in Salem. And Mary said your father and Goody Proctor hurt her! Are you saying we're lying? Do you believe I'd do this to myself?"

Lydia couldn't answer. She didn't know what to think. The marks were real.

"Ann, do you realize this isn't one of your games? My father could hang!"

"Lydia, if he's innocent, he won't. If he's guilty of witchcraft, do you really want him to live?"

Lydia pushed Ann backwards and slammed the door. She heard Ann yelling on the other side.

"Watch out, Lydia! You'll be next!"

Was that all it was to it? Ann could just say Lydia was a witch, and then Lydia would be in jail, too? What was happening? Those accused thus far had no recourse of action. They had no defense. Was this justice?

She opened the door again and yelled at Ann's retreating back. "Go ahead, Ann. Accuse me! Just remember that Tituba was accused and now they're saying she's a victim! I can play victim and name names, too!"

Ann stopped in her tracks, but didn't look back. Lydia watched her until she disappeared through the path in the woods.

Sighing, she sat down and ate some bread, hoping to fill the emptiness she felt. Worry gnawed at her stomach. Surely they'd release her father. The trial would reveal his innocence. The guard at the jail had told her they owed money for her father's shackles and chains, and also for the food and water. Lydia had heard what kind of food they offered in prison. She doubted it was worth what they charged. Her father was innocent! And now they actually had to pay for him to be shackled like some wretched, evil criminal. It wasn't fair. Why was this happening? How could God be so cruel?

Rebecca's words came to her. Words she had said over and over to Lydia since she was a little girl.

This world is a cruel place because of sin, not God. God offers peace, not pain. Pain is here because we invite it through our choices. Pain is here because sin cursed the world. God never wants pain for us, but He can use it to draw us closer to Him, and to make us stronger in our faith. Never forget that, Lydia. Always let Him use your pain for good.

Lydia didn't know how any of this could be for good.

Another knock at the door startled her. Surely Ann wasn't back. Did she want another shove? Or maybe she would be arrested now. When she opened it, she saw a strange woman there, though the lady looked familiar. She had a lovely face, and kind eyes.

"Lydia Knapp?" the woman asked.

"Yes, I'm Lydia." Who was this woman?

"I have some shocking news for you so do you mind if we sit for a moment?"

Lydia didn't know if she wanted to let this stranger in her house, but something compelled her to. She stepped aside and the woman entered. She immediately sat in one of the chairs near the fireplace. Lydia sat in the other. She didn't speak as the woman looked her over.

"So like your mother, but I see your father, too." Sadness filled her expression.

"You knew my mother?"

"Yes, I did. I wish…well, I don't know what you know about their past, but they had a troubled beginning, your mother and father."

"Yes, I know. So you must have known them in Groton, then?"

"Yes, I knew them in Groton. Lydia, I'm your Aunt Elizabeth, or Aunt Eliza. I'm called Eliza now."

Lydia stood. "You're my father's sister? The one who-who-"

"Yes, I'm afraid so. Word reached me about what's going on here. I wanted to check on you and my brother."

Lydia sat back down. "He won't want to see you. He wants nothing to do with you."

"I was afraid of that. What about you? Do you want to see me?"

"I don't know. I'm not sure how I feel." She thought of Ann. Could she forgive Ann and Mary for what they were doing to Goody Nurse and her father? Now she could see why her father felt this way about his sister.

Her aunt looked at her a moment, then nodded."It's best to be truthful, and I understand. Where is your father?"

"You don't know?"

"Know what, Lydia?"

"He's been arrested. He's in jail for witchcraft."

Her aunt brought her hand to her mouth."No! Oh, my poor brother. For it to happen twice." She looked back at Lydia, and took her hands. "You need to come with me. Come stay with me in Boston until this whole thing is over. I have a daughter a bit younger than you. You would enjoy getting to know her, and her father, my husband."

"No. I'm not leaving father. And I don't even know you." She pulled her hands away. Her aunt put her hands back in her lap and stared at them. Lydia wondered if she'd speak again. Would she just leave Lydia now? The silence hurt.

Finally, she spoke again. "Lydia, I just want to keep you safe. I'm sure your father would want you safe as well, even if it is with me. You may not know this, but I'm different now. I changed my story. I know your mother wasn't hurting me back then. It was a deception of Satan."

"Then why would you say that? Why are these people saying all of this about their own neighbors? About my father?" Lydia started crying. Her aunt pulled her into her arms. She didn't resist. While she didn't know her aunt, she had felt an immediate connection. Now she knew why she was so familiar. She reminded Lydia of her father when her mother still lived. The same smile, and kind, gentle eyes. The same silent strength.

"I had been deceived, Lydia. Fooled by the devil. He came to me in your mother's likeness. I don't know anything except that I was terrified and knew what I saw. The only thing is, the image of your mother often changed."

"Changed? Changed into what?"

"Creatures. Ugly, red-faced creatures with snake noses and mouths with sharp teeth. Their eyes glowed."

"Aunt Eliza, you're frightening me."

"I'm sorry. It was more frightening in person." She shivered with the memories. Rubbing her arms, she turned her attention back to her niece. "Lydia, I think it's happening here. I heard about the afflicted girls. They act in much the same way I did. You need to come with me, and get far away from this madness. People act hysterically when faced with fear."

"No. I will not leave my father." She stared hard at her aunt.

"I thought you might say that. Do you mind if I stay a day or two, and go see your father?"

"They wouldn't let me see him. I'm not sure if they'll let you see him, either."

"We'll see about that. Now, would you like something to eat? I brought some things from Boston. Probably some goods you haven't had in a while. Would you like some tea?"

Lydia perked up some, but not much. She didn't know what to think of her aunt's visit. She seemed happy to meet Lydia, but as soon as Lydia had mentioned her father's arrest, she had been ready to drag Lydia to Boston. She could not leave. No matter how afraid she might be. And she was afraid. She was always afraid.

⌒

Paul sat alone in his cell. He had given up on counting the large stones on the walls, but since he was the only man in the jail, he

164

contemplated talking to them. Odd, he thought. He had never been one to talk much, but now that he couldn't, he longed for conversation. He could hear the women now and then in the cells nearby. He wondered how Goody Nurse was doing. These conditions were hard enough for him. How could a woman her age handle it for long? He counted his blessings that it was spring, although at night it was cold in the dark, damp prison. He heard Sarah Osborne coughing at night. She cackled so loudly that it had woken him several times. How could the guard listen to such suffering and not offer her some measure of comfort? Instead, she had been beaten every day. They had all been whipped with the strap, in hopes that the lashing would bring about confessions. The judges and ministers had maintained that a confession meant repentance, while claiming innocence meant guilt. Absurd. Paul couldn't confess to something he was not, or to something he didn't do. No matter how much the whippings hurt. He turned over on the hard, stone floor and winced. Those lashings sure did burn. They didn't allow their lashes to heal before they strapped them again the next day. His raw flesh stung and his filthy clothes stuck to the dried blood. He would endure it ten times over, though, as long as his Lydia stayed safe. He supposed he'd be more comfortable if he had some straw, but like everything else, they'd just add it to his bill. Paul didn't know what would happen after his trial, but he didn't want to chance leaving Lydia with any debt. What would happen to her if he went to the gallows?

The kick in his side woke him the next day. "Get up, Knapp. Ye have some visitors." The guard jerked him to his feet. He swayed, but he quickly steadied himself. He must keep some of his dignity. The guard led him to a common area in the jail. There, at the table, sat Lydia with…no. It couldn't be.

"What is she doing here?" he yelled.

"Settle yourself!" The guard hit him behind his knee and he crumpled to the floor.

"Papa!" Lydia ran to him.

"Away from the prisoner!" the guard yelled. "Get back to the table."

Lydia backed away and sat down next to her aunt.

The guard jerked Paul up again and shoved him to the bench across from them. Paul glared at his sister.

"Why are you here?" he spoke through his closed teeth. "I told you I never wanted to lay eyes on you again."

"Paul-"

"You dare to show your face in such a time as this? And you dare to approach my daughter? Her mother is dead because of you!"

"Papa! That's not true. She died of smallpox."

"She was never the same after what this woman did to her. She never recovered. She had weakened, and the fever took her because of what your aunt did to her."

Eliza bowed her head. No one spoke.

"Are you praying?" Paul sneered. "You? You're wasting your time. I doubt God hears a liar."

"God hears everyone." she answered.

"You need to leave. I've no wish to see you."

"I think I can help, Paul."

"No thanks. You've done enough. First my wife, now me. You stay away from Lydia."

"Papa-"

"Paul, I really think I can help. Please just hear me out."

"Why? So you can stab me in the back like you did before? Did you not get enough attention the first time, dear sister? Well, guess what? I'm already in jail. So you missed your opportunity. Now go back where you came from, and leave us alone. Lydia, you will not have any more dealings with this woman. Is that clear?"

Lydia looked at her aunt with indecisiveness.

"Don't fret, child. We tried." She patted Lydia's hand, then she looked at her brother. "I've paid wages to the guard so you can have proper food and some straw. Before you protest, think of your daughter. She lives in agony at the thought of your suffering." She reached out to touch his hand. He jerked it away. Tears filled her eyes. "I really am sorrowful about what happened, brother. I wish you could understand. The devil…he…well, I was deceived. I know that now, but if you could have seen what I saw, just maybe you'd understand. Your sweet Emily understood, and I am forever grateful she did."

"I'll never understand. You didn't deserve Emily's understanding. Or her forgiveness. And you certainly don't deserve mine or Lydia's."

Eliza nodded resignation. She reached out as if to touch him again. Instead, she touched Lydia's chin gently before she walked out.

⌒〜

It was visiting day at the jail, for a fee. John fought not to embrace his Elizabeth when he saw her. How he wanted to hold her, to comfort her and tell her everything would be alright.

"Are ye resting, my love?" he asked her.

"Aye."

"Don't be false. You know I can see it when you are."

She smiled. "You could always read me, John."

"Yes, and I know there's something you want to say now. So say it."

"I don't like to tell you like this."

"Tell me what?"

"It isn't the kind of news you want to say in a jail, under these circumstances."

"News? What else could be new, or even important, in light of the fact that you are here and not at home where you belong?"

"What's important is who else is here, and not at home."

"What do you mean? I know everyone who's here, don't I? Has someone else been arrested, and it got by me?"

"Yes."

"Who?"

"Your baby."

His eyes widened, but he said nothing.

"Did you hear me, love?"

"Yes. You aren't telling me you're expecting a babe? Not now."

"That's what I'm telling you."

It hit John in the gut. This should be a happy moment. A baby. Imagine that. Another child at his age.

"John?" Elizabeth's uncertainty sounded in her voice. "Are you upset?"

"Upset? That's not the word, sweet woman. I'm angry."

"I'm sorry."

"No, love. I'm not angry at you. I'm angry because if we were at home, you would have just made me the happiest man alive. Having another child with you is a gift. But you and my child do not belong in this filthy jail. I can't be happy with you two stuck in here, with no righteous cause."

"Oh, John, please don't blame yourself for this. Whatever this is, it isn't your fault."

"I'm supposed to protect you."

"There's nothing you could have done."

"I should have gotten you and the boys out of Salem right when this thing started. I had a bad feeling, but I ignored it. Now, my family suffers."

"You listen to me. They won't hang me while I'm pregnant. And if I do hang, my baby will have a brave, strong man to raise him, and a mother who went to her grave, thanking God above that she had these precious years with his father."

"Please don't talk like that, Elizabeth."

She reached out and touched his forearm. The guard walked over and popped her hand. John jumped up and knocked the guard to the floor.

"John, don't!" Elizabeth said.

The guard threatened to arrest John, but he didn't care. He grabbed his wife and kissed her desperately before running out of the jail.

As he walked home, he prayed to himself. *God, please, do something. Anything. Save my wife, and spare my child. No matter what it takes.*

CHAPTER NINETEEN

Oh thou my soul Jehovah bless,
And all things that in me,
Most inward are, in humbleness
His holy Name bless ye

The psalm fell flat on Lydia's ears. She had always hated Sunday meetings. The sermons frightened her, and the psalms bored her. Now, this meeting tortured her. She couldn't focus on such mundane things like psalms and passages, and Reverend Parris' monotone voice at a time like this. Those she loved most were in jail! She would have to be careful, though. Any time now, it could be her next. Her father had told her not to stir suspicion upon herself.

She saw Mercy Lewis staring at her. Mercy was now an afflicted girl. Apparently, Goody Proctor tormented her as well. Lydia wanted to go sit with Goody Easty and Goody Cloyce. Apart from her father and Goody Nurse, they were her only family here in Salem. Her aunt hadn't left, but thought it best if she didn't attend meeting. Lydia didn't bother asking why. Everyone suspected every one and every motive these days. Lydia feared for her father. What would happen to him? What would happen to Goody Nurse?

She looked back at Goody Easty. The older woman already had

her eyes on Lydia. She smiled and nodded at her. Then, she motioned for Lydia to look forward. Reverend Parris started speaking.

"Why does the devil feel so at home here? We must ask ourselves this difficult question. We must look around as the disciples looked around at each other when Christ remarked that one of his chosen was a devil. It is our duty to seek out any Judas in our church. Some of you have already taken this duty seriously, and for that you have God's favor."

Someone stomped out of their pew in the back. Lydia jerked her head around to see. Goody Cloyce! She stomped right out of the meetinghouse and slammed the door behind her. Goody Easty looked as though she wanted to follow, but she remained still, her eyes on Reverend Parris. Murmurs and whispers spread throughout the congregation. Reverend Parris spoke louder, commanding attention.

"Christ's church consists of good and bad, and are either saints or devils. If one partakes of communion and is a devil, the result is the subjection of God's hottest wrath."

Lydia shivered. Hell. Witches burn in Hell. The bad burn in Hell. She didn't think she'd been good enough to go to Heaven. Hadn't she partaken in rituals that had brought about all of this madness? Her father and Goody Nurse and the others suffered because of what she did. She could never go to Heaven now. But Goody Nurse had said God's forgiveness is for all. Reverend Parris said they are either saints or devils, and if she wasn't a saint, then that made her a devil. Devils couldn't go to Heaven. Devils couldn't take communion or Hell would be even hotter.

Lydia shook with fear. She couldn't stop it. She wrapped her arms around her body to still herself, but her body had its own mind, and in seconds, people around her jumped away.

"She's afflicted! A devil torments her!" somebody yelled. Lydia swooned and fell back on the pew. Someone grabbed her arms.

"Don't touch her! You'll get the devil's mark!" someone else shouted. Lydia closed her eyes, hoping to ease the sick feeling in her head. She could hear voices around her, but they sounded muddled. She opened her eyes, and screamed.

⌒∾

Carreau floated over the girl. Semiel fought to reach her, but several large and nasty demons snarled and held him at bay. They were too strong for him alone. Where were the others? He needed back up. The creatures pinned him to the floor at the back of the meetinghouse. He hoped Uriel or Raguel would arrive.

⌒∾

Samuel Parris jumped down from his platform and rushed to the girl's side. It was happening again! In his church! He would not allow it.

"Who harms you, child? Who do you see?"

Lydia slapped at the air above her. The face didn't move. The creature's hot breath singed her skin. Was she on fire? She screamed again. Her body stuck to the pew, as if someone had placed the blacksmith's anvil on her chest. Could they not see him? What did Reverend Parris want from her? He was asking her something. To name someone?

"Who is your tormentor? Tell us who afflicts you."

Lydia couldn't tell him. She didn't know what this thing was. She tried to move, but the creature placed his claw around her neck. She screamed with pain.

She heard something, then. Something different. Prayer. She heard someone praying. Goody Easty prayed for her! The pressure on her chest lightened. The ugly face pulled back and hissed toward

Goody Easty. She continued to pray, and placed her hand on Lydia's head.

"I said do not touch her!" Reverend Parris said. "Goody Easy, do you ignore the instruction of your minister?"

She continued to pray. The hideous demon shrank back, howling and hissing his odious breath. Lydia breathed easily again. She saw a bright light, then the creature fled. Goody Easty pulled Lydia to her, and Lydia sobbed relief.

Goody Easty spoke to Reverend Parris. "She needs to go home."

"She's an afflicted girl now. She needs to be questioned."

"She needs rest, Reverend."

He looked at the girl, sobbing in Mary's arms, and consented.

As Mary escorted her out of the meetinghouse, Lydia saw a bright light swoop down over them, and then it vanished. Did Goody Easty see that?

"Lydia!" Abigail Williams caught up to them. Lydia didn't want to talk to Abigail.

"Lydia, I must ask you. Did you see him? The monster?"

"What do you mean?"

"The creature with the hot breath, and eyes like a snake's. Was it him that tortured you?"

"How did you know that?"

"Because that's who I saw. It's who we all saw. At first. Except Ann. She's the only one who didn't see him. We saw him before we saw the other faces."

"Other faces? You mean like the face of my sister?" Mary Easty asked.

Abigail looked ashamed, but nodded.

"I see." Mary Easty took her hand. "Abigail, no frets. I understand. Lydia was terrified back there, and though we could not see what tormented her, it was real. I'm sure of it. But I'm also sure it is not my sister who did it, and you girls won't be in any trouble if you admit it."

Abigail's face changed. "Admit what? It was your sister! She joins the devil in his work!"

Reverend Parris came out the meetinghouse and his eyes landed on the three of them. Abigail ran to join her uncle. She didn't look back. Lydia watched her retreat.

"Goody Easty, what does all of this mean?"

"It means we have enemies, Lydia."

"Abigail? Or do you mean Ann Putnam?"

"Neither."

Lydia felt confused. "Then, who?"

Mary stared after the reverend as he departed. Lydia barely heard her whisper, "The devil." She shook her head sadly. "They are just his pawns." She patted Lydia's arm.

"Come. Let's get you home. We have some praying to do."

John Proctor and Giles Corey hadn't always gotten along, but the two men seemed to have bonded the past few days since both had wives in prison. Neither went to meeting that morning, but sat at one of John's tables, sipping cold cider. John loved spring, when the barrels of frozen cider thawed to a slushy drink, cool enough for a warm spring day. The treat didn't please him like it usually did, not without his Elizabeth here, to share it.

"John, I've been thinking. These arrests have turned this whole community into a pack of hens, pecking at each other. People have gone mad."

"Yes, that much is obvious."

"Well, these hearings have been no more lawful than I am. I suspect our women won't get a fair trial."

"So what are you proposing?"

"I say we break them out. We plan an attack, and we escape."

"Giles, I've thought about that. I just don't see how we can manage it. My Elizabeth is expecting. I can't ask her to risk herself like that."

"But you can ask her to hang?"

"She won't hang.' He stood, running his fingers through his salt and pepper hair.

"Ye can't be sure, man. People are thirsting for their hangings. The judges are convinced they have the devil in them."

John sighed. "Even if we could manage to get into the jail, we'd be dead in minutes. There are men with muskets surrounding the jail, Giles. Besides, you and I aren't exactly in our prime youth anymore."

"Are ye saying we shouldn't try?"

"Giles, I'd die for my woman, and I know you would, too, but what good is being dead if they're still sentenced to hang after we're gone?"

"So what are we supposed to do? Sit by and let our women get the noose?"

"No. I say we put ourselves to better use. Fight the only way we know how."

"If you say prayer, I'm going to slug ye."

"I wasn't going to say that, although prayer is our most powerful weapon, Giles. And I wager you're like me and could do with a bit more of it."

"Aye, I suppose so. What were you going to say?"

"I think we should start a petition for Goody Nurse."

"For her? Why not for our own women?"

"Think about it, Giles. She's the most likely to get off. Everyone has been a recipient of her good deeds at one time or another. We could get a load of signatures on her behalf."

"How does that help our women, John? Make some sense."

"I am making sense. If we get Rebecca out, then people will look at the accusations with more scrutiny. Just maybe we can put an end to this whole thing."

Giles rubbed his whiskered face and stared at the floor. "You might have an idea there, John." Then, he smiled. "Yep, you just might have a good idea."

John slapped him on the back. "Well, that's the first time we've agreed on anything in quite in a while. Must be a good sign."

Giles sobered. "I sure hope so. We could use something good around here."

In two short days, the men had acquired ninety-one signatures on Goody Nurse's behalf. John whistled as he walked into Ingersoll's tavern, more hopeful than he'd been in weeks. He had stopped to see if Goodman Ingersoll or any of the other men had heard any news on the charter. Instead, he heard more disturbing news. Goody Easty and Goody Cloyce had now been arrested, along with Giles Corey, and the sheriff was looking for him.

CHAPTER TWENTY

May 1692
Salem Village

"I need my salary, Goodman! This is the third month it has been deferred."

Thomas Putnam had not looked forward to this confrontation. He couldn't blame the minister. He should expect to get paid every month. "I'm sorry, Reverend, but now may not be the time to push the agenda. The witch trials are coming up. People are in jail, and some of the families are enduring hardships because of it. They're having to pay for the jailing accommodations, and now that there are more arrested, we will see more of this hardship in our church." While this was true, Thomas didn't mention that many just didn't want to pay the reverend. Even before the girls had been afflicted, the reverend had angered many in Salem village, and they weren't giving to the church anymore.

"I still need to care for my household. How do you expect me to do that?"

"Don't you have the slave, John Indian? Can't you hire him out in surrounding counties?"

"He has to pay for Tituba's jail fees with his hiring money."

"Ah. Well, at least it's not coming out of your pocket, Reverend."

"It is coming out of my pocket! His hiring money should be invested in this household."

"Of course. My apologies. How is young Betty and Abigail?"

"Betty seems to be coming out of it. Removing her from the area was the right thing to do."

"And Abigail?"

Reverend Parris stared hard at him. "She still suffers from time to time, but she serves a better purpose here. She's stronger than Betty. She can withstand the trials that are to come. Speaking of which, we need to get the proceedings under way."

"The judges informed me that we absolutely are prohibited from trying capital cases until we have the new charter for government. We must wait on the governor to return with it."

"Madness! We have evil in our midst, and the devil doesn't wait to do his damage. I suppose it will takes months to follow the Crown's requirements to reorganize our government."

'I'm afraid so, sir, but once we have the new charter, we can begin trial proceedings, and even punishments if necessary. That will occur shortly."

"The sooner the better, Goodman Putnam. With all of the new arrests and accusations, we must get on with the business of the trials."

"If I may, sir. I have my misgivings on some of the accused."

"What is this, Thomas? Is the devil giving you doubt?"

Thomas bristled. "Of course not! It's just that-"

"Speak your mind, Goodman."

"Well, Goody Easty and Goody Cloyce have now been arrested. That's all three sisters. Those three women have the reputation of being the purest, and godliest in the community. Sir, that petition for Goody Nurse had ninety-one signatures on it!"

"I'm well aware of the petition, Goodman. It means nothing. The devil uses piety to serve his motives. Do not be deceived. Did your wife not accuse all three women, the first being Goody Nurse?"

Shame flushed his cheeks. "Yes, she did, but I'm afraid her viewpoint might be slightly slanted due to past confrontations with her."

"I know your wife's tendencies, Goodman. Yet, she is not the sisters' only accuser. If that were so, they might be in a different position. As I said, the devil walks about, seeking whom he may devour, and he will use any means in any way to do so. Now, that's enough on that matter. See to my salary as best you can."

Thomas Putnam knew it was futile to argue with the reverend. He wished he could talk to someone about his doubts. Something just wasn't right. He knew his wife didn't like the sisters, but he had always thought them to be respectable and kind. What did that mean? He had watched those girls, including his Ann, as they convulsed and screamed, writhing in pain. They couldn't be pretending. Could they?

$\sim$

The jail had filled up so fast that many of the women had been crowded into cells together. This made the conditions that much more deplorable. Rebecca Nurse tried to rouse Sarah Good. Since the death of her infant, she had not spoken, not even to little Dorcas. Dorcas cried for several days, calling Mercy's name. Now, she just sat near her mother, linking her fingers together, then unlinking them. She did this over and over again. Even the wails of Dorcas had not stirred Sarah's emotions. She had just stared at the stone walls surrounding them. Now, she lay on the hard floor, gazing at the ceiling. She had not eaten since the morning she discovered little Mercy was stiff and blue.

Mercy wasn't the only loss in the jail. Sarah Osborne didn't wake up two mornings after Mercy had passed. This jail meant death. Rebecca was sure of that.

"Leave her be, Rebecca. Give her more time." Martha Corey whispered not far away. Martha had been dealing with a raw throat for several days now. All of them were sick in some way or another. Some had dysentery, including Rebecca, some had blocked noses and sore throats, with coughs, and others were just weak from malnutrition. Everyone in the jail was plagued with lice. That was the most miserable condition of all.

Little Dorcas screamed. Rebecca turned around to see a rat attached to her hair by his teeth. She picked up her chains and thrust them at the rodent, but it clung to Dorcas. Dorcas' screams woke something in her mother. Sarah blinked and gasped as Rebecca swung her chains at the rat to no avail. She reached down and grabbed hold of Dorcas' hair with one hand, and the rat with the other, then jerked the rat free. She smashed the rat down on the stone floor. Rebecca watched as the rat's head oozed blood. Sarah held Dorcas and the little girl clung to her mother.

"Thank you, Lord, for bringing our sister back to us," Rebecca said.

Sarah looked up with tears in her eyes. She smoothed her daughter's hair. "I'm sorry, child. I'm sorry."

"Mother, I want Mercy." The child wailed.

"Me, too, daughter. I want Mercy, too."

Rebecca couldn't help but think that the child's sentiment echoed throughout the jail. They all wanted mercy.

～

Tituba watched Sarah hold little Dorcas. She wept with guilt. She had started this with her customs. She never should have allowed the girls to participate in them. It looked like the reverend had been right when he first bought her in Barbados. *Your customs are not welcome in my house, Tituba. They are the devil's playground.* The devil was certainly having fun with all of them. Evil resided in this place.

So many more had been brought in. Bridget Bishop, Susannah Martin, Rebecca's sisters, and others now joined them in the dark place. The guard had told them about Reverend George Burroughs, the former minister of Salem Village, and Giles Corey, Martha's husband. The men were separated from the women so Martha didn't get to see Giles. However, for a fee, they could use the common room from time to time to visit. There was a time when Tituba would have gloated over all of their misfortune, but not now. She didn't want this. The whole thing was like a long nightmare, and Tituba hoped to wake soon.

She dozed off, and woke to the sisters whispering.

"She is faking." Mary said.

"Of course she is. So is her daughter. I'd wager they both conspired together after the first accusations," said Rebecca.

"What about the others?"

"I don't believe they're all faking."

"So you still believe in your theory, then." the youngest sister asked.

"Yes, I do."

"But, Rebecca, demons?"

"Yes, demons. The girls act as the maniac in the Scriptures. I've heard of things like this. I'm certain that Betty and Abigail have not been faking, and maybe some of the others are truly afflicted as well."

"Some would say the witches and demons are working together."

"That's not the case here. There is not one in this jail who has practiced witchcraft, save one."

"Yes, but she comes from a foreign place, and they have strange customs."

"Those customs are still witchcraft, Sarah."

"Yes, I suppose so. But do you think she is knowingly a witch?"

Rebecca sighed. "No. Just ignorant of the wiles of the devil. Just like the girls that partook of her rituals, which started this whole ordeal."

"I still can't believe Lydia had anything to do with any of it. She should have known better."

Rebecca sighed. "She doesn't understand Christ's love the way we do. She has no comprehension of grace, only harsh punishment and impossible rules. To her, God is a strict being who sits on His throne, watching for imperfection, ready to punish any wrongdoing. That, coupled with a difficult home life, led to her needing and craving acceptance. That craving can lead some to do things they wouldn't normally do."

"But now look at the mess it's created."

"Yes. You can't invite the devil and expect him to come alone. Destruction always accompanies him."

Tituba couldn't believe what she heard. Their religion had always confused her. Reverend Parris talked about salvation as if it was earned, that if you didn't follow the rules, you'd go to Hell. Goody Nurse spoke differently about her faith than Reverend Parris did. She spoke of salvation as a free gift, and as if she didn't just practice her faith, but that her faith was who she was. All three spoke compassionately about Tituba. The times she had been outside the jail for questioning, she had been spat upon, and some of the villagers threw rotten vegetables at her, and at the others accused. Those who had been accused later hated Tituba. They blamed her for their imprisonment. These ladies had never mistreated her. Would they mind if she approached them and asked about their God? She drifted off to asleep, dreaming of Heaven. In her dream, Heaven looked like her beloved Barbados.

The next day, the guard came in to deliver their morning porridge, or "slop" as the prisoners had called it. Always cold, the mush never excited them, and the portion was never enough to fill the aches in their stomachs.

"Got some news for you witches." He dumped the cold porridge into the pans. Little Dorcas scrambled to hers, and gulped eagerly. Her mother gave her half of hers as well. No one wanted to eat it, but did so because their stomachs demanded it.

The guard continued. "Governor Phips has arrived in New England, and is in Boston now. He is commissioning a special court, just for you folks. You're going to trial."

He walked out with their water bucket and came back with it filled. He looked at Bridget Bishop. "Looks like you might be first."

"You shouldn't have stood up for me, Goody Bishop. It's why you're in here, and why you're going to trial."

"No, Goody Good. That's not so. I'm in here, same as you, because folks don't like me. It's easy to believe someone is evil if you don't like them."

"Then how do you explain the three sisters being in here, and Goody Proctor, too?"

"Well, I suppose even the saints have enemies. Didn't Jesus himself have Judas and the Pharisees? I mean, if Jesus can't make everyone happy, then no one has any hope of it."

Sarah Good looked at her a moment, than cackled. Goody Bishop laughed with her. The other women joined in, except Tituba.

"What is wrong with all of you? How can you be laughing at a time like this?" Tituba asked.

"Well, woman, we've cried and screamed enough. We might as well try laughing now." Bridget said. She wiped her teary eyes on her red apron.

Tituba smiled for the first time since she'd been arrested.

～

183

Giles and Martha sat together in the prison common room. He had not seen her since his arrest days ago.

"Oh, Giles. How did you end up here?"

"I suspect it had to do with that petition."

"I heard about that. It was for Rebecca?"

"Yes. We'd be happy to get that dear woman out of here, but we had hoped it would help you and Goody Proctor, too."

"I see. Stir some doubt, eh?"

"Exactly. It was a good plan, but it just got turned on us. We ended up here just because we publicly supported Goody Nurse, and made it known we disagree with the afflicted children."

"It seems that anyone who disagrees or shares a different view becomes accused of being a witch themselves. Even a simple woman like me knows that's not lawful logic."

"You're not a simple woman, Martha."

"Why, Giles. Is that sentiment I hear from you?'

"It's past due. Martha, I know I haven't been too generous with words, but I'm glad ye said yes to becoming my wife all those years ago."

"I'm glad, too, Giles."

"Are ye? Because you shouldn't be."

"Why?"

"I should have let you keep your boy, Martha. It wasn't right the way I asked you to send him away."

She nodded, but said nothing.

"I'm sorry about that. It's funny what these trials have done. They make a man think."

"I understood then, Giles, and I understand now. My boy has the mark of shame."

"It isn't his shame to bear. Nor is it yours."

Martha smiled through tears. "Thank you for saying that, Giles."

"I should have said it long ago." He looked at the guard, who was carving a piece of wood, and took his wife's hand. "Anyway, if God spares us this calamity, we'll be bringing Thomas to the farm. That is, if he'll come."

Martha let the tears fall down her cheeks. "You've given me a great gift, my husband. For that, I'll love you 'till I die."

CHAPTER TWENTY-ONE

Magistrate Hathorne thanked God for the timing of Bridget Bishop's arrest. Alice Putnam did act maliciously in her accounts, but he supposed it didn't matter when it came to witches. They deserved malice. That petition the men had presented with all of those supporters of Rebecca Nurse had many people questioning the validity of the accusations, even giving the men on the bench pause to consider it. Therefore, they might question the validity of the trials altogether. Goody Bishop didn't have the support of Goody Nurse. Most women despised her. Men were ashamed of what she knew about them. Oh, Magistrate Hathorne didn't put stock into the rumors that she was a loose woman. He himself had visited her tavern on occasion and saw no evidence of that. No, the only guilt men had associated with her involved their loose tongues when drunk with the ale. Her reputation suffered not because of what she did, but what she knew others did, and what she often made others think she did. Her bold tongue and constant disregard for propriety would cost her in this court today. Magistrate Hathorne needed this legal win. If he could persuade the jury that she needed to hang, then the others wouldn't be as difficult to pass off as witches, maybe even that pious Rebecca Nurse. He walked into the courthouse and greeted Judge Corwin, and the presiding ministers.

"Are we quite certain we should proceed with the spectral evidence in the trials?" Reverend Hale asked, when the constable left to get the prisoner.

"Yes, Reverend Hale. We are quite certain. These girls and these girls alone know who hurts them."

"Aye. I suppose so, but there is a marginal chance for error, even with mature, reputable witnesses. These girls are young, and quite impressionable, Your Magistrate. I suggest we reconsider how much weight we place upon their accounts."

Magistrate Hathorne's blood boiled. This minister challenged his authority before the other men. He cleared his throat while trying to generate a response. He must remain calm, and appear to be in charge. He would be in charge.

"Reverend, my hope is that you'd want to eradicate this evil from our midst, just as I'm sure your fellow ministers desire to do. We should all agree that to delay ridding ourselves of those that would harm children should only serve to magnify the evil that reigns. We do not wish for evil to triumph, do we?"

Reverend Hale conceded, but reluctantly. Magistrate Hathorne smiled. He was still in charge. He'd make sure it stayed that way, starting with Goody Bishop.

⁓

Constable Herrick escorted Bridget to the Salem town courthouse. She didn't walk in submission. She decided she'd make it difficult for him. If they wanted to try her based on this pathetic evidence, then they could drag her. She'd not go compliantly.

Her attitude did not please the judges. "Constable, is there a problem?" Judge Corwin asked as he pushed Bridget into the box.

"Aye. She made me drag her all the way here by her chains. Dug her heels in, she did."

Magistrate Hathorne frowned. "Is this true, Goody Bishop?"

"I'll not walk willingly into Satan's trap."

Hathorne narrowed his eyes. "You speak of Satan in a familiar tone. You are bought before authority to give account of your conversations with the devil. What witchcraft have you dealt against the afflicted?"

"All of the people know I am clear, and should speak of it as witness for me." She looked around the room. The afflicted girls screamed.

"You are accused by five of the afflicted. What do you say to it?"

"I don't even know some of these persons, and I know nothing of it." Her anger increased with every question, and she knew it sounded in her tone, but she just could not help it. These liars should get their just due. They should be in this box, not I. Dare she say this aloud?

"Are the rumors true, Goody Bishop, that you bewitched your first husband to death?"

She laughed and shook her head back and forth. The girls wailed. Bridget ignored them.

"Why do you laugh? Do you not care that you hurt these children?"

"I do not hurt them."

"Well, do you have concern for their condition?"

"I do not think anything of it."

"You're telling me you do not think anything about their suffering?"

"I don't know what to think of it. I only know I am not causing it."

"Your very motions of your body cause it."

"By your opinion and their statements. That is not truth."

"It seems you have familiarity with spirits, and with the devil."

"If I were a witch, trust me, you'd know it." She challenged him with a stare. Judge Corwin dropped his quill.

Magistrate Hathorne clenched his jaw. "Goody Bishop, you can threaten, but you can only do what you're permitted against an ordained official of the court. Now, I ask you again, will you admit to your crimes of witchcraft?"

"I will not say I am a witch so you can take away my life."

"Confess, and you will not hang, but serve your days in jail. Alive."

"That's not life."

"You'll not confess then?"

"I won't lie."

"Oh, Goody Bishop. I think you would. I think you do. It is clear in this courtroom that you intend to inflict harm on these children, and perhaps even your judges."

"If I wish to inflict harm, 'tis only in my own defense."

"You admit your own guilt then."

"I did no such thing. Which are you, judge or prosecutor?" The room gasped at her audacity.

"Hang her!" someone yelled.

Hathorne reprimanded the outspoken onlooker, then turned to Corwin, and they spoke in whispers for several minutes. Low murmurs carried across the courtroom. Bridget felt eyes on her, but she stared straight ahead. She no longer felt like laughing.

~

Lydia's aunt asked her to stay home and not attend the trial. She said it would be enough to attend Goody Nurse's trial and her father's.

Lydia had never known Goody Bishop well. She had spoken to Lydia a time or two, but her father had warned her to keep her distance. Goody Bishop's reputation didn't bode well for her. Lydia feared the outcome of her trial. Would she hang for witchcraft? And if she was found guilty, what did that mean for her father or Goody Nurse?

"You need to eat, Lydia."

"If Father knew you were here, Aunt, he'd be displeased."

"You need me now. I won't leave you. I owe your mother that. Besides, I want to help you."

"What about your family? Won't they miss you?"

"I sent word. They'll understand." Her eyes filled with sadness. She must have told them about her history with her brother."Now eat. That is fresh fish from Salem Town, and I must say, it packs a flavor."

"I'm not very hungry." In fact, her stomach had rejected food since her father had been arrested. She had barely managed to keep anything down.

Aunt Eliza patted her hand. "Don't fret. We'll pack it away for later. Maybe you can bring your father some."

"If it's from you, he might not accept it."

She frowned. "Maybe he will. After all, he's had little sustenance since his arrest. 'Tis a shame I don't have enough for all of the prisoners. It must be dreadful the way they practically starve them, and then charge the families for it. You must go to him tomorrow, child, and tally up the bill. I can continue to pay for it while I'm here. And you'll bring him the fish."

Lydia didn't ask how her aunt could afford the jail fees, and the food she had bought them. She had gathered that her uncle was a merchant of some sort in Boston.

"How long can you stay, Aunt Eliza?"

"As long as you need me, Lydia."

"Do you think they'll let my father go?"

She bit her lower lip. "I can't be certain. I'll do all I can. I'm going to write a letter to the new governor. Perhaps we can persuade others to do the same."

"But so many believe my father is guilty. They believe the others are guilty."

"Do you believe he's guilty?"

"Of course not!"

"Neither do I, and that's a start."

Lydia hoped her aunt was right. She wondered how Goody Bishop would fare with so many against her. Did she have anyone to care for her?

CHAPTER TWENTY-TWO

They came to the jail for Bridget. Two judges accompanied the sheriff and constables, along with several guards appointed to escort her to the gallows.

"You have one last chance to confess your crimes of witchcraft, Goody Bishop. Denounce the devil and you shall live."

Bridget gripped her chains and spat at their feet. "You would have me confess a lie just to ease your conscience. I am no witch."

The constable slapped her across the face.

"Enough, constable. Take her to the cart." Sheriff Corwin said.

The women in the jail started grabbing for Bridget's red petticoat. "No! She's innocent!"

"This is wrong! You can't hang an innocent woman!"

Constable Herrick ignored them and loosened the shackles around Bridget's wrist. She bravely stood and walked out.

Outside, people had gathered to see the first of the witches brought to justice. They spat on her as she climbed into the cart. Once again, the constable shackled her wrists, then chained her to the cart. The villagers and townspeople followed behind all the way to the hanging site. The cart stopped at the bottom of the hill. Bridget looked up and saw the rope on the tree. She trembled. This was real. She was about to die. She started to vomit.

"The devil's with her! Look how he afflicts her now that she failed him!" someone shouted from the crowd. Someone else threw a stone and hit her in the head. She fell backwards, but didn't dare cry out. She wouldn't give them the satisfaction. Blood trickled from her forehead.

Constable Herrick walked her up to the ladder that had been placed against the tree from the other side. Easy enough to kick away. Bridget's stomach heaved again. She gagged now, as she had already emptied her stomach of what little contents it had. The constable pulled her up to the first step. She pulled back.

"Wait! I'm innocent! I am no witch! You are damning an innocent!"

He pulled her back onto the ladder. "Climb, witch!" He forced her up the rungs, and wrapped the rope around her neck. Panic hit her with as much force as that stone did minutes earlier.

"Wait! I don't want to die! I'm innocent!" She hated this begging, pitiful version of herself, but she couldn't stop it. She didn't want to die this way.

Reverend Noyes prepared to pray. He looked at Bridget with no emotion. "Your cries of innocence are ignored, Goody Bishop. Your chance to confess your guilt has passed. You will die, but perhaps you'll be saved from eternal damnation if you tell the truth now."

"You are an evil minister. It is you who does the devil's work, not I." She would have kicked him, but that would just hurry her death along with shame. If she had to die this way, she'd try to keep what little dignity she had left.

Noyes addressed the crowd. "See you not how she blasphemes the man of God? The devil is in her still. Let us pray. Father in Heaven, may this act of justice today be the beginning of a cleansing here. Purge us, Oh, Lord, of the manifestations of evil that have wrought ill will upon us. Have mercy on the afflicted children, and we thank you for revealing those who do the devil's bidding. Amen."

The judges said some official words, but Bridget wanted to have her say, so she stared speaking Scripture over them. "Yea, though I walk through the valley of the shadow of death, I will fear no evil."

The judges spoke louder, but she didn't falter. "Thou preparest a table before me in the presence of mine enemies."

"Hush, you witch!" The constable yelled.

She ignored him. "I will dwell in the house of the Lord forever."

"Hang her, Herrick!" Hathorne yelled.

The crowd watched as her neck snapped.

～

Lydia had told her aunt she wanted to visit Goodman Nurse, then she slipped away to the hanging. She didn't know why she wanted to be there. Her father had never allowed her to attend a hanging. She had always been curious, but terrified. Today, she was more terrified. She arrived while they were loading Bridget onto the cart outside the jail. Lydia looked longingly at the jail. Her father was in there, but visiting would not be allowed at this time. She wondered how the sisters were doing. Lydia followed the procession to the hill where Bridget would be hanged. The procession seemed endless. Lydia watched as people she had known for years treated their neighbor with such cruelty. Many had brought items to toss at her in the cart. Eggs were the crowd favorite. It was spring, and nearing summer, so the hens were laying nicely. Eggs were not only plentiful, but they made a satisfying sound for the blood thirsty crowd. Every time an egg would crack, the crowd laughed. Goody Bishop didn't move a muscle as egg ran down her face from her head. More laughter rang out as a radish thumped her back and bounced back into the crowd. Someone picked it up and tossed it back at her. Still, Bridget did not move. She did not shout or cry. She just stood and stared straight ahead in the direction the cart moved. The path to her death. Lydia shivered. How could Goody Bishop be so calm? Would someone stop this? Surely God would stop this. If she is innocent, God wouldn't let her hang. When you follow the rules, you're rewarded. When you break them, you're punished. Lydia figured she'd find out whether Goody Bishop would be rewarded or punished.

When they arrived at the site, Lydia barely resisted turning and running back to Salem village as fast as she could. The rope hung from the tree. She looked at Goody Bishop who bent over and spilled the contents of her stomach over the side of the cart. Constable Herrick grimaced and waited for her to finish. Then, he dodged as someone threw a rock and hit Goody Bishop in the head. She swayed. The constable said nothing to the crowd, but spoke harshly to Bridget and basically drug her to the ladder where the noose dangled above.

Goody Bishop protested. Lydia cried. This couldn't be happening. Someone needed to say something. Goody Bishop is innocent! She knew it. She didn't know how she knew, she just did.

Say something, Lydia. Stand up for her. Be her voice. She couldn't see the angels gently whispering in her ear. She also couldn't see the fear demon reaching into her mind and blocking out all courage.

The minister talked to the crowd and Bridget loudly proclaimed the twenty-third psalm. Surely they'll see she's no witch now, Lydia thought.

"How can she quote the Holy Bible when she serves the devil?" someone shouted. Others joined him.

"It's a trick!" The minister Nicholas Noyes yelled. "The devil knows Scripture! He can use it to deceive us. Don't be fooled by her ramblings!" Bridget voice grew louder and louder. "I will dwell in the house of the Lord forever."

"Hang her!" The magistrate shouted.

"No!" Lydia screamed as the constable kicked the stool and Bridget's neck snapped. Black birds flew from the tree.

The crowd fell silent. Bridget's body dangled there on the hilltop, the onlookers dazed at seeing her swinging and twisting in the air, in her signature red bodice. The rope creaked on the tree limb. Then, as if all emotion for humanity had left them, the crowd started chatting excitedly.

"One down! Many to go yet."

"We should just take care of them all today!"

"No, there must be a legal process."

Someone else spoke up. "You call what's been going on in court a legal process? It's insanity, that's what it is. Better watch out, or we'll all be on that rope!"

Arguing within the crowd ensued, and Lydia turned to run. There, right behind her, stood the afflicted girls.

"Where are you going, Lydia?" Ann asked.

"I'm heading home."

"Yes, I've heard tell your aunt is visiting you."

"You've heard correctly, and now I must go. She's expecting me."

"Wait. What did you think of the hanging?"

"I thought nothing of it, Ann."

"Oh? I thought I heard you cry out just before Goody Bishop started swinging. Didn't you, girls?"

The other girls nodded.

Abigail spoke. "Lydia, be careful. You don't want to be on the wrong side of this thing." She spoke in a sinister voice, and her eyes looked strangely brilliant. Bumps rose upon Lydia's arms.

"I'll be careful. I must bid you goodbye, and return home at once." She didn't wait for a reply, but darted to the path in the woods that would lead her home. She wanted desperately to talk to Goody Nurse about what she saw, but she couldn't. Goody Nurse could be next. Lydia fell against a tree and sobbed, with her mind replaying the image of poor Bridget Bishop's body dangling in front of her.

~⌒~

"Bridget is experiencing fullness of joy now." Raphael said.

"Yes, Captain, that is a comfort, but how much of this will we see?" asked Semiel.

"I'm afraid this is only the beginning."

"I just don't understand the purpose."

"It's not our job to understand. We obey."

"Yes, but so much sorrow is here."

"As long as there is sin, there is sorrow."

Uriel joined the exchange. "When do we fight these evil forces?"

"Soon. We must be patient. The battle always belongs to the Lord."

"Lucifer thinks he's winning."

"As usual, the prince of air is wrong. He might succeed in winning many men, but the ultimate victory has never been his, nor will it ever be. Take comfort in that, my soldiers."

Raphael left them, then, and flew over Goody Bishop's body, sprinkling particles of light over her. Uriel and Semiel followed, and showered her with more of the same. The human eyes couldn't see it, but the angels felt better, knowing the demons could.

Sonneillon laughed from the tree. "She's still dead, Raphael! Now, come fight!"

Raphael waved at him, and soared high into the clouds. "Our time will come, oh servant of Lucifer. Our time will come."

CHAPTER TWENTY-THREE

"I can say before Christ Jesus I am free." Mary Easty said.

Abigail Williams screamed. Reverend Hale couldn't believe it. The accused said Jesus' name. That shouldn't be. Witches denied Christ's name.

"She's innocent! Let her go!" someone shouted from the crowd.

"It's a trick!" Reverend Noyes said. "The devil deceives!"

"Reverend Noyes, this goes against my training-"

Magistrate Hathorne interrupted. "Reverend Hale, we'll discuss this at a more appropriate session. For now, we'll proceed with the questioning." He looked at Judge Corwin and nodded. Judge Corwin began again.

"What are you doing to these children? What are you doing to the child Abigail?"

"I've done nothing." Mary Easty answered.

"How can say you've done nothing when they are tormented so?"

"Would you have me accuse myself?"

Hathorne answered. "If you are guilty, then yes."

Corwin asked, "Why do you comply with the devil?"

"I do not comply with him. I have prayed against him all of my days. I am clear of this sin." She folded her hands in front of her chest as she began to pray silently.

Mercy Lewis wailed and frantically tried to pull her own hands apart. The demon next to her held them tight.

Mary looked up in surprise, releasing her hands. Mercy Lewis stared numbly at her own hands as they loosened. The demon laughed after he let go. He loved these games.

"See, her hands! Your hands are open now, and her hands are open! Are you not the one tormenting her now?"

"No. I cannot confess what I do not do."

Ann Putnam screamed out, "You are the woman, Goody Easty! You know it! You are the woman who afflicts us!"

Mary lowered her head. The girls' necks snapped forward in unison. The crowd gasped.

"Grab her head!" Magistrate Hathorne shouted at Constable Herrick. "When she lowers her head, she attempts to break their necks!"

"Goody Easty, if you do not hurt these children, then how do you explain what's been happening to these girls?" Judge Corwin asked.

"I cannot explain it."

"Would you say it's witchcraft?"

"I cannot tell."

"Why do you not think it's witchcraft?"

"I know it's an evil spirit, but I know nothing of witchcraft."

The girls cried out again in agony.

The constable led Mary back to jail.

⁓

Molly Warren turned fitfully in the jail, bemoaning her situation. She had been brought in the day after John Proctor's arrest when she refused to join the other afflicted girls and testify against him. When asked why, she said she had seen the truth.

"Hush, Mary!" Elizabeth Proctor scolded. "If little Dorcas can quietly endure, then so can you."

"I'm sorry, Goody Proctor! This is all my fault!"

Rebecca spoke. "It's not all your fault, child. More had a say and a hand in it, and an unseen hand is instrumental as well."

"Don't make her feel better for what she did, Rebecca." Sarah Good hadn't stopped eying the young girl since she arrived.

"I was deceived, Goody Good! I really saw Goody Proctor, and Goodman Knapp, too! I felt the pain!"

Sarah Good reached out to slap Molly Warren, but the shackles didn't reach.

"You liar! You will not speak your lies here!"

Molly shrank from Sarah's sharp tongue.

"Sarah-"

"No. Don't you cut me off, Goody Nurse. I'll have my say. We're stuck here, in this earthly hell, and she's part of the blame, and she dares —now that she suffers, too- to attempt to draw our sympathy for her plight. I'll not have it. Not when my babe lies buried in an unmarked grave, snatched from my arms by death, she was, and now my little Dorcas suffers for this girl's lies. As far as I'm concerned, she murdered Goody Bishop, and my babe, too. You can forgive her if you want, Goody Nurse, but not I."

Molly Warren started sobbing into her apron, and no one moved to comfort her. Not even Rebecca. The anger in Sarah's tone didn't mask her grief. The women didn't want to disrespect that. They had all felt the loss of little Mercy, and Goody Bishop, too. They missed Bridget's laughter. For the short time she had been in jail with the women, she had brought a little life back to them.

Rebecca turned away from Molly Warren's sobs.

"You should get to sleep, Rebecca. You need to stop mothering us all." said Mary.

"I will. Soon I won't be mothering anybody."

"Don't talk like that, Rebecca."

"You know me well, sister. I'm not afraid to die. I just wish it was under different circumstances. I don't want the devil's mark upon my good name. And I don't want to leave Francis." She ached at the thought of her husband, alone in their house, worrying over her. If she could just reach out to touch him one last time.

"There's still hope."

"Yes, there's always hope. That's why I'm not afraid. You're not afraid, are you, Mary?"

"I won't lie to you. I'm afraid of the rope. I'm not afraid of what comes after, though."

"Aye. The rope doesn't thrill me, either."

"I'm going to write to the judges."

"Oh?'

"Yes. I don't know if it will do any good, but I must try. If it doesn't help us, then perhaps it will give them pause for others."

"I think that's a good idea."

Mary put her head on her sister's shoulder. They both looked at their younger sister, who slept for the first time in days.

"Yes." Rebecca whispered. "It's a very good idea."

CHAPTER TWENTY-FOUR

Lydia's aunt baked her a small cake to encourage her to eat. The honey flavored crumble didn't please her as it should. Nothing tasted good these days.

"You're losing weight, child. You need to eat."

"I'm sorry, Aunt. You are being so kind to stay with me, and I'm afraid I'm not pleasurable company."

"Nonsense. This isn't a normal visit, so you do not have to act in a normal fashion. I just wish we had met years ago, and that your father-" She shook her head and let it drop. Lydia felt for her. She seemed to be genuinely sorry for the past. Yet, Lydia understood her father's perspective. Lydia hated the afflicted girls now, for what they'd done to her father and the sisters. She didn't let it show, of course. She couldn't. Anyone who defended the accused, or went against anything the afflicted claimed, was then accused themselves. No. Lydia had to keep quiet. Just as her father said.

"Lydia."

She looked up at her aunt.

"You look so like your mother, you know."

"I've been told that."

"By your father?"

"No. By the sisters."

"They're right. You have her eyes, and her creamy white skin."

"I look like her, but I don't act like her."

"What do you mean?"

"My mother was brave. Goody Nurse told me."

"You don't think you're brave, Lydia?"

"I know I'm not. I'm afraid. I'm afraid of what will happen to father. I'm afraid of what will happen to the sisters, and I'm afraid of what could happen to me."

"Being brave isn't about not being afraid. Being brave is doing what's right, even when you are afraid."

"What do you mean?"

A knock interrupted them. Aunt Eliza opened the door and gasped. The constable stood there.

"I'm here for the girl."

Lydia jumped up. "Am I under arrest?"

He held up a summons. "No. You are being summoned for questioning as an afflicted child. That's it."

Aunt Eliza sighed with relief. Lydia's stomach threatened to reject the cake she just ate.

"I'm coming along. Please give us a minute to gather our wraps."

Constable Herrick nodded. Aunt Eliza shut the door.

"Now you listen. I know all about this. You watch what you say. Don't let the judges intimidate your answers. Don't let the atmosphere intimidate you, either. Just answer truthfully, but wisely, keeping in mind what they seek."

"Aunt Eliza, I don't understand what I should do."

"Just answer truthfully, Lydia. Stay calm. I'll pray. Now, come along before the constable thinks we've bolted."

"Aunt Eliza?"

"Yes, child?"

'I'm so glad you're here."

"Me, too, love. Me, too." She squeezed her hand.

⁓

Lydia didn't like Magistrate Hathorne. She preferred Judge Corwin's soft tone to Hathorne's cold stare and sharp tongue.

"Witnesses say you are afflicted. Why haven't you come forth with names?"

"I have no names, sir."

"Were you not afflicted in the meetinghouse?"

"I don't know, sir. That is, I only saw a-"

"Yes?"

Tell the truth. "I saw a creature."

"What did this creature look like?"

"Hideous. Ugly. His breath was hot."

"It was a man?"

"No."

'You said, 'he'."

"Yes, but he wasn't a man."

"What are you saying, that he was the devil himself?"

"I don't know, sir. He looked like what I'd imagine the devil to look like."

"Did he talk to you?"

"No. He burned my skin with his breath. He held me fast to the pew so I couldn't move."

"Was this creature your father?"

"No! Of course not!"

The magistrate twisted his mouth. He wrote something down, then spoke to the constable. "Bring in the girls."

Ann Putnam, Abigail Williams, Mercy Lewis, and the other girls walked into the courthouse.

"Afflicted children of the court, I must ask you, has your tormentor ever been a creature rather than a person you know?"

They all shook their heads. Ann stood up. "They are who we said they are, sir."

"You're saying that each time you were afflicted, your tormentor had a human face and body?"

"Yes, of course."

"You may sit down. Abigail Williams? Do you attest to the same?"

Abigail looked at the floor. Ann nudged her. "Yes, of course." Did Magistrate Hathorne not notice her hesitation? If he did, he didn't show it.

He looked back at Lydia.

"You are the first not to identify your tormentor, Lydia Knapp. What reason have you to hide the identity?"

"I have no reason. I'm telling the truth."

"Goody Good claims you and these girls have something to hide. Is this true?"

Lydia looked at Ann Putnam. She slightly shook her head at Lydia. If Lydia spoke up, Ann would accuse her, too. She'd be in jail just like her father and the sisters.

"Goody Good wishes ill upon me and my friends." The lie tasted bitter upon her tongue.

"What say ye of your father's accusation?"

"My father is innocent."

"Are you saying these girls are falsely accusing him?"

Lydia bit her lip. She looked at the girls. Ann silently dared her to speak against her.

"No, sir. Only that the devil perhaps uses his shape to torture them. It is not my father, but perhaps looks like him."

"By your logic, are we to presume that all of the accused are innocent then? Are we to release all of the accused? Have we hung an innocent woman?"

Lydia's mind replayed the hanging of Bridget Bishop, of Bridget quoting the twenty-third psalm.

"I-"

"You see the problem we have, don't you? Either these girls are lying, or your father is guilty. Which is it?"

Semiel whispered to her again. *Be brave. Speak truth.*

The fear demon assigned to her hissed at Semiel. "She's mine!"

Lydia hung her head. She couldn't speak.

"Lydia Knapp, is your father guilty, or are your friends lying?"

"I guess he's guilty, sir, but-"

"If you see this creature again, perhaps he'll reveal his identity. I trust next time you'll be inclined to reveal him or her promptly to this court, am I right?"

"Aye, sir."

⌒

Semiel grieved for the girl as she cried all the way home. Her aunt couldn't console her. He needed to ask for more support. They needed a larger army of angels for this assignment. These fear demons had great strength. He shot to the sky, hoping Raphael could gather some worthy warriors.

CHAPTER TWENTY-FIVE

"I told the children not to visit me anymore, and not to bring their father, either."

"Rebecca, why on earth would you do that?" Mary asked.

"It's too hard to see them cry and carry on so. They do not need to see me decline any further in my physical state. Each time they see me, I look more dreadful, and closer to death."

Sarah Cloyce grabbed her hand. Tears dropped down her dry, chapped cheeks."Don't say that."

"We have to face reality. My hanging date is set. And so is theirs." She nodded to the other women in the cell with them. Sarah Good slowly rose from her lying position. "You have a man who loves you, and children who are safe, and you turn them away. Some people don't deserve what's been given to them."

Sarah Cloyce faced Sarah Good. "You're grieving, so I'll ignore how you speak to my sister. But know this. She is more deserving than any of us."

"Sarah." Rebecca gently scolded her younger sister in her tone. "Truth is, none of us are deserving of anything."

"There ye go, with ye preaching again," Sarah Good said, "It's not enough that I have to be in this filthy hole in the first place, but I have to listen to you go on about the grace of God, and His unfailing love. What love? What wrongs have we committed that we're suffering so, and that my little babe had to be birthed into these conditions, with no hope of seeing her first birthday? And my little Dorcas, she's gone mad. You see it. I know you all do. Every day the light goes out of her eyes just a bit more."

It was true. They had all watched little Dorcas slip into another reality. She just sat dazed, and when she spoke, it was as if she spoke to an invisible force. Rebecca didn't dare speak her suspicions aloud, that little Dorcas had gone insane from shock. Sarah Good had been through enough.

"Goody Good, I know you're suffering. We all suffer, but perhaps you have suffered most. God understands your anger."

"Does He? I thought I'd be condemned to Hell for daring to speak against Him. Isn't that what our religion says?"

"It might be what religion says, but it is not what the Bible says."

"Make sense, Goody Nurse. Or are you starting to go mad like my Dorcas? Religion is the Bible."

"Not necessarily. Not man's religion. You've heard nothing but rules. For too long, we've had ministers that preach what the Bible says not to do. We've had ministers preach that if we do not follow these rules, we incur the wrath of God."

"Well, I guess it's true. I didn't follow the rules, and here I am. Of course, that doesn't make sense for you, Goody Nurse. You have always been a pious woman. Why are you here?"

"Suffering is no respecter of persons. Neither is death."

"So if I'm here, and you're here, that just means it doesn't matter what we do. So what difference does it make if one is godly?"

"Exactly. It isn't about our outward actions. It can't be. It has to be about what Jesus did on the cross."

"We've all heard the story, Goody Nurse. There's nothing new there."

"Isn't there? I see it as new every day. I wake up in this filthy hole as you call it, and wonder at the injustice of it all. Then, I remember Jesus suffered greater injustice than this. Sure, we're innocent of witchcraft, but we're not innocent of sin."

"You sin?" Sarah said. "What do you know? The saintly Goody Nurse sins."

"Yes, I do. I don't seek to follow rules to be good enough, or Christian enough for Heaven, Goody Good. I seek to follow Jesus because He paid my way for me. I want to love Him, and walk in His ways because of what He did for me, not to mention that His ways are best for me, anyway."

"Are you saying that if I accept what He did for me, then it doesn't matter if I curse William Good for the miserable wretch he is?"

Rebecca grinned. "Well, it matters, of course, but it won't change your eternal destination. Our eternal destination isn't determined by what we do. It's determined by what He already did. The only involvement we have is accepting it."

"And how would I do that?"

"Do you believe you're a sinner, Goody Good?"

"Well, there's no question about that, is there?"

"Do you believe Jesus died and rose again?"

"Aye. I believe."

"All you need to do is admit that you're a sinner, believe that He died on the cross for your sins, and then confess it publicly. That is all there is to it."

"How can I confess it publicly when I'm stuck in here?"

"Well, you have a crowd of witnesses in this jail, Sarah Good. Pray with me, then all you have to do is shout it to these women."

Sarah smiled. "Imagine that. Goody Good of Salem, a brand new woman. From witch of the devil to a woman of God. We'll see if they believe it."

"Do you believe it?"

Sarah did something she hadn't done in years. She reached out and took Rebecca's hand and grasped it. "Yes, Goody Nurse. I think I do believe it."

Then, she bowed her head with Rebecca and prayed.

⁓

Sonneillon screamed his fury and shook the jail. The little demon had frantically chased after him, urging him to get to the prison immediately. Now he knew why. Sarah Good believed in Christ! She might hang, but she'd live eternally with Him.

He cursed and looked around for Belias. The demon cowered behind other demons, who readily moved aside to reveal him to Sonneillon.

"What happened?" Sonneillon roared.

"It happened so fast. There was nothing I could do. The angels surrounded the women, creating a strong barrier."

"You should have immediately called for reinforcements. You know better! You pitiful, pathetic little excuse for a demon."

"I'm sorry, Sonneillon." He tucked his head, fearing the larger demon's wrath.

"Don't tell me. Tell Lucifer." He picked Belias up, and threw him hard into the dark abyss.

CHAPTER TWENTY-SIX

The Reverend Jonathan Hale hadn't been sleeping. Pontius Pilate must have felt just this way, he thought. He had tried to reason with the others, but they seemed to thirst for blood. This use of spectral evidence did not sit well with him. While he had seen it used before, and had even been an advocate of it in the past, he felt it being abused in this case. Oh, he didn't doubt the legitimacy of the afflicted girls, at least most of them, but he felt there was more going on.

He sighed relief that he'd soon be discussing his concerns with Cotton Mather. A highly respected authority on witchcraft, surely Reverend Mather could shed some light on the situation. Reverend Hale just wanted to be sure things were being handled correctly in Salem. One woman had already died, and now more were sentenced to hang. He saw Goody Nurse's kind eyes in his mind. Most of the villagers had nothing but good things to say about her. When he had witnessed a petition on her behalf being presented to the court, he thought perhaps he should work to ensure these trials were authentic and fair to the accused.

Boston moved with its usual bustling activity. It was warm now, but not too hot yet, so occupants of the city were roaming about, working at various activities. Merchants tended to shoppers, while fisherman worked on their boats at the docks. People stood in the streets, talking about whatever fancied their interest.

He arrived at the reverend's residence. A servant saw to his carriage and another escorted him into a sitting room and served him tea and biscuits while he waited. The reverend had affluence, for his writings had become popular, giving him great demand for speaking and caused his parishioners to treat him nicely in order to keep him. He also served on committees for courts, both in the new land and in England. His father had quite the reputation before he did, so he essentially had his path paved for him before he had started in ministry. Jonathan looked around in envy. He knew he shouldn't covet, but his paltry salary didn't provide for such luxuries he witnessed here in Reverend Mather's home.

"Reverend Hale. How good to see you. Is the tea to your liking?"

"Aye. Thank you." He stood and shook the man's hand.

"I trust your journey was nice and uneventful?"

"It was. Not an Indian in sight."

"Splendid. As our government improves, perhaps we can see to the savage slaughtering of innocent people."

Jonathan said nothing. It would do no good to go into a discussion about the savage acts on both sides. He had more important matters to discuss.

"You wanted to speak to me on behalf of the Salem trials, is that correct?"

"Yes, Reverend. I have concerns about the evidence being presented in the proceedings."

"Ah, yes. I have expressed those same concerns."

"This spectral evidence. I'm not so sure it is as helpful as it should be in these cases. I know we've relied on it in the past. The spiritual nature of evil is definitely a factor, but how reliable is it? Should we trust all spectral evidence?"

"That is the question, isn't it?" He held out his cup as his servant poured in more tea. He offered more to Jonathan, but he declined. Reverend Mather sipped the hot liquid for a moment, then continued.

"Reverend Hale, this is a dilemma. As you know, I am a strong believer of witchcraft."

"Yes, as am I. However, I just don't know if I believe all of the evidence presented is completely accurate."

"Of which part are you uncertain exactly?"

"Well, regarding the spectral evidence, how can we be sure the girls are really seeing who they say they're seeing?"

"I've thought that same thing. But then there's the validity of the afflictions when the accused are brought into the courtroom. I read in the reports how Goody Nurse, a respected and most pious woman by her reputation, looked at them, and they twisted and writhed in pain. I did not understand it to be a false affliction."

"No, I was there, and I did not see it to be false, either." Jonathan rubbed his chin. He wasn't certain how to continue. It seemed as though this trip could be wasted.

"That doesn't mean I don't share in your concern, Reverend Hale. I am making notes and speaking with others about this issue. We just can't jump in and proclaim that spectral evidence is wrong just because we like the accused, you know."

How did he know how Jonathan felt about Rebecca nurse? Of course, her reputation was widespread by now.

"I would never initiate such a thing, Reverend."

"Of course not. I know you desire that which is right and just. That is all any of us wants. We will have to examine this thing a bit more before a decision is made."

"Is it possible to delay the trials, or at least the hangings, until that time?"

"We cannot ask that. To do so might cause a communal uproar, which we should try to avoid. Don't concern yourself. I will begin discussions and observances right away. I had already been contemplating all of this before you sent your message that you wanted to discuss the trials."

"I understand the proper cautious procedures, but sir, people's lives are at stake. There are to be several hung on the 19th. That's days away."

"Yes. I suppose we do need some urgency. I'll write to the judges Hathorne and Corwin immediately, and express my concerns. In the meantime, perhaps it will help if you and the other area ministers come together and report your concerns on the matter. Present it in an official report and I'll add my thoughts as summary. Does this suit you?"

Reverend Hale wanted to say what would really suit him, but thought better of it. He shook the reverend's hand, and departed, declining the offer of an afternoon meal. He didn't want to spend another minute in that man's company. That was the Lord's servant? He didn't seem too concerned about the souls that would soon be sent to an ill-timed eternity. He also switched back and forth on the spectral evidence issue. Reverend Mather had been polite and cordial, but Jonathan sensed a pompous attitude. He knew Reverend Mather was an important and influential religious leader, but Jonathan wondered how authentic his faith could be if he disregarded the lives of possibly innocent people. He had wanted to tell him apathy served Satan well. Did that make him the devil's servant? Reverend Hale chuckled to himself as he climbed into his carriage. Imagine that. Cotton Mather on trial for serving the devil. As if that could happen. The most religious man in the new world. Again, he saw Rebecca Nurse, her face turned upward in the courtroom, praying with tears rolling down her face. At this point, he guessed anything could happen. With his doubt in spectral evidence coming to light, Reverend Hale supposed that even he could be in danger of accusations of witchcraft.

He shivered in the midday heat.

CHAPTER TWENTY-SEVEN

Rebecca didn't know how much more she could take. She could barely stand when they ordered her up and released her from her chains.

"What is this?' her sister Sarah demanded.

"Where are you taking her now?" Mary asked.

"She gets to be formerly excommunicated like a good little witch." Constable Herrick jerked her back up when she slumped. "Come, witch. If you have enough strength to torture those girls, you can walk."

"Why you-" Sarah jumped up, swinging at the constable. Her chains stopped her attempts. Constable Herrick turned and pushed her backwards. She fell, but did not cry out. He frowned at her and mumbled, "Witches. Can't wait to be rid of all of ye."

At the meetinghouse, the constable led Rebecca to the front of the church, Lydia sat in front, tears streaming down her face. Rebecca couldn't look at her. Instead, she looked around at the friends she had known for years. Friends she had worshiped with, prayed with, and led in Scripture studies. Surely none of them could possibly believe she was a witch. Rebecca held on to the wood in front of her. She didn't dare fall. Not here. This humiliation demanded what little dignity she had left to hold fast.

Reverend Parris began. "Goody Nurse, as you know, you are a convicted witch. As such, this church cannot allow you to remain a member of its congregation. Do you understand that you are being excommunicated?"

"I understand, and I contest it."

"No matter. Had you been a sinner of any other kind, then perhaps we could give you time to get yourself in order with God. As it is, you are under an official sentence by the court to hang. Repentance will not matter in this case."

Someone spoke from the congregation. "Why does repentance not matter? What about forgiveness?"

The reverend clicked his tongue in annoyance. "It only matters if we can witness a changed heart. In Goody Nurse's case, we will not be afforded that luxury. She is to be hanged, and therefore cannot show any proof of a changed heart."

A changed heart? Repentance? Oh, how easy it'd be to confess of this evil slander, and be done with it. She'd spend her remaining days in jail, but at least she'd not die with a reputation of an excommunicated, unrepentant sinner. She heard Lydia's sobs again. What was she thinking? She couldn't die confessing to something she wasn't. She already had a reputation as a witch. At least Lydia and those who knew her best would always remember she held fast to the truth. No matter the cost.

"Rebecca Nurse, you are hereby excommunicated from Salem church, and are no longer a member of our congregation. We take your name from our records, and any mention of you in association with this congregation is hereby forbidden. Let us pray for your soul."

"You do not need to pray for my soul, Reverend Parris, for I know where my soul rests. It does not rest in this congregation or in a church membership. My soul rests in Jesus."

The reverend's face flushed.

"See? She says the name of Jesus! How can you stand there and do what you are doing to this fine Christian woman?" A lady in the meetinghouse said. Rebecca didn't know who it was. She was a lovely woman, and sat with Lydia. Curious.

"Constable Herrick! Hand her off to Constable Locker, and bring in Giles Corey!"

Rebecca turned as the constable led her out of the church. She met Lydia's tearful eyes, and smiled at her. As she passed her, she reached out her hand to touch Lydia.

"Keep moving, witch!" Constable Herrick pushed her. Rebecca tried to keep her balance, but she lost her footing and landed on the floor.

"Get up!" Constable Herrick pulled on her arm. Lydia reached out to help her up.

"Goody Nurse, I'm so sorry. Please forgive me. If I hadn't-"

Rebecca put her wrinkled hand over Lydia's mouth and whispered so only she could hear. "Don't grieve so, child. God is working all of this for your good."

Lydia shook her head. "No, Goody Nurse. I don't want anyone to die for my sake."

The constable pulled Rebecca to her feet and dragged her away from Lydia. Rebecca looked back and spoke as clearly and loudly as her sore throat allowed.

"Someone already died for your sake, child."

～

"John, this can't be happening. Others were arrested before you. Why are you hanging so soon?"

John couldn't bear to see his wife sob for him. "My love, I'm so sorry. I'm sorry I couldn't help you."

Elizabeth shook her head. "No. Don't you do that. This is bad enough without your unfounded guilt. You did nothing wrong. I did nothing wrong."

He decided to drop it. "I saw the boys."

"Did you? How are they?"

"Distraught. It's to be expected. They're still quite young. This is a lot to take on, and also trying to hold on to the farm and tavern."

"They're strong men, like their father. They'll endure."

"I'd say they have their mother in them, too." He touched her cheek. The guard didn't object this time. John doubted it came from a place of compassion, but probably from intimidation. He couldn't see the angel who discouraged the guard from approaching John and Elizabeth.

"This can't be the last time I see your sweet face. I won't accept it." How could he leave this woman?

She grabbed him and pulled him tight to her. "Just promise me something, John. Please."

"Anything."

"Let them pray for you when it's time."

He pulled back from her embrace. "Elizabeth, I can't do that. Their prayers are no good, for the lies they spew."

"Please, John. Please don't go from this world listening to those hateful mobs screaming. Let them pray for you."

Her eyes implored him to agree. How could he deny her anything?

"Alright, my love. I'll have them pray. Now, you promise me something."

"Anything."

"If you get out of here, you live your life. Don't fret over me. Just live your life, and take care of our child. I would want no less, do you hear?"

She pulled him to her again. "I will, John. I will." He brought her face to his and kissed her one last time.

Back at the jail, Sarah Good waited for Rebecca to return. She didn't know why, but she longed to be excommunicated from the church. She knew it was utter humiliation at its worst, even more than the trial and sentencing, but she felt like it'd be a proclamation that Sarah Good was a gospel woman, like Rebecca. Oh, she knew it wasn't so, at least not in the same way. Rebecca had been godly for years. Sarah had only just come to really know Jesus, but the Bible said that's all that mattered in the eyes of God. Sarah might still be just as filthy on the outside, but she was clean on the inside. She'd like to leave a legacy of some sort. That was over now. Her name would forever be sullied by the identity of witch. Her little Dorcas, too. Dorcas just didn't act the same these days. Sarah didn't know what to do about it, except pray. The old Sarah would curse God for allowing such torment on her children. Yet, as heartbroken as she was, and in all of her misery, she didn't feel the emptiness anymore. They could hang her body, but they wouldn't take her soul. That belonged to Jesus now.

The cell door creaked, and the constable shoved Rebecca inside. Her sisters tried to catch her, but the older lady hit the dirt hard. Her hands were wet with perspiration, so the dirt stuck to them. She wiped them on her filthy apron that not long ago had appeared white. She, like all of them, had scratched her skin raw, and it was pale from lack of nutrition, which made her look ghostly, and frightful. Sarah assumed her face looked just as pale since all of them looked the same way. Those tiny pests of bugs had gotten worse, and tormented their heads, bodies, and private areas so much that they all had been bleeding on the skin surface. When little Dorcas relieved herself, she cried out in pain and agony because her privates were so raw. They had finally received bundles of rags from Rebecca's daughter so they could be more comfortable on their monthly flow times. By now, they were all on the same schedule, which helped with embarrassment. They had only taken a handful of cloth baths since being imprisoned, and families were charged for the lye and water. Sarah didn't know who paid her fees, for she knew William didn't. She heard he'd disowned her and little Dorcas. Sarah didn't care anymore. She only worried about Dorcas. She hadn't had her trial yet. What would happen? Surely they couldn't hang a child! But this same child suffered in this jail, and no one cared.

"What happened, Rebecca?" Mary gently pulled her sister beside her.

"The church officially rejected me as a member. Imagine that." She laughed. "All those faithful years." She wiped the tears from her wrinkled cheeks.

Martha Corey kicked the water bucket. Water splashed over the rim.

"Martha Corey! That's our only water for the day!" Elizabeth said. She constantly worried over her nutrition for the babe she carried in her womb. Sarah swallowed her envy. If this babe was born in this jail, it might not survive, either. She didn't wish that agony on anyone.

"I don't care! I'm sorry, but this can't go on! We have to do something! Why are we letting this happen?" Martha said.

"What do you propose we do? Most of our men are in jail themselves, and there are guards with muskets out there."

"We need to formulate a plan. Philip and Mary English already escaped!" Elizabeth's sons had told her about the couple who managed to flee during their attempted arrests. The sheriff and constables had looked everywhere, but they weren't found. Goody Good didn't know much about them, only that they had been quite wealthy. Apparently, the accusations no longer held bias on monetary status.

"Martha, their escape only happened due to the right circumstances at the right time. We'd only be dead sooner, probably shot to death. Besides, Goody English is a young woman. Most of us aren't."

Martha sat down in defeat. "Aye. I suppose you are right."

Rebecca touched her hand. "Remember, friend. For me to live is Christ, and to die is gain."

Sarah Good was glad to finally understand that verse, but she wasn't sure she embraced it the way Rebecca did. If she thought there was the slightest chance of escape, she'd do it, and take Dorcas with her. She'd love to know what happened to Philip and Mary English. She hoped they got away.

~

July 19, 1692
Salem Town

The morning clouds darkened, hinting at rain. Rebecca didn't know if rain would make it better or worse. On the one hand, it'd be cooler. They had been so miserably hot. If they could just feel rain, and get some relief before it happened. Yet, Rebecca had hoped for a clear day so she could speak to everyone. Maybe she could say something profound that would save her sisters' lives, and others.

The cell was silent, except for occasional sobs. Most of the women just didn't want to leave their families. Rebecca knew her children would be able to recover soon. They had their spouses and children. Francis would be alone. She didn't want to look at his sorrowful face, knowing how he'd suffer. She hoped he didn't come for his sake, even though the selfish part of her wanted to look at him as it happened. How would it feel, to have her neck snapped by the rope? Would it hurt? Would she choke, or suffocate, or just die instantly? She wasn't afraid of what came next. She would see Jesus. She just didn't want to feel great pain. How weak she felt, fearing the pain of death. She supposed the others felt that way, too. There was so much grief in the jail. Her sisters had clung to her and cried the night before. She wished she could know what would happen to them. Maybe she'd be meeting them soon at Heaven's gate. Sarah Good sobbed silently all through the night, holding her little Dorcas.

The door creaked open and Sheriff Corwin walked in with Constable Locker and Constable Herrick. The men released the shackles, but for the first time, Rebecca wished she could keep them on. This was really happening. Now she knew the personal dread Goody Bishop had felt that horrible morning when they watched her go to her doom. First, the sheriff led Rebecca out, then Martha Corey, Susannah Martin, Sarah Wilde, and Elizabeth Howe. Finally it came time to unshackle Sarah Good.

"Just give me one minute!" She pulled Dorcas to her, and rocked her.

"Where are you going, Mother? You can't go." Dorcas' little fingers touched the sides of her mother's face. She pulled Sarah's head to hers, holding her tight.

"We talked about this, remember? I must go, daughter. Mercy needs me. I must see to Mercy. She is just a babe, not a big girl like you." Her voice cracked and she struggled to hold back the sobs.

"No! Mercy is in Heaven. She can't come back! You have to come back, Mama!"

"I'm sorry, child. I can't come back. You know I wouldn't leave if I didn't have to. I'd never leave you on purpose, but I must go now."

"No!" Dorcas' voice level rose. Rebecca and the others heard her outside. The sounds of that little girl's agony silenced the growing crowd.

"Let's go, witch!" Constable Locker pulled at Sarah and pushed her through the jail door.

"Leave her be! Can't you hear that child's horror?" John Proctor said.

"Silence, Proctor! Goody Good, get in the cart!"

"I need more time! Please, just let me go explain it to her again!"

"You've had enough time." Constable Herrick came over, and together they pulled Sarah into the cart. Her daughter's screams and sobs followed Sarah out of the jail. She hadn't been chained to the cart yet, so she jumped down and ran inside the jail. A guard knocked her down at the cell door and pulled her away. Sarah looked back, and saw Goody Easty embrace her baby girl, a child who had seen so much misery in just four short years of her life.

She couldn't leave her girl yet. Dorcas still needed her. Sarah tried to force her way back to the cell, but the men were too strong and she was incredibly weak. They moved her out of the jail. She screamed at them. "How can four years be enough time? I didn't have enough time!" They said nothing, just shoved her next to the other women in the cart, and chained her. The cart rolled away from the jail. Five women and one man were on their way to hang.

⌒‿

Rebecca, Martha, and Sarah held hands all the way to the hanging site. When they arrived, the judges and ministers stood near the tree where the rope dangled.

"That rope killed Goody Bishop," Susannah Martin said. "If she could bear it, we can, too."

"Aye. That's the spirit," Rebecca said. She didn't know if her feelings matched her words. Her eyes roamed the crowd for any sign of Francis. She saw her children, weeping and holding on to each other. She hoped Lydia didn't come. She didn't want that child to witness this.

"Rebecca, I can't be watching you hang. I'm going to shut my eyes."

"That's fine, Sarah. Shut your eyes, and pray."

Sarah had calmed on the ride to the ledge. Rebecca had quoted Scripture, and had prayed for their loved ones who would be left to grieve that day, including Dorcas.

"Becca!" She heard his voice. He had come. She searched for his eyes. The bluest eyes she'd known. She spotted him. He was too close to the cart. The sheriff shoved him back as he pulled the women down, one by one. Francis bounded back, grabbed Rebecca's arm and pulled her in for a quick embrace.

"I'll see you soon, my love. I won't tarry here long."

"You stay as long as God Almighty wants you, Francis. He has a purpose. Live your purpose."

"I can't live with purpose if you're not here."

"I'm not your purpose, Francis. Look up. There's your purpose. Now please go, and don't watch this."

"I must watch. 'Til death us do part, remember?"

Sheriff Corwin yelled at him to get back, and he grabbed Rebecca around the waist to pull her away from her husband. They held on to each other's hands until they couldn't hold on anymore. When their hands broke away, Rebecca felt as if that very moment she had begun to die.

⌒

"Hang the witches!"

"Hang them now!"

Shouts from the crowd angered Lydia. Goody Nurse had not seen her yet. Should she alert the older woman to her presence? Would it be harder?

She watched the constables drag the women up onto the rocky ledge. There was only one tree, with one noose, so these hangings would take a while. Lydia couldn't stomach all of this. Could she really watch them hang her beloved friend? It was bad enough to watch Goody Bishop die. She had not been close to the woman, but the shock and despair of that day still lingered with her.

"Let Goody Nurse go! She's innocent!"

"You cannot hang a gospel woman!"

"Witches aren't gospel! Hang them all!"

The shouts were as different as people in the crowd. It was much bigger than the last crowd.

People had come from all over to get a good look at the witches and to watch them die.

CHAPTER TWENTY-EIGHT

"Goody Nurse goes first." Magistrate Hathorne told the sheriff.

"That crowd's getting excited." Sheriff Corwin said.

"Exactly. Get her on that ladder. Now."

"Aye." He pulled Rebecca toward the tree.

Rebecca didn't like that her Francis was in that crowd. He heard their friends supporting her, but he also heard the angry, hateful shouts that thirsted for her blood. Rebecca had never attended hangings. Even when she thought them just, it didn't sit well with her to watch a man die.

When they reached the tree, the crowd fell silent. She didn't fight. God had appointed her time to die, and it had arrived. She just wished it didn't have to end this way. Would her name forever be marred by witchcraft?

She climbed the ladder. "That's far enough." The sheriff climbed up with her and placed the rope over her head and onto her slim neck.

"Do you have any last words, Goody Nurse? Now is your opportunity to confess and absolve yourself for eternity." Reverend Noyes said.

"She has nothing to confess, you swine!" John Proctor yelled. Constable Herrick brought the end of his musket down onto the back of John's neck. The blow forced him to his knees. One of John's sons tried to get to him, but the armed men stopped him.

"All is well, John." Rebecca voice sounded calmer than she felt.

"Will you confess, Goody Nurse?"

"I am no witch. A sinner I have always been, but a witch I am not. My eternity is sound because Jesus absolved my sins long ago."

"She refuses to confess!" Reverend Noyes shouted to the crowd.

"Hang her!"

"Let her go!"

"Stop this madness!"

Rebecca caught Francis' eyes in the crowd, tears streaming down his face. He mouthed, "I love you."

She fought the urge to beg for her life. She managed a small smile and nodded at him. He collapsed with grief. Rebecca lost the battle with her own grief and started sobbing then. How she wanted to run to her husband. Where were her children? She spotted them, sobbing on their own. They had their spouses with them. Her dear Francis stood alone. Someone rushed to his side and wrapped her arms around him. Lydia! That sweet child! She wished she could have more time with the girl. She needed to see the light amidst all this darkness.

"Sheriff Corwin, proceed." Magistrate Hathorne's voice rang loud and clear. The sheriff secured the rope on her neck, and began to climb down the ladder.

This was it. In minutes, she'd see Jesus.

"Turn away, Goodman Nurse! Don't watch it!" John Proctor yelled once again.

Rebecca didn't look at the crowd anymore. Instead, she closed her eyes and prayed.

Goodman Nurse went home with his children. He had begged to carry his wife's body to their land and bury it, but the officials denied it. She had been a convicted witch and didn't deserve a respectful burial. Lydia felt numb. Her beloved Goody Nurse was gone. She hadn't watched her hang. She had clung to Goodman Nurse and buried her head into his shoulder. Somehow their shared grief comforted her.

"Lydia, let's go." Her aunt touched her shoulder. Lydia saw the sheriff leading Goodman Proctor to the ladder. He didn't make it easy for the sheriff, so the constables joined the effort.

"I can't go, Aunt Eliza."

"You don't need to see anymore."

"Yes, I do. It's the least I can do."

"Lydia, we talked about this."

"Please, leave me be." She shook her aunt's hand from her shoulder and focused on Goodman Proctor. She didn't know how to make her aunt understand.

Someone yelled from the crowd. "He has a babe on the way! Have mercy!"

Someone else yelled, "Look how he fights! He stalls so the devil will come. Hurry up and hang him or we'll all be doomed!"

John Proctor stood tall and proud on the ladder and faced the crowd. Sheriff Corwin tightened the noose, and John's face changed. Lydia had only seen his face look like that once. The day his wife had been arrested. The day their whole lives had been changed.

"Do you have anything to say, Goodman Proctor?" Reverend Noyes asked.

"No."

"You do not wish to confess?"

"No."

Reverend Noyes shook his head and started to speak to the crowd.

"Wait," John said.

"Yes?"

"Get Reverend Hale."

"What?"

"I want him to pray for me."

"Reverend Hale is not available." Reverend Noyes' voice held no emotion.

"Then you pray for me. I want to hear praying when I go."

"I'm sorry, Goodman Proctor, but your request is denied."

"Are you saying you won't pray for a dying man?"

"I won't pray for a lying servant of the devil."

John spoke so low the crowd had to lean in to hear his next words. "The devil's servants aren't on this side of the rope."

Everyone gasped, then started shouting. Magistrate Hathorne raised his hand to silence them. He motioned to the sheriff. Just as he raised his leg to kick the ladder away, John yelled, "I love you, Elizabeth!"

Goodman Proctor didn't die instantly. Aunt Eliza shielded Lydia from the sight of his kicking feet while he strangled for air.

"Lydia, let's go home." Lydia jerked away from her embrace and ran to some nearby trees to empty her stomach. Should she leave with her aunt? How could she watch anymore? She had known these people her entire life. Because of what she did, they were dying. One by one.

She spat the vile taste from her mouth and turned to follow her aunt home. The crowd shouted again.

"She's a filthy witch!"

"Finally! We're rid of her! Give her the rope! It's what she deserves!"

Lydia had to look. Sarah Good stood on the ladder. No one in the crowd yelled in her defense. Not one. At least Goodman Proctor and Goody Nurse had support in the crowd. Goody Good had no one. Lydia looked at the woman she had despised for years. There was something different in her face. There was peace where there once was bitterness. Still, Goody Good stood falsely accused. Lydia was partly to blame. What could she do? If she spoke up, would she be accused next? Everyone expected Goody Nurse and Goodman Proctor to have supporters, but not Goody Good. She had been either ignored or hated by all in the village. Her reputation had only worsened with her trial and conviction. No, Lydia couldn't speak. They'd assume she associated with the devil, too. Only a devil's servant would defend Sarah Good. Yet, Rebecca had defended her. She and John Proctor had stood up for everyone.

Reverend Noyes asked the same question. "Do you wish to confess your sins of witchcraft, Sarah Good?"

"I am no witch."

"I happen to know you are."

"You are a liar! I am no more a witch than you are a wizard."

"She won't confess!" Noyes shouted to the crowd, then he turned back to Sarah. "It seems you will receive your just punishment."

"If you take away my life, God will give you blood to drink."

The crowd turned into a mob at that statement.

"She dares to tell fortunes and curses!"

"Look how she speaks to a minister, a servant of God!"

Reverend Noyes smiled eerily at Sarah. "We'll see who drinks blood."

The sheriff tightened the noose. The crowd continued to shout. Some threw vegetables at Sarah. Lydia wanted just one person to shout for Sarah. Just one. Sarah looked at the crowd. Tears flowed from her eyes. She met Lydia's stare. They looked at each other for what seemed an eternity. The sheriff started to climb down from the ladder. Lydia couldn't bear it.

"Wait! No! Please, wait!"

"Who shouts there?" Magistrate Hathorne yelled.

Aunt Eliza hushed her, but Lydia couldn't stop now. She stepped forward.

"I do."

"It's Goodman Knapp's daughter, Lydia." Reverend Parris said from nearby. "If you recall, she has been one of the afflicted, though she has never given a name for her tormentor."

"Oh? Why do you shout, child?"

"I want to speak for Goody Good. I think she's innocent."

The crowd erupted in shock. Reverend Noyes laughed.

"What is this? Why would you claim this now?" Magistrate Hathorne asked.

"Because they're all innocent! This is not their fault! We were playing with witchcraft. All of the afflicted girls and I were playing with Tituba and her games. They're not witches! We aren't witches, either, but we have been deceived! We've all been deceived!"

"Who is in charge of this child?"

Aunt Eliza stepped up. "I am, Your Magistrate."

"Take her away. We'll deal with her later."

Lydia would not be dismissed. "No! You can't hang her! She's innocent!"

"Silence!" Magistrate Hathorne looked at the sheriff. "Now, Sheriff!"

Goody Good smiled at Lydia. That was the first time Lydia had ever seen Sarah Good smile. And it was the last. Sheriff Corwin kicked the ladder.

Lydia didn't stay to watch Martha Corey's hanging. She couldn't. The constable arrested her for witchcraft.

The jail cell smelled so foul that Lydia's eyes burned. There were women piled in, chained to the wall, and most barely looked up when the guard brought her in.

"Lydia!" Sarah Cloyce reached out for her. The guard purposely led her to the opposite side of the room. He chained her arms to the wall, and he bound her feet with rope.

"There's so many of you witches we don't have enough chains. We should hang more of you more often."

The heartless comment pierced Lydia's grieving soul. She wondered if Papa knew she had been arrested. The guards liked to torture the prisoners any way they could so he probably did.

She looked at the woman beside her.

"Tituba!"

"Hello, Lydia."

"Oh, Tituba. What have they done to you?" The slave bore no resemblance to the beautiful woman she had been. Her matted hair stuck to her face, which had a nasty rash on the cheeks and forehead. She had lost weight, and didn't possess the energy Lydia had always admired about her.

"Have you seen my husband, Lydia? It's been a while since he's visited. He's not been arrested, has he?"

"Oh, no. He's been working extra jobs. Reverend Parris has him making up for the wages he isn't receiving from the church. At least that's what I heard."

"He already worked hard enough. But I suppose it's better than jail. This place will change you, Lydia. How did you come to be here?"

"Yes, Lydia, what happened?" Sarah Cloyce asked.

"I tried to stop the hanging."

"What?" Tituba said.

"Oh, Lydia. For Rebecca?" Sarah asked.

"No. I wanted to, but I was afraid, Goody Cloyce. I'm sorry. I couldn't help her." Her voice broke.

"No, Lydia. I'm sure you helped her. She saw you before she died." Mary Easty said. "Did you see Francis?"

"Yes. We were together."

"Praise God." Mary said. "Rebecca worried the most for him."

"Who did you stand up for?" Tituba asked.

"Goody Good."

All of the women just looked at each other.

"I know. Of all people-"

"No. That's not what we're thinking, Lydia." Mary said.

"It's not?"

"No. We're glad you stood up for her. Sarah Good didn't leave this jail the same as when she came in."

For the first time, Lydia noticed Dorcas on Goody Cloyce's lap.

"What's wrong with Dorcas?"

"She's grieving. In her own way." Mary said.

Dorcas didn't look at anyone. She just stared at some unknown thing or person. Her eyes appeared empty of any life or light.

"Tituba, you're right. This place changes people. Even little girls. What will happen to me?"

The slave surprised her by placing her thin, chained arm around Lydia's shoulders. "Goody Good changed for the better. Maybe we need to change like she did."

"How did she change?"

Tituba pointed to Mary. "I think we need to ask her."

CHAPTER TWENTY-NINE

"Surely you can see this is ludicrous!"

Reverend Hale pleaded with the judges the morning after Goody Nurse's hanging. "This is getting out of hand. What evidence is this, that anyone who speaks up for the accused is then accused? Or anyone that questions the validity of the afflicted is accused? Are we all to assume then that those who say nothing are innocent? How is this logic possible in this official court?"

"Mind your tongue, Reverend Hale."

"Is this warning that I myself might be accused, Your Magistrate?"

"I only implore you to mind the tone you use with your officials."

"I admit I'm a bit incensed, sir, but surely you can see that spectral evidence cannot be our primary source of evidence. Why, those girls could be delusional."

"Am I to understand that you are blaming the victims? Do you propose they lie?"

"Of course not, sir. I do believe someone—or something, the devil, I'm certain—afflicts them, but I'm not so certain that it's those they accuse. Why Rebecca Nurse-"

"Don't speak of the guilty dead, Reverend. No good can come of it."

"Someone must speak of them! We must ascertain if we are

dealing with these trials in God's wisdom."

Judge Corwin cleared his throat. "Well, perhaps we can discuss it more before we proceed with any more trials or punishments."

"We'll do no such thing. No servants of the devil will rule this land as long as I'm able to stop them. This is precisely what he wants. He means to deceive us all, with doubt. No, we'll go on as planned," Magistrate Hathorne said.

"I agree with the magistrate." Reverend Parris said.

"Of course you do. I would expect nothing else, Reverend Parris," Reverend Hale said. He straightened and pulled at his waistcoat. These men embodied pride. There was no reasoning with them.

"If I can't change your mind, then maybe this will." He laid down a parchment and stormed out of Judge Corwin's house. Judge Corwin picked it up.

"What is it?" Magistrate Hathorne held out his hand. Judge Corwin didn't hand it over. He just stared at the parchment. "It's a written petition. From Goody Easty."

"A petition? Well, go on. Read aloud."

To the honorable judge and bench now sitting in judicature in Salem, and to the reverend ministers, your humble poor petitioner being condemned to die doth humbly beg that you take into your pious consideration that I, knowing my own innocence, which is blessed by the Lord, am wrongfully confined and now condemned to die. The Lord above knows my innocence, and one Great Day it will be known to both men and angels. I petition your honors not only for my own life, for I know I must die, and my appointed time is set, but if it be possible that no more innocent blood be shed, I petition you to question the course you go in. The Lord alone, who is the searcher of all hearts, knows that I shall answer it at the

Tribunal Seat that I know nothing of witchcraft, therefore, I cannot belie my own soul to confess. Please do not deny this my humble petition for a poor dying innocent person, and I question not but the Lord will give a blessing to your endeavors.

    Signed,

    Mary Easty

Mary hung a few days later.

"Do you still refuse to enter a verdict with this court?" Magistrate Hathorne asked.

Giles Corey stood tall and proud, and mute. He would not speak.

"Do you understand that refusing to speak or to enter a verdict refuses you the right to a trial?"

Giles still did not move an inch. He showed no emotion, and his eyes stared straight ahead, just above the heads of those on the bench.

Reverend Hale admired his resolve. He didn't know much about the man, other than the testimonies he'd heard during questioning. Apparently, Goodman Corey had killed a man during a fight on his land. Many claimed he had a hefty temper, although there were no accusations of wife abuse. His wife had just been hanged with Goody Nurse, and she had many friends in the crowd that day. The guard testified that Giles wept on the day of her hanging.

Goodman Proctor and Goodman Corey had worked hard to gather names on Goody Nurse's petition, for what good it did. Reverend Hale didn't understand Giles' motive for not entering a plea, unless he just wanted some measure of control over this hysteria.

"Why did you deed your land to your son-in-law? It is understood that you two do not share common interests and opinions."

Reverend Hale rather enjoyed Magistrate Hathorne's frustration with Goodman Corey's silence. This was something he couldn't control, and the man definitely had to feel in control at all times. This should get interesting.

It made sense that Corey didn't want to leave his land to fall into the hands of the court. The sheriff had seized a great deal of property since the trials had begun, all in the name of the law. Reverend Hale knew what really happened to it. The court took what value it wanted from the goods, and held the property to sell at a later date. Whatever they didn't use, the sheriff and constables took as their own. Even if these people were released, they wouldn't have those things restored.

Reverend Hale didn't even know why he attended this questioning today. After their refusal to heed Mary Easty's petition, he couldn't stomach much more of this hysteria. Last week, someone had actually accused his wife. Reverend Hale knew with absolute certainty that the claims made against her were pure folly. He would make it known to the governor that the court of Oyer and Terminer no longer had his support for these trials.

"Goodman Corey, as you have no wish to speak by admission of guilt in these accusations, this court has no other recourse but to sentence you according to English common law with the torture of death by pressing." Reverend Hale stood up.

"Surely you can't kill a man when you don't even know his plea. Do you want that on your conscience, Your Magistrate?"

"He's knowingly choosing his sentence, and foregoing a trial."

"That's because no one who has been tried has been given a chance, or even a voice!"

"Reverend Hale, must we endure this tiresome debate each time we meet? If he's choosing suicide over a trial, then he's guilty. So even if he is not guilty of witchcraft, he's guilty. Either way, justice will be served. Now, this hearing is dismissed." He banged the gavel twice.

That was it. The other ministers and judges said nothing. He would see no support from them. Reverend Hale shoved the table and stormed out of the court.

The following day, he decided to attend the pressing. Maybe he could offer comfort to Goodman Corey through prayer. The sheriff escorted Giles from the jail to a nearby field. Like the hangings, there were different voices in the crowd. Some couldn't wait to witness the gruesome torture of their fellow neighbor. Others were there, pleading with Giles to change his mind.

"Goodman Corey, just enter a plea! You don't want to do this!'

"You deserve this torture, after all the times you afflicted our children!"

"Anyone who could hurt a child deserves to die!"

"Just say you're guilty! Then, you'll live!"

Giles ignored them all. He didn't look at anyone, not even family members or friends. The constables forced him down on the ground and staked his arms and legs. Then, they placed a large board on top of his body. A pile of large stones had been prepared nearby. Someone had taken the time to stack them high. It was enough to erect a small outbuilding.

Reverend Hale was the only minister in attendance. The others weren't required to be there. A death by pressing was considered most undignified, for that person had actually chosen it, thereby committing the shameful act of suicide.

"Well, Goodman Corey, you can confess now, and save us all of this trouble, even save yourself this miserable death," the sheriff said.

"I'll die on my own terms, Sheriff."

The sheriff frowned. "Stupid man. Have it your way. Constable Locker, you and Herrick start placing the stones."

Reverend Hale watched as the constable placed the first stone on top of the board, right above Giles' chest. He blinked, but did not move. They placed the next stone on his belly, and then Reverend Hale saw him wince.

"Goodman Corey, are you sure you want to do this?" he asked him.

He spoke in broken breaths, "Reverend, if the Good Lord wanted to take me, I'd have no say, and I'm fine with that. As it is, they are going to take my life without just cause. At least this way, I have a say."

"I understand, Goodman. Don't talk anymore. Would you like me to pray?"

Giles smiled through the pain, and nodded.

The next day, Reverend Hale went back to the field. The sheriff and the constables were still there, looking fatigued. The pile of stones had almost dwindled, and the pile on top of Goodman Corey stood as high as a small wall. If Reverend Hale hadn't know there was a man under there, he wouldn't have seen him. He moved closer, and stilled in shock. Giles' face was unrecognizable. Blood vessels colored his face blue and red. The swelling distorted his features so much that Reverend Hale couldn't tell if his eyes were open or closed.

"Is he still alive?" he asked.

"Oh, he's still alive. Stubborn man, he is. He won't confess, and he won't die."

"How can you tell if he's still alive?"

"Ye can hear him, if you get close. Go on. He takes a pained breath every now and then. Don't see how, though. His ribs are broken clean through."

"Careful, sheriff, your callousness won't go unnoticed."

"My callousness is warranted, Reverend. The man tortured children. This is his just due."

Reverend Hale saw blood trickling out of Giles' mouth.

A young lady ran up to him. "Please, father, just confess! End your misery!"

Reverend Hale pulled her away. "It's too late. Even if they stopped now, the damage is done. Let him be."

She knelt to the ground and sobbed. Her husband came and took her away.

Reverend Hale reached down and held the man's hand. He was too weak to grasp in kind, but Reverend Hale knew he provided comfort with just that small gesture. He listened as Giles' breaths became a bit raspier each time.

"Goodman Corey, I ask you again. Will you confess? Do you have anything to say before you die?"

Giles tried to open his mouth. "Silence! He's trying to speak!" The sheriff yelled to the crowd.

"More—weight." Giles whispered.

"What did he say?" someone yelled.

"I think he said, 'more weight'. The man is mad with agony," Sheriff Corwin said.

"No, he's not mad." Reverend Hale said. "He's asking for you to end it. Add more weight, and end this now."

"I'm supposed to prolong his torture."

"I don't care what you're supposed to do! Be ethical, and end his pain! Now!"

The sheriff didn't argue, but nodded to the constables, who started picking up the heavy stones from the pile. It was no doubt a decision brought on by his great fatigue.

Reverend Hale squeezed Giles' hand once more as the next two stones were stacked on top. Giles gave a little hiss, and then his raspy breaths stopped.

"Another victim has died." Reverend Hale said.

"What did you say?" The sheriff asked.

Reverend Hale didn't answer. He didn't know why he had called Giles Corey a victim, but when he had watched that man die such a gruesome death, with no clear justice, that's exactly how he saw him.

～⌒

The magistrate frightened Lydia. She didn't want to hang. All of those who had hung had been innocent of witchcraft. She had dallied with it, just as the afflicted girls had. If anyone should hang, it should be her. Why should she beg God to spare her? She heard Goody Easty's voice in her memory. *All God does is contingent upon His love.* How wonderful that she really understood that now. She didn't have to be perfect to earn His love. She didn't have to earn His love at all. She missed Goody Nurse and Goody Easty so much, but she was so thankful that they taught her the truth, and that she finally accepted it.

"Lydia Knapp, why do you serve the devil?"

"I do not, sir."

"Then why defend his servants?"

"I do not believe they are —or were—his servants."

"Are you saying we are guilty of hanging innocent people?"

"Probably not intentionally, sir."

"So you are saying they were innocent of witchcraft?"

"I believe so."

"Then do you also believe that the afflicted girls—your friends—are lying?"

"No sir. I believe they are afflicted by an evil assailant."

"What assailant? Can you name him?"

"Satan, sir."

"Are you saying he acts alone?"

"I don't know, sir. I'm not familiar with how the devil works, only that I do not work for him, and I do not believe the accused have, either."

"Do you believe your friends are suffering?"

"Aye, sir."

"Were you close to the deceased, convicted witch Goody Easty?"

"I was."

"Then you know how her petition reads?"

"Yes."

"What do you make of it?"

"I agree with it."

"So you hold to its argument? That the accused are innocent and the afflicted are deceived?"

"I do."

"Have you ever practiced witchcraft?"

"I have, sir."

"When?"

"Several times in the last year, at Reverend Parris' residence, when Tituba played some forbidden fortune telling games with us."

"Is Tituba a witch?"

"I don't believe so, sir."

"Did she not confess?"

"Yes, but she is not a witch."

"How do you know?"

"Because she believes in Jesus now."

Magistrate Hathorne visibly flinched, but continued.

"Are you a witch?"

"No, sir."

"You have practiced witchcraft. Doesn't that make you a witch?"

"I don't know, but I know I'm not one now. Jesus' blood has covered all that I have done."

Magistrate Hathorne narrowed his eyes. Reverend Hale smiled at her.

Hathorne didn't smile. "Never mind that. You have practiced witchcraft, therefore, you must be a witch."

"If that's true, then the afflicted girls are witches, also. They practiced it with me."

Alice Putnam started screaming. "She's tormenting my daughter! There, she pinches her arm!"

Ann looked at her mother in surprise.

Judge Corwin yelled at the constable. "Examine her arm!"

Ann pulled away, but the constable grabbed her wrist and turned her arm over.

"There's no mark, Your Magistrate. Nothing on her at all."

Alice panicked. "You can't see it! It's invisible! It's a trick of the devil. That girl is using his powers to deceive you!"

Magistrate Hathorne looked at the other girls. "Are you not harmed?"

Abigail spoke up. "No, sir. I feel nothing."

"Liar!" Alice screamed. "Ann, speak up! She harms you!"

"Silence, Goody Putnam! Ann, do you see anyone's specter in this courtroom?"

Ann looked at her mother, then stuttered when she spoke. "Yes-I see Lydia. She-she holds a sewing needle. She wishes to harm me."

The other girls slowly chimed in their agreement.

"Are you changing your statement?" Magistrate Hathorne asked Abigail. She nodded.

Reverend Hale spoke up. "Clearly, this testimony is influenced."

Reverend Parris jumped up. "Are you claiming that my niece isn't being truthful?"

"I'm claiming that the afflicted children have no real evidence against this girl."

Alice Putnam stood up. "You're a liar! Perhaps you're the one influenced, by the devil himself!"

Reverend Hale ignored her. "Your Magistrate, with the governor's reservations, and with today's display, I advise that we reexamine these accusations, not just for Lydia, but for those in jail as well."

Alice Putnam stomped her foot on the floor. "The governor! Why his wife is the one whispering in his ear! Her specter came to me in the night and she pinched me, and told me she'd harm my husband if I didn't do her bidding! That's why he has reservations! His own wife is a witch!"

Magistrate Hathorne stared at her. "Are you claiming that you are now afflicted, and that your tormentor is the governor's own wife?"

"Yes! She's here now! Girls, tell them!"

The girls stared at her, then they nodded in agreement, Reverend Hale coughed. "Goody Putnam, surely you want to revise your statement."

"I want to revise nothing! Goody Phips should be arrested!"

Magistrate Hathorne tapped his quill on the table. "We will focus on the case at hand. Lydia Knapp, with the strong evidence against you, this court hereby condemns you to hang for the crime of witchcraft. Considering the danger of your association with these girls, I recommend that your hanging be set on the morrow. This court is dismissed."

Lydia's aunt jumped up from the back of the room. "No! You can't do that!"

Judge Corwin started whispering frantically to Magistrate Hathorne, but the man waved him off and rose to leave. Lydia just stared straight through the constable as he approached to take her back to jail. What just happened?

Aunt Eliza rushed to Reverend Hale's side, pleading with him to intervene. "You must do something! Please!"

Lydia looked at him, the only official in that room who had been on her side. He looked from her aunt to her, and then back at her aunt. He shook his head sadly and fled from the room.

⁓

"Papa! I heard you're getting out!"

"Lydia, you shouldn't be here." Paul sobbed into his hands. "I'm so sorry." He wanted to grab her and hold her, but the guard watched. All of those wasted years where he could have held her more, been more attentive. Now, he wouldn't have any more chances.

"Papa, Aunt Eliza has been taking care of the homestead. She has paid the jail fees with her own money. You still have a home."

"I told you not to mention her."

"You're not going to make her leave, are you? She's done so much for me. Besides, you need her, Papa. Please don't send her away." Her voice cracked with the tears in her throat.

"Don't cry, daughter. I'll let her stay." Right now, he'd do anything for his daughter. "Why did you do it, Lydia? For Sarah Good? Of all people. I could understand if it was for Goody Nurse, but why for Sarah Good?"

"You don't understand, Papa. She had no one. She hung because of me."

"That's not true, Lydia. It's those girls telling tales."

"I don't think they're all telling tales, Papa. It's because of what we did. That's why the devil torments them."

"Even so, it's not your doing."

"Still, all of the others had supporters in the crowd. People threw things at her. And even though they threw things at the others, at least they had people who shouted for them. Goody Good only had people shouting against her."

"But surely you knew this would happen. That they'd accuse you of witchcraft, too!"

"Aye, Papa, I knew. I had to do it. I had to shout for her. I just couldn't let her die that way."

He smiled at her. The guard looked out the small window, so Paul reached across the table and embraced her face with both hands.

"You are a brave girl, Lydia. Your mother would be so proud."

"I accepted Jesus, Papa. Did you know?"

"I thought something was different. It's in your eyes."

"Why didn't you tell me, Papa?"

"Tell you what?"

"About Jesus? About who He really is? I always thought He was like Magistrate Hathorne, just sitting on his throne, waiting to hand out harsh punishments whenever we messed up. I never really knew about His grace."

"I'm sorry. Grief blinded me, child. I just figured Goody Nurse and the meetings were enough."

"I needed to hear it from you."

"Aye. I guess you did."

"It's alright, Papa. It's alright that I'm going to hang."

"How can you say that?"

"If it was a good enough death for Goody Nurse, then I suppose it's good enough for me, too. Besides, I finally stood for something, Papa. I'm not afraid anymore. I'm not afraid to live, and now, I'm not even afraid to die. I do not fear eternity any longer."

"You're too young. It should be me."

"No, Papa. Don't say that. Forgive your sister. Marry again someday. Please, Papa. Say you will. Say you'll live. For me."

Paul wiped the tears from his eyes and nodded. "I'll live for you, Lydia." He squeezed her hand.

The guard yelled. "No touching!" Paul ignored him and pulled his daughter into a tight embrace before the guard's club came down on his back.

When he woke, he was at home, in his bed. It was morning, and the day his daughter would hang.

Like Bridget Bishop, Lydia would hang alone. No one threw food at her. Paul stood at the cart and threatened that anyone who did would have to answer to him. The sheriff didn't dispute it, probably because he had grown tired of the stray food hitting him.

When they reached the ledge, Lydia didn't look at the rope. She looked at her father. She couldn't see her aunt. Lydia thought she'd show up, but maybe she didn't think Paul would want her there. That might be true, but Lydia wished she could have said goodbye. She'd grown to love her.

Sheriff Corwin led her to the tree, and Lydia climbed up the ladder.

"No! Stop! Take me! Hang me!"

Paul rushed the guards, knocked them over and appeared at the bottom of the ladder. He grabbed Lydia's foot to pull her down. The guards were on him again, but his adrenaline provided great strength and movement. He punched both guards, and the constable, then knocked the sheriff from the ladder.

"Papa! Don't! You can't get into trouble again!"

The men ganged up on him and held him to the ground. He screamed out in agony and grief.

"Enough!" Magistrate Hathorne yelled. "Keep him quiet! Chain him and take him back to prison for obstructing justice!"

"No! Please, sir, he is just taken with grief for his only daughter. I'm not causing trouble. See?" Lydia stepped up the ladder.

"No!" Reverend Hale raced to Lydia's side. "You can't hang her. It's time to stop this madness!"

"Reverend Hale, not you, too. That will be enough of this nonsense. This is about justice. Now move aside."

"I'll not move. This is not justice. If you hang her, you'll have to hang me as well."

"Don't be ridiculous."

"What? I'm not exempt, am I? Anyone who defends a witch must indeed be one as well."

Magistrate Hathorne narrowed his eyes. "Reverend Hale, I know you're well acquainted with Reverend Mather, but I have friends in high places, also. You don't want to do this."

"I have a friend in a high place, too, Your Magistrate. In fact, I have the highest friend in the highest place. And I have it on His great authority that these trials are of the devil, as are these hangings. We cannot proceed and hope to regain His favor."

Raphael had seen all of the demons gathered at this hanging. Sonneillon knew what was at stake with this girl. Gabriel had given him the order to fight, so Raphael had recruited his best, including Uriel, Semiel and Raguel. They pulled their swords as the demons approached. Finally, the battle they had been waiting for.

Sonneillon squared off with Raphael. He didn't waste any time.

"You can't have this girl. She might be a believer now, but she'll hang. I know what He wants to do with her, and I can't allow it, Captain of Heaven."

"You have no say in it, servant of Lucifer."

"We'll see about that." Sonneillon drew his flaming sword, and jabbed at Raphael. He darted away just in time, and dived down on top of the demon, pulling at his large reptilian wings. The demon screamed in a fit of rage, and swung around, clipping Raphael with the tip of his sword. Raphael gasped at the sharp pain. He had been stabbed before, but Sonneillon had increased in strength since their last fight.

The women in the jail prayed, so Raphael felt his own strength increase, and he swung his sword of light into Sonneillon's side. The demon shrieked in agony. Raphael looked at his angels Semiel and

Uriel. They struggled against Carreau and Verrier, but they held their own. The prayers were building. He looked down over the jail and could see the women, including Tituba, holding hands in a circle, lifting up the name of the Lord, and lifting up their fellow believers, including Lydia. That's all his army needed. His angels all across the sky lit up, shining brighter than they had since this mission started.

Sonneillon came at him again, but in minutes, it was over. The large demon escaped, with his many minions flying away in shame behind him. Lucifer probably heard the angel army's victory cry all the way in Hell. Now, they could focus on the Salem saints.

⁓

Magistrate Hathorne stared at the bold minister. "Are you telling me God told you we must end these hangings?"

"That's right. I am. Hang her, and you'll have to hang me, too."

Sheriff Corwin looked conflicted. He whispered to his uncle. "Reverend Hale is considered in high esteem by many. Surely we can't hang him!"

Judge Corwin hushed his nephew. He started to speak to Reverend Hale when Lydia's Aunt Eliza rushed through the crowd, waving a piece of parchment paper.

"Stop the hanging! You must stop the hanging by order of Governor Phips!"

"This is absurd! What are you shouting, woman?" Magistrate Hathorne said.

Aunt Eliza climbed up the ledge to the judge and handed him the parchment. "Read this!"

As he read, the magistrate's face flushed red. He shouted to the crowd.

"This hanging is postponed until further notice! Go home! Sheriff, take her back to the jail for now."

Reverend Hale walked over to the magistrate. "What is it? What's happened?"

Irritated, Magistrate Hathorne turned around to face him. "The governor has ordered a suspension on the trials and hangings for an assessment of the proceedings. He wants a thorough examination of the cases against those arrested." He looked at Alice Putnam, who stood motionless in shock. "I'm sure it has everything to do with his wife being accused." Her eyes widened as he stomped away.

Reverend Hale walked over to Paul, who still lay on the ground, and helped him to his feet. "He won't be going back to prison, guards. I'll bring him home."

"No, Reverend. He's my brother. I can take him," Eliza said. Lydia expected her father to argue, but he didn't. Instead, he asked, "How did you manage that?"

"I didn't. I stopped at Ingersoll's for a moment. A constable from Boston came in, asking where the hanging was taking place. He said he had an order to stop any further hangings." She laughed. "I didn't blink. I grabbed that parchment with the order on it, and ran to my horse. I didn't even look to see if the constable followed me. Then, a bit down the road, my horse went lame, and I had to run all the way here. I suppose we'll have to pick up the horse on the way home."

"You were almost too late."

Eliza frowned at him. "But I wasn't."

"No, you weren't. You did right this time, Eliza."

"Paul-"

"There's no need, Eliza." He turned and hugged his daughter before allowing his sister to escort him to the carriage.

The reverend smiled at Lydia. "We've seen a miracle here, today, child. You'll be going home soon, too." Lydia nodded at him, but as the constable led her away from the hanging site, she felt deep sadness for those who had seen no such miracle.

CHAPTER THIRTY

Elizabeth Proctor carried her baby out of the jail. She squinted against the light and looked down at little John. His eyes opened and shut as he tried to adjust to being outside. He'd meet his brothers soon. If only he could meet his father. She pushed her grief down into the depths of her heart. She would not cry today. She was out of that horrid cell. She couldn't go home. The boys had to sell everything to pay for their parents' jail and court fees, and to pay for their father's execution. They weren't the only ones in that predicament. Some were already moving away, and those that weren't were trying to figure out their plans to regain a future. After settling up with the jailer for her release, her boys had taken what was left to purchase a small house in Salem Town. They had decided to work on the ships at port so they could earn enough money to buy back their father's property. That was the hope, anyway. Elizabeth had one thing on her mind. Survival. She'd do what she could to raise her newest son to be the man his father was. Grief would not win. John would want her to move on.

As she walked on the road away from the jail, a child spat at her. His spittle landed on her bare foot.

"You're a witch! Go away, witch! Take your devil baby and go away!" The child's mother raced up to her boy and pulled him with her.

"Don't anger her! You don't know what she'll do to you!" They scurried away, the mother looking back at her with frightened eyes.

If John had been there, he'd tell that child and his mother just what he wanted to do to them, but Elizabeth didn't dare. Not now. She knew all too well how easily words could be misinterpreted. No, she'd stay quiet. She'd survive. Little John would survive, too. She'd make sure of that. He already had his father's spirit, and while Elizabeth wouldn't let anyone stifle it, she couldn't let anyone exploit it, either. Even if she had to move away from Salem, no one would ever harm little John Proctor. No, that name would be respected again someday. Her husband had stood up for those he cared about, and his name should be honored. One day, she thought, it would be. John Proctor would once again be known as a man of courage and honor. She smiled, and as she snuggled her son to her breast, she was positive he smiled back.

⌒‿

Tituba remained in jail for weeks. The reverend did not come to settle her jail fees. She heard he moved away from Salem, and took her husband with him. She had not even been allowed a goodbye. Those who hadn't been hanged, had all gone home, or at least to a new home. Lydia visited her once a week, and brought her food. No one else came to see her. Then, one day, the guard surprised her with a visitor.

"Hello, Tituba."

Her old master! "What are you doing here, sir?"

"My ship docked in Boston last week. I heard all about the trials here. A man told me the whole sordid story. When I heard your name, and that you were still in jail, I had to come. Where's your husband?"

"I don't know. Reverend Parris took him when he moved away."

"I shouldn't have sold you. I've often regretted it. I'm so sorry."

Tituba didn't know what to say. She believed in a different way now, so hate had no place in her heart.

"Would you like to come with me, Tituba? I could pay your jail fees, and you could work on the ship."

"You're buying me back?"

"No. I'll pay your fees, but once you earn those back, you're free to go. You can stay on the ship and earn wages, or you can go back home."

"Home. Do you mean Barbados?"

"Yes."

"What if John comes looking for me?"

"I have an idea for that, too. I'll find out where this Parris has moved, and I'll offer him a nice fee for John, one he cannot refuse."

"I don't understand. Why would you do this for us? We're just slaves."

"Tituba, that's another story, and I'd like to tell you about it, but first, let's get you out of here, and go find that husband of yours."

She almost hugged him. Only God could have brought such a beautiful gift to her. She was going home to Barbados! With John! Why her? She should have hung on that rope, not the others. She had caused so much grief. Dare she expect such happiness? Then, she remembered what Goody Easty had told her the day she and Lydia had found their faith. *There is no condemnation in Christ.* She had to remember that. Jesus had absolved all she had done. Besides, if the witch trials had not occurred, she wouldn't have known Jesus, and Lydia wouldn't, either. She knew if Goody Nurse was here, she'd tell Tituba to go in peace. If Jesus forgave her, and Goody Nurse would forgive her, then she must forgive herself.

After her old master paid her fees, she walked out of the jail. Like Goody Good, she walked out a different person, in a good way. She would never forget what this horrible place did for her. Not to her, but for her. She wouldn't forget, but she wouldn't linger on it. God offered her a new future, and she would take it.

She had no time to tell Lydia, so she asked the guard to tell her when she came to visit.

Minutes later, she left Salem, and she didn't look back.

⌒～

Lydia's father wanted to move away again, but she convinced him not to. The people of Salem needed them. So many were hurting because of the witch trials. Even those not accused suffered the effects. They had missed days of work attending the trials.

"Where are you going? We visit with Goody Proctor and Little John today," Paul asked. He smiled more these days, especially on the days they visited the widow Proctor. Lydia didn't mind at all.

"I know, Papa. I just have something else I have to do first. I won't be long."

The angels followed her as she went door to door, carrying eggs, cider, bread, and canned goods in a large basket. She talked and prayed with her neighbors. Her last stop wasn't a residence. The little abandoned shed sat on the side of Ipswich road.

"Who is that?" A voice bellowed.

"It's me, Goodman. I came to visit with little Dorcas."

"I told ye she's not right in her thinking. She can't understand what ye say and she won't remember what ye do."

"I know. I just wanted to see her."

"Suit yourself." As he walked out of the shed, he muttered, "Stupid witch."

"Hi, Dorcas."

The little girl sat on a straw bed, holding a corncob. She hummed softly to herself.

"Dorcas, I brought you a honey cake."

Dorcas didn't look up, just kept humming. Lydia set the cake down beside her, and then moved closer. She began to comb her fingers through Dorcas' matted hair, and then she dipped a cloth in the bucket of water outside the door, and wiped the child's face clean. She dipped the cloth again and wiped her arms, legs, and feet clean. When she finished, Dorcas looked better than Lydia had ever seen her. Still, the child did not look up.

"Dorcas, your mother loved you very much. You know that, don't you?" Lydia asked.

Dorcas hummed.

"I bet she'd like you to eat the honey cake. Will you take a bite?" Lydia broke a piece of the cake and brought it to Dorcas' mouth. She opened her mouth and chewed slowly. She stared down at the corncob.

"Well, I'll come see you again, Dorcas. Would you like that?"

Dorcas hummed again.

"Goodbye, little Dorcas."

"Say goodbye to Mercy."

Lydia turned back to the soft, sweet voice. Dorcas looked at her now. She held up the corncob.

"Mercy says goodbye. Tell Mama that Mercy says goodbye."

Lydia nodded. "I'll tell her, Dorcas."

William Good stood outside, smoking a pipe.

"I told ye. Her mind's gone."

Lydia wanted to scream that it was his doing. She knew he had testified against his own wife, and he hadn't stood up for his little girl. Did he even care that his baby had died in prison? Still, if she spoke to him that way, he wouldn't let her see Dorcas.

"Goodman, do you mind if I come once a week and look in on Dorcas?"

"If you want to waste your time on her, then that's your decision. In the meantime, you can bring us some eggs and bread. Her mind is gone, but she still eats."

Rage filled Lydia's chest, but she pushed it away. If it was up to her, Dorcas would come home with Lydia, but William Good already turned down Sarah Cloyce's offer to care for the child. Papa had said he wanted the girl to help him with his begging. Folks would feel sorry for the child and give him lodging and food. She would just have to do what she could for Dorcas, with the opportunities God gave her.

"I'll be happy to bring food, Goodman."

She started the walk back home, vowing that as long as she could, she'd see to Dorcas' care. That child would never go hungry or lack for love, not as long as Lydia had breath in her body.

She realized she had been humming the same tune that Dorcas hummed moments ago. It was a song Lydia had heard many times in her childhood. She sang the words aloud, and as she did, she could hear Goody Nurse's voice instead of her own.

Shine thy light in the darkness, Oh God
Let not the enemy harm me
Reveal thy plan in the trial, Oh Lord
Thy glory the world to see

Raphael and Uriel watched the girl walk home.

"Now you see the purpose," Raphael said.

"I don't understand."

"The girl has changed. She's no longer afraid and focused on herself. She is confident, and caring. A strong and true warrior, like Rebecca."

"So all those people died to transform this one girl?"

"Is that ever how it works, Uriel?"

He thought for a moment. "No. Other lives will be effected."

"They already have."

"Yes, but Satan's plan worked. The courts will change. They are already restructuring the system and removing many of the former proceedings. They will use fewer spiritual methods, including the use of ministers and Scripture. How can that be good?"

"It's not. It is a manifestation of man answering his own will, and Satan using it for his. However, we must remember, Uriel. Satan does not win in the end. The Most High is still working in hearts. There is always hope, and we see it in her." He motioned to Lydia.

"I'm guessing you know more than I do, Raphael?"

"Not much. I only know a descendant of hers will lead many to Christ."

"So all of this pain brings triumph after all."

"Like I said, The Almighty always offers hope. Come. There's a celebration in Heaven for the newly welcomed saints. We don't want to miss it."

The angels spread their wings and flew to the sky, disappearing over the clouds.

EPILOGUE

August 25, 1706
Salem Village

Ann walked to the front of the church, her stomach in nervous knots. She knew she had to do this. She should have done this long ago. She wished there wasn't a need for it, that it had never happened, but wishing that for all of these years had not changed it. Not long after the trials, Lydia had tried to rekindle their friendship, but Ann couldn't bear it. Not after all she had done. Spending any time with her former friend constantly reminded her how pure and good Lydia had been through the trials, and how utterly corrupt Ann had been. Lydia had finally moved on. She had become so like Goody Nurse, pious, and good and kind to all.

Ann turned and looked at the faces of the congregation. Some were compassionate, mainly the few afflicted girls who had remained in Salem. They understood the guilt she endured. Others, including the Nurse family, looked back at her with emotionless eyes. She didn't blame them all, but it stung anyway.

Her mother had not wanted her to do this so she wasn't in the congregation today. She had never been humble enough to admit her wrongdoing and didn't accept the shame that had been placed upon the Putnam name. Ann didn't care about their reputation. She just longed for a reckoning. Maybe today would be a start.

She cleared her throat and began her formal confession to the church.

"I desire to be humbled here today, before God, and before you, for that shameful happening that befell us all in the year of ninety-two. I, being but a youth, allowed myself to be an instrument in accusing several persons of a grievous crime, whereas their lives were so sadly taken from them. I now believe I have just grounds to believe they were innocent of such crimes, and that it was a great delusion of Satan that deceived me in that sad time. As I was a chief instrument of accusing Goodwife Nurse and her sisters, and the others, I desire to lie in the dust and be forever humbled by it, that I caused such a calamity to them and their families. I hereby earnestly beg forgiveness of God, and of all of those I have caused great sorrow and offense."

Ann walked back to her seat, and prayed that she'd finally find some peace after years of heartache and grief. None of the family members of the victims spoke to her after the service. She didn't really expect them to, but she had so hoped for it. She supposed it would take time.

Salem Village, 1716

Ann gripped her chest with her fist. The pain didn't last long. Unmarried and alone, there was no one in her house to hold her as she took her last breath. When she reached the light, she finally saw the reckoning she craved in the faces of the victims who welcomed her home. The first to step toward her was a woman holding a child. Ann knew her instantly. Goody Good embraced her, then stepped aside for a woman who wore a red petticoat.

December 13th, 1717
Salem Town

Reverend Noyes couldn't wait to present his new written reflections to the other ministers. He needed another publication. It had been a while since he'd published his poem, and even longer since he'd published *Election Sermon*. It had been fairly popular, and brought him great esteem in his circle of ministers. After years of repairing his reputation from those pesky witch trials, he'd finally restored his name with those publications, especially when Cotton Mather allowed him to write some verses for his book. Some of the family members were still angry that he hadn't formerly apologized for his part in the trials, but he didn't plan on doing that. He had only been doing his duty after all. What did he have to apologize for? Besides, he had joined the effort to assist those families with any charity he could offer, and the court gave all the prisoners amnesty after they paid their jail fees. What more could they want?

He stood up from his chair, and placed his newest collection of writings on the table. A cup of tea would be a nice treat this afternoon. He had no servant for the evening. The man had gone to visit relatives in Boston. Reverend Noyes had always thought he liked being alone. Now, at almost seventy years of age, he regretted never marrying. How nice it would be to share some tea in the evening with a lifelong companion who understood and respected him.

He walked to the cupboard, but stopped and grabbed his neck. Pain sliced through his throat, and he began to cough. The spasms took his breath, and he continued to cough violently. He dropped to his knees, gasping for air. As he fought for breath, he saw the hangman's noose of years ago, wrapped around Sarah Good's neck. He spat blood onto the floor, then choked and gurgled as the thick, red liquid ran out of his mouth.

Sarah Good's voice echoed in his mind. *If you take away my life, God will give you blood to drink.*

He gasped for air one last time, and fell to the floor, choking on his own blood, nine days shy of his seventieth birthday.

Present Day

A man stared in awe at the results of his family tree. He had no idea after all of these years that his mother had stored this trunk in her attic, filled with treasures of family history. Now, days after her funeral, it sat opened in his office. He flipped through old documents, which smelled of mildew and moth balls. He couldn't wait to show his wife. She loved history, and this new discovery would thrill her.

He stared at the name again. Lydia Knapp. She had been a victim of the Salem Witch Trials, and had also been instrumental in having the accusations and convictions reversed. He had studied about the trials in college, and had even written a paper on the topic, never once imagining that he could be connected to it. Had his mother not known? Lydia Knapp was his ninth great grandmother!

A knock sounded at the door and it opened.

"Pastor? They'll be here in a few minutes to take you to the airport. Are you ready?"

"Yes, Kathy, thanks."

"Oh, and they have a final number on attendance this time."

"Oh yeah?"

"Yes. They'll be 62,000 attending the conference."

"Wow."

"This movement has really taken off, hasn't it?"

"I prefer to call it a revival. The Lord knows we need it. Are the other pastors arriving on time?"

Kathy nodded. "As far as I know. What's with the chest?"

He smiled. "Just a bit of family history, that's all."

"Cool. Anything interesting?"

"I'd say so." He chuckled.

"Well, it'll have to wait." She looked out the window. "Looks like your ride is here. I'll be praying that it's even better than the last time in Dallas. How many lives were changed at that one?"

"We had six thousand salvations, and thirty-three hundred re-dedications."

His secretary whistled. "Amazing."

He put the items back into the chest, and latched it. He thought about Lydia, his ancestor, and wondered if she was a Christian. He had a long line of a godly heritage, but he wondered just how far back it reached.

He grabbed his suitcase, and slid his phone into his pocket. Forgetting momentarily about Lydia Knapp, he turned his attention to the *Alive!* Conference in Memphis. He couldn't wait. God had used his small seed of an idea, and brought it to greater heights than he could have ever imagined. Who would have thought that a man who was once just a young kid, so mixed up and confused about Jesus, and so afraid, would one day be chosen to lead such a large movement, or revival, as he liked to call it.

He walked out, singing an old song that his mother had said her great grandmother sang to her:

> *Shine thy light in the darkness, Oh God*
> *Let not the enemy harm me*
> *Reveal thy plan in the trial, Oh Lord*
> *Thy glory the world to see*

Raphael and Uriel sat on opposite sides of the old cedar chest and watched the pastor leave.

"This is the best part of being an angel." Raphael said.

"What?"

"Watching the results."

"That is good, but I like a few other things as well." Uriel said.

"Oh? Like what?"

"The celebrations. Looks like we'll be rejoicing in Heaven again."

Raphael beamed with joy. "What are we waiting for?" He spread his wings wide, and shot out of the church, with Uriel flying fast behind him.

A Letter from the Author

Dear Reader,

I first encountered the story of the witch trials almost twenty years ago while researching for a project for a college class. While reading, the behavior from the afflicted children intrigued me. The cause is still debated today. With all of the theories circulating, I didn't see my own theory, which is that the girls were experiencing demonic influences. I am not convinced that all of the afflicted were demonically influenced or possessed. I believe some were influenced by suggestion and paranoia, or by ill intentions; however, some of the girl's antics point to this theory, based on what we know of demonic activity.

When I formed this opinion, the idea for this novel planted itself in my mind, and then in my heart. I knew God wanted me to write this story. Yet, I wasn't ready. I needed time to grow as a writer, and as an adult Christian, before God allowed me to take it on. I have gathered research over the years, and it has never been far from my mind. Finally, God told me it was time, and I began to write *Afflicted*. I have written other books, in a different genre, but this is my favorite so far. It challenged me, and helped me to grow in my own faith and as a writer. There were days when I didn't think I'd ever finish, but by God's grace, here we are.

Lydia and her father are the only fictional characters in this story. Lydia's aunt, "Eliza", is based on the real Elizabeth Knapp, who was indeed an afflicted girl from Groton, several years prior to 1692. It's interesting how God brought her to me. As I was trying to come up with a last name for Lydia, I researched different last names of the period. When I saw Knapp, I knew it was the one, because it happens to be my husband's mother's maiden name. Then, as I researched, I came across the story of Elizabeth Knapp, and knew I had to include her as a relative of my main character.

As for the other real characters in the book, I included many true life facts about them into the story, such as Sarah Good's words to Reverend Noyes at her hanging, and the fact that he really did choke on his own blood.

You may have noticed that some of the characters had the same names. Normally, I'd never write characters with the same names, but in this case, I left their names as they were, to honor the victims. However, I did change a few names. For instance, Ann Putnam's mother was really Ann, Sr. I changed her name to Alice to avoid confusion.

Obviously, I took a few liberties with the non-fictional characters based on what I know of them. I did my best to honor their memory and sacrifices. The hardest part of writing this story was deciding who to put in the novel, and who to leave out. There were over 200 people accused, with the hysteria reaching far and beyond Salem village. Nineteen were hanged, and one pressed to death. Four died in prison.

When I asked God what he wanted me to say through this story, He immediately told me to warn about the dangers of Pharisee religion. Pharisee religion is a legalistic way of Christianity, based on the way the Pharisees in the Bible practiced their faith. It simply means to focus on outward practices to earn favor with God. This is not in line with the teachings of Jesus. We can never be good enough.

The Bible says in Romans 3:10, that "There is none righteous, no not one." None of us can earn our way to Heaven. We are all sinners, in need of what Jesus did on the cross. In my story, Sarah Good, Lydia, and Tituba had to come to this understanding before they could discover the peace of Christ, and allow Him to secure their souls' eternity in Heaven with Him, forever.

Another theme of this story is fear. Satan uses our fear. The Bible says there is no fear in love, and that perfect love drives fear away (I John 4:18).

When we don't rest in the assurance of God's unconditional love, we invite fear into our lives. God's love is our security. Without it, we live by our insecurities rather than His peace. Pharisee religion encourages this fear because it brings us to rely on ourselves or others for our salvation or purpose, instead of Jesus, who is our only source of salvation.

If you have never personally accepted Jesus as your Savior, and you want to know more, please email me at faylaott@gmail.com. I'd love to help you understand how you can do that. I would never disclose anyone's name. I value your privacy and your trust.

Thank you so much for reading *Afflicted*. If you enjoyed this story, please consider posting a review. Also, if you just want to drop me a line by email, I'd love to hear from you.

To stay updated about my future books, follow me on Facebook. I'll have a new website soon, but until then, you can check out my current one at www.faylalindseyott.com.

Fayla Ott
Isaiah 41:10

Salem Photos

My friend Marcia Nelson and I are posing at the statue of Samantha, the fictional witch character from the television show *Bewitched*. Surprisingly, despite the history of the trials, this is the most popular tourist attraction in Salem.

Above: Judge Corwin's house. This is the only house that is still standing in Salem (Town), which is directly related to the witch trials.

Below: The inside of Judge Corwin's house. The table is where official business would have been conducted, including arrest warrants, etc.

Above: The Salem Witch Trials memorial.

Below: This picture shows one of the stones with the victim's name engraved on it.

Above: This is Proctor's Ledge, the actual hanging site.

Below: This picture shows how the victims' names are engraved on the stones.

Above: The Rebecca Nurse Homestead in Danvers, formerly known as Salem Village.

Below: Rebecca's fireplace in the "keeping room".

Above: More of Rebecca's "keeping room". I imagine her reading her Bible and praying at the table by the window.

Below: This picture is the monument for Rebecca that her descendants had erected in her honor. It was rumored that her family dug up her body and buried it on the Nurse property, and this monument is directly over her remains.

Above: An exact replica of the meetinghouse. This was built before they tore the original down, and they moved the replica to the Rebecca Nurse homestead.

Below: The gravesite of Magistrate Hathorne.

Here, I am pictured with Jessa Moyer. She is a direct descendant of Susannah Martin, one of the Salem witch trial victims. What's interesting is that I met her in my own hometown while visiting my local bookstore. She even showed me the copy of her family tree, and how it traces back to Susannah. How amazing it is, that I traveled all the way to Salem, Massachusetts, but I met a descendant when I arrived home in East Tennessee.

Discussion Guide

1. Why does Sonneillon tell the other demons they have been invited to Salem Village?

2. Do you think Reverend Parris is a bad minister? Why or why not?

3. Does Lydia change in the story? If so, in what ways?

4. How are Reverend Noyes and Magistrate Hathorne alike? How are they different?

5. How are Bridget Bishop and Sarah Good alike? How are they different? Why are they drawn to one another?

6. Discuss the deaths of both Ann Putnam, and Reverend Noyes. What did you feel when reading Ann's death scene? What did you feel when reading Reverend Noyes' death scene? What is the difference between the two, and why are they different?

7. Discuss Rebecca Nurse and how she influenced the other victims. How did she influence Lydia?

8. What is the difference between Ann Putnam and the other afflicted children? Other than protecting herself, why would she go to such lengths to accuse innocent people of witchcraft?

9. The angels talk about prayer as if it gives them strength. Do you agree with this concept? Why or why not?

10. Sarah Good has great bitterness toward God, the people of Salem village, and her husband. Name three incidents that begin her journey of change, leading up to, but not including, her salvation experience. Discuss how those incidents contribute to her change.

11. Discuss John Proctor's heroism. Does his sacrifice make a difference?

12. Why do the people of Salem not care for Bridget Bishop? What can we learn from her attitude, concerning their opinions of her? Is she wrong to speak to Alice Putnam the way she does? Discuss her thoughts on how the people of Salem worship and how they relate to Rebecca's thoughts on the same subject.

13. How does Giles Corey change in the story? Discuss why it is so important to Martha that he tells her Thomas can live with them, even though she knows they will most likely die. What does he say specifically that gives her peace?

14. Compare and Contrast Martha Corey and Tituba, regarding their rape experiences.

15. What does Reverend Hale mean when he talks about ideas being contagious?

16. Discuss similarities between the witch trial accusations and our political climate of today.

17. Why do Pharisee religion practices encourage fear? Can you think of times in your own life where you have focused primarily on your outward obedience, rather than the status of your heart? How does Pharisee religion affect how we look at others? Does it alter our view of them, and ourselves?

18. The afflicted children aren't the only ones afflicted in this story. Can you think of some ways that others are afflicted?

19. What can we learn from Alice Putnam? In what ways does she and her daughter help Satan's mission? How do Christians in the church compare to her?

20. Tituba and John Indian are slaves. How does this contribute to their behavior in the book? How does it contribute to Tituba's part in the trials?

21. There is more than one type of slavery in the book. How many forms do we see, and discuss how they affect society, and the individual.

22. Discuss the scenes which stand out to you personally. How are you touched, or challenged by them?

23. Why does God not intervene in tragic moments? Do you think he has a purpose in suffering? Discuss a modern tragedy, and see if you can point out something positive that came from it.

24. Why do you think Reverend Parris' household is vulnerable to Satan's attack? How could he have protected his family?

25. Paul and Lydia both dealt with fear. How are they alike in their fear? How are they different?

26. Elizabeth Knapp brings a minor theme to the story. Do you know what it is? If so, discuss it. Does her relationship with her brother change?

27. There are several incidents of physical violence in this novel. Discuss those acts, and why you think the characters are driven to use it.

28. How should Christians think about spiritual warfare? In what ways can we prevent a demonic attack? In what ways can we strengthen the cause of Christ?

29. If you could be like any character in this book, who would it be? Why?

30. Has this book inspired you to change in any way? If so, how?

About the Author

Fayla Ott began writing at an early age. Before she could even read, she would look at picture books, and make up her own stories to match the pictures. As a teen, she filled notebooks with poems, short stories, and essays. She graduated with a Bachelor of Arts degree in English from the University of Maryland, and then with a Master of Arts degree in English from National University.

Fayla is married and has two boys. She lives in the Great Smoky Mountains of East Tennessee. When she is not writing, she is homeschooling her sons and helping her husband with his martial arts school. Her hobbies include reading, cooking, hiking, singing in her church choir, playing piano and guitar, and spending time with her family. She enjoys the adventures of traveling, too, and does so any chance she gets.

Fayla's desire for her writing is that it draws others closer to Jesus Christ, and that she can worship Him through her stories.

If you'd like to contact Fayla, email her at faylaott@gmail.com, or follow her on Facebook, Amazon and Goodreads. You can also visit her website at www.faylalindseyott.com.

10/19

55165478R00162

Made in the USA
San Bernardino,
CA